GHOSTWRITER

DON RICH

Library of Congress PCN Data

Rich, Don

GhostWRITER/Don Rich

Florida Refugee Press LLC

Cover by: Cover2Book.com

This is a work of fiction. Names, characters, and incidents are either the product of the author's imagination or are used fictitiously. Any resemblance to actual persons, living or dead, businesses, companies, events, or locales is purely coincidental. However, the overall familiarity with boats and water found in this book comes from the author having spent years on, under, and beside them.

Published by

FLORIDA REFUGEE PRESS, LLC, 2020

Crozet, VA

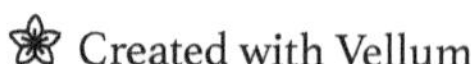 Created with Vellum

ABOUT THIS BOOK

This book is based on the out of print book *"AI Politics"* by Don Rich. This is the first book centered around Colt Toffler, a character who originally appeared in the **Coastal Adventure Series.**

For the best background of *Chesapeake Bayside Resort*, Rikki and Conrad Jenkins, Cindy Crenshaw, Casey Shaw, and Dawn McAlister, I would suggest reading the Coastal Adventure Series by Don Rich, available at Amazon.com.

Additional background, including photos, facts, and inspiration that I find in my pre-writing research are available to members of my Reader's Group. You can sign up on the home page of DonRichBooks.com

You can also follow the series and get release updates on Facebook as well at https://www.facebook.com/DonRichBooks/

FOREWORD

"It doesn't matter if justice is on your side. You have to depict your position as just."
— Benjamin Netanyahu

I've never been measured for a tinfoil hat (at least not yet), and I don't normally see conspiracies everywhere. Just because I hear one person say something doesn't mean I believe it, and I guess that's the cynic in me coming out. But while I was writing Coastal Cheats, for whatever reason I started hearing a lot about AI, or Artificial Intelligence. I dismissed it, thinking it was just another overused buzzword. Then as I finished writing that book I saw that John Roberts, the Chief Justice of the US Supreme Court, had given a speech to his daughter's high school graduating class. This wasn't some passing remark, or cocktail party circuit chatter in DC. It was something he had given a lot of thought to, and what he strongly wanted to instill in his daughter's class before they moved on to their institutions of higher learning. This was something not intended to be taken lightly. What he said was chilling:

"Beware the robots." Addressing the eighty-three young women, Roberts warned that Artificial Intelligence and "big data" can alter

the way people perceive the world. He stated machines advise law-makers about *"... what their constituents think, how strongly they feel about particular issues, how best to appeal to them, and so on. Any politician would find it very difficult not to shape his or her message to what constituents want to hear,"* Roberts said. *"Artificial Intelligence can change leaders into followers."* He said private companies can *"tell you what to read, watch, and listen to, based on what you've read, watched, and listened to,"* and match customers to their preferred people and ideas. *"The result,"* he warned, *"can be a narrowing and over-simplification that is contrary to individuality and creativity... I worry that we will start thinking like machines."*

That made me sit up and take notice. I started talking with friends about it, and the basis for this book started taking shape in my head. The more I thought about it, the more concerned I became. I finished reading the 5th novel in a series, *Duty & The Beast*, written by an email acquaintance and author from Australia, Chelsea Field. In it, two people are murdered by an AI-based alarm & protection system. It now really felt like the stars were aligning.

The final straw during this time period was finding out about a memo sent out by the then Deputy Secretary of Defense, Patrick Shanahan. In it, he stated: *"In support of our National Defense Strategy, this week, I directed our department's Chief Information Officer... to stand up the **Joint Artificial Intelligence Center (JAIC)**. The JAIC will enable teams across DoD to swiftly deliver new, AI-enabled capabilities and experiment with new operating concepts in our military missions and business operations. You know what we need here: speed and agility. We also need to evolve our partnerships with industry and academia. This department **will** lead in this arena. Plenty of people talk about the threat from AI; we want to **be** the threat."*

You only have to hit me over the head a few times before I get the message. Then I found a picture in a defense news feed of a laser-aimed pistol shooting robot in Russia which was directed by AI. Not something from the future, not science fiction, it is real, it exists now, and it is a fact. After seeing that, I let my imagination run wild. The Prologue that came out of my keyboard stunned and frightened me.

It's no wonder I'm drawn to old historic wooden Chesapeake sail-boats and vintage cars with carburetors and no computers. The simpler they are, the better I like them. I even have an inherent distrust of autopilots on boats and aircraft. Now old Ford F-150 trucks in pole barns have made the list. You'll see why in the Prologue...

Don Rich
    July 8, 2018
    Crozet, VA

This book is dedicated to the man who inspired 'Colt Toffler.' For reasons that will become obvious as you read this, he's a very private person, so I'm omitting his name. He's a friend who has helped shape my writing, and I am deeply indebted to him for that. But more than that, he has risked his own life and come close to losing it in hell holes across the globe losing blood, limbs and buddies along the way. All sacrificed for those of us who love living our lives in freedom. He continues to serve our great nation today, in some unknown location, and unnamed capacity.

Like Colt, my friend remembers almost everything, so he was a great help in proofreading my earlier books, comparing facts. He pointed out when one of my favorite author's lead character's boat had three different speeds at wide-open-throttle in three different books. THIS is why I will never play cards with him. But some of my favorite and most interesting conversations have been with this man. He has experienced more in his lifetime than most people could in ten. He's also the one who picked out the forty-seven-foot Fountain Lightning model as Colt's mode of water transportation. Nice choice, pal!

"Colt", thank you for first being an inspiration, but most of all for being a friend. Wherever you are now, thank you for what you and your brethren have done and continue to do for every freedom-loving person in America. We all owe you a debt we'll never be able to repay.

PROLOGUE

C rozet, *Central Virginia, Present Day*

The "security fence" was a joke. Six feet high and made of plain old chain link, with no concertina or barbed wire at the top. The gate was even worse, a standard four-foot-high pipe gate from the farmers' supply in Charlottesville. It was secured by a chain and lock smaller than Joe Shifflett would have used for a bicycle. His compact bolt cutters snapped right through the first link of the loose chain with little effort, and he put both halves of the link in his pocket. There would be no forensic evidence left behind to match up to his bolt cutters.

With his gloved hands, he pushed the gate open as he scanned the area beyond it. There were no cameras, alarms, or motion sensors that he could see, either on the fence or the building. Surrounded by woods and tucked back behind a sawmill between Route 250 and I-64, he was far out of sight of any passing motorists. In the twilight, he could see several deer grazing in the grassy field beyond the parking lot and the small open-sided pole shed at the end of the gravel drive-way. They had no problem either jumping the gate, or heck, maybe there was even a hole in the fence back toward the woods.

Joe chuckled as he thought to himself that for such a high-tech business, these people sure were low tech when it came to security. He figured they depended on most folks not knowing they were back here. These must be some really dumb eggheads; book smart but lacking in common sense. The truth was most of the 9,500 residents of Crozet had seen one or more of their automated cars running around the roads during testing. They were kind of hard to miss, each with a rack similar to a cop's light bar on top loaded with a bunch of weird-looking instruments. Funny looking things on the front and back bumpers, too. And it was hard not to notice that the people in those cars didn't have their hands on the steering wheels. Just another bunch of computer geeks cashing in on some government grant money he guessed.

He walked past a large concrete block building on his right, which turned out to have a huge carport in the back with half a dozen Tesla sedans under it, all of them loaded up with those same instrument packages. These were the cars he had seen out testing on the roads around Crozet. He figured the carport must be their charging station since most had cords attached. But he wasn't interested in the cars. He shook his head and smiled. Even with around half a million dollars' worth of automobiles here, there still was no sign of any cameras or security systems, though the cars would no doubt still have their factory alarms. Not that anybody was around to hear them if they went off.

Under the pole shed just ahead sat an older model Ford F-150 pickup, loaded with more of those same instruments on top. Joe saw there was a charging cord connected to it, so they must have converted it to electric like the Teslas. But again, he wasn't interested in the pickup. What he was after was the construction equipment to the right of the shed. There were two large tracked excavators, a few bulldozers, track loaders, and on the end was the first thing on his list for this afternoon, a brand-new tractor-sized front end loader and backhoe combination. This one was already pre-sold, and he had a good prospect for one of the track loaders. He knew about all the equipment here because a buddy of his was a driver for a national shipping company, and Joe paid him well for leads on where he might find equipment to steal. Nobody pays attention to their package delivery guy when he walks back to his truck and is busy texting on his phone. Only in this case, he was secretly taking video for Joe instead of texting.

The construction equipment all had those same instrument packages attached to them but Joe knew he could quickly strip it all off after he got back to the shop. He had left his nondescript semi-truck and its lowboy trailer on the gravel entrance road with its loading ramps down. The truck was backed in for a quick getaway in case he ran into trouble, not that he was expecting any. It was late Sunday afternoon, and the sawmill next door was closed. The nearest occupied house was a half-mile down the road, and he was just over a minute and a half away from the on-ramp to I-64. This section of the interstate is loaded with cameras and radiation sensors because of being a main feeder to Charlottesville. Unbeknownst to most of the populace, Albemarle county is packed with clandestine government defense and intelligence agency outposts. Because of the cameras, Joe had replaced his license plates with some from another identical semi. Any recordings from the cameras would lead the cops to that truck, which was based two towns away from Joe's shop.

Joe climbed up into the cab on the backhoe/loader and pulled out a ring of construction equipment master keys from his pocket. He found the one that fit and tried starting the engine. Nothing. It was like the batteries were dead. He figured that the egghead engineers must have disconnected the batteries since he'd seen that done many times before as a theft deterrent. This was why he'd brought along a crescent wrench in case he had to reattach and tighten the terminal clamps. Joe climbed down out of the cab and unlatched the cowls over the batteries. He never heard the semi-autonomous Tesla moving up behind him until some of the gravel drive crunched under its front tires. The custom metal front instrument rack pinned him against the backhoe's chassis as he tried to spin around toward the Tesla. He screamed as the car continued to move forward, crushing both of his knees. As it backed up, Joe fell to the ground, still screaming. He didn't even notice as the backhoe started itself, moving just beyond him. He was now in the range of the backhoe bucket which slammed down onto his head, crushing his skull and killing him instantly.

The backhoe scooped up Joe's body and drove out into the field as the deer slowly walked away, since they were used to the unmanned equipment moving around and realized the machines posed no threat to them. The backhoe stopped at a predetermined point and dug a deep hole. Once completed, it dropped Joe's body in and returned the dirt to the hole. The machine compacted the dirt in the same way it had dispatched Joe, using the flat part of the bucket to mash it down. Once finished, it dragged the front loader backward across the area, smoothing it out. The raw, red Virginia dirt matched so much of the disturbed area where all the equipment was continually undergoing testing. It returned to where it had killed Joe after picking up a front scoop of gravel from a nearby stockpile. The backhoe distributed the gravel across the area which still had a large red pool and spatters of gray matter. It spread and smoothed the gravel as it had the dirt over Joe's final resting place. Once finished, through its cameras and sensors, it determined there was no visible trace on the property of Joe ever having been there. The backhoe returned to its place in the line of construction equipment and shut down.

Joe had made some false and ultimately deadly assumptions. The first was that since there were no obvious standard security devices, the business and the equipment were unprotected. The second and most lethal was that the old Ford pickup under the shed had been converted to electric power. In fact, it no longer ran at all and was actually the sentinel. The large cable was only partly for power but mostly for data, coming from an array of lidars – a laser based radar, microphones, motion detectors, heat sensors, and other detection devices mounted on the old truck. It had sensed Joe's presence just as it had the deer, and it had fed the raw data to what was dubbed the "Mini Brain" in a room underneath the adjacent building. The electronic brain recognized the security threat, came up with a plan of defense, and uploaded instructions to the backhoe and the Tesla, all in a fraction of a second. The autonomous part of the backhoe took it from there, sending updates back to the Mini Brain wirelessly at the rate of sixty times per second. Mini Brain would only overrule the backhoe if the situation exceeded its preset parameters.

A few minutes later a black late-model Range Rover pulled up outside the gate, soon followed by a new black Navigator. Lloyd Heatherton, CEO of Contour Auto Tech climbed out of the Rover and met up with Will Rinehart, his chief of security, and one of Will's men. The Mini Brain had already texted numeric codes to both Lloyd and Will which represented a perimeter breach, equipment targeted, intruder neutralized, and situation normal. In these days of metadata storage, neither man wanted anything sent "in the clear" that might be obvious to a law enforcement agent.

Lloyd looked over the semi, turned to Will, and said simply, "Make it disappear." Will nodded and motioned to his companion to get into the cab while he raised the two rear ramps. The driver hot-wired the ignition, and the diesel clattered to life with a cloud of black carbon spewing from each stack. Without a word, Will headed back to the Navigator and took the point position, leading the semi to a rough neighborhood in Charlottesville where it would be left on the street, still idling. It would find a new home within a half-hour and be in someone else's parts inventory within a day.

Lloyd walked over to the gate and opened the padlock, re-fastening the now slightly shorter chain. He climbed back into the Range Rover knowing the property along with its biggest secret was still secure.

$$1$$

THE OFFER

My custom white and red Fountain 47 Lightning "go-fast" boat, *Blitz*, has become even more important for my work than it used to be. To be honest, I bought it for recreation. It was an expensive toy, but in my mind, it was also a necessary tool to blow off steam because my job is at times... stressful. *Very* stressful. Most of the time in fact. Explosions, flying lead, and "bad guys that are the basis for nightmares" kind of stressful. So, as a forty-five-year-old bachelor with only a condo to maintain and a semi-serious girlfriend, Nancy, who as a medical resident doesn't have a lot of spare time for herself or me, *Blitz* fits in well with my life.

My number one customer needed me to do more work from their Norfolk location starting back a few years ago. I live in Woodbridge in Northern Virginia, or as we call it here in the Old Dominion, NOVA. It's convenient to Washington DC where I do a fair amount of work. But driving to Norfolk means taking I-95 south to I-64, then east. One hundred eighty-five miles of Interstate for a trip that should take just over three hours. You've got about a one in ten shot of making it in that amount of time or less. There are usually long stretches of slow or stopped traffic on either Interstate. By water, even with all the twists and turns of the upper Potomac, the same trip is ten miles shorter. But going by water also means no traffic jams, no speed limits between NOVA and Norfolk, and a lot less stress. *Blitz* cruises at over fifty miles per hour, and at wide-open-throttle her brand new twin Mercury 1350's can push her beyond a hundred and twenty. So, if I need to get down there in a hurry I can while burning a tad over a gallon of fuel per mile. Still, she's almost as fast as a helicopter, and while she's loud, she still draws less attention. Plus, I have a "floating apartment" when I get where I'm going. She's equipped with a vee berth, a small galley (kitchen), a "head" (bathroom), a stereo and a small flat screen TV.

I work in the "security" business. My customers are corporations, though probably not in the sense you are thinking. You'll never see their names on a race car, or on your kid's peewee baseball team's jersey. If everything goes well, you'll never hear their names, period, because they don't advertise. They specialize in handling things that aren't either black or white, operating in and concentrating on the gray areas of the world.

My customers also have a lot of government business from those "Alphabet Soup" agencies. The ones that are better known by only a few initials. Washington plays by strange rules, and it seems that the fastest way to make a name for yourself there is by dragging someone else's name through the mud. The best way to avoid that happening to you is to be able to say truthfully under oath, "I have no knowledge of that, Senator." It's the golden "get out of jail free" phrase for the DC elite. Our job is to provide them with plausible deniability, and it doesn't come cheap. And since I lack that luxury, I charge a lot of money for risking my neck to cover some politico's butt. My customers then get to charge the government even more for my services. Let them deal with the creative billing headaches; that's why I like having a middleman. You can't send Homeland Security an invoice that says, *One Russian mobster dispatched, one private aircraft destroyed over deep water, one pound of C4, one detonator, hazardous waste disposal fee (additional C4). Tax exempt. Please remit this total and Thank You for your repeat business!*

My customers take care of the issues that would be, well, embarrassing if they were dealt with through normal channels. Heaven forbid we should make the Russian president blush over one of his out-of-control plutocrats running wild in the US with diplomatic immunity and traceable Kremlin connections. Not that the Russian president has ever blushed in his life. But by handling things in a low-key manner on our side, it allows everyone to save face and avoid an international incident. Okay, so maybe a pound of C4 going off onboard a private jet isn't all that low key, but it is compared to certain other solutions. Like a radioactive "Mickey" slipped in a drink in a Georgetown bar by a foreign operator working on US soil. Or a Russian nerve agent administered uncontained in public. These are two of their favorite "solutions" which also tend to create a public panic and are eventually traceable back to their source. Not something we need to have happen within our borders.

My customers help our government avoid that kind of nightmare, so all the Washington agencies can semi-truthfully swear, "It wasn't us!" Do laws get bent or broken in the process? Maaaybe... That's why we are in business, why we charge so much, and why *Blitz* is paid for. Because sometimes the best solution isn't always the neatest or cleanest one. But before you get the idea my customers and I will do anything for a buck, you need to know my customers are all patriots. Most of the people I work for and with have served our nation in the armed forces, just as I did. We all swore an oath to defend the USA. We meant it then, and we still mean it now. I won't work for or with people that don't share that dedication. And while we may do work for the government, we also don't play politics, nor will we let either party play us. Never have, never will.

Today is a beautiful and calm early morning on the Potomac. *Blitz* is purring like a kitten at cruising speed with her two new power plants. I'll turn that purr into a roar when I reach the Chesapeake. It's Thursday, and instead of Norfolk, my destination today is *Chesapeake Bayside Resort* on the Eastern Shore of Virginia. That part of the peninsula is more commonly referred to as ESVA. *Bayside* is one of my favorite places; a year ago, it was just a defunct inn and marina, but then it was bought by a guy named Casey Shaw from Florida. He and the group he put together have renovated and expanded it, and it's becoming the best place to chillax on the Chesapeake. Casey's become a good friend in a short amount of time; he's a lot of fun to fish and hang out with. But I'm not headed to *Bayside* to relax or fish today, I'm headed to see a customer.

Maybe I should rephrase that. I'm headed there to see my largest customer, the one I do over ninety percent of my business with, my old friend Conrad Jenkins. He sent me a cryptic text asking me to meet with him today and offering no explanation. But in this business full of secrecy and surprises, a text like that isn't really unusual.

Conrad is in his mid-sixties and has built his company into a stealthy powerhouse. It's become the "go to" group in DC when things get out of control and there's a need for swift and quiet solutions. His "right-hand person" is his daughter Rikki, his only living relative. She's one of my favorite people in the world, and like a niece to me. She's now just over thirty, and I've been working with Conrad for almost twenty years. I've watched Rikki grow up, get into this business, and become one of the best field operatives out there. I know Conrad plans on passing his business to her at some point. She was on her last field assignment several months ago when she ended up getting shot in the shoulder, right at *Bayside*. If Conrad hadn't already decided to pull her out of the field, that would have done it.

Like Conrad, Rikki now lives aboard her own boat in *Bayside's* marina on the private South Dock. Conrad just leased space for his business in a new building on site that also houses Casey Shaw's offices. Sounds like a strange place to operate from, except that it's only a little over an hour away from Norfolk by car (faster by *Blitz*), and half an hour from DC via one of Shaw Air's charter aircraft, an offshoot of the resort. The local airport is only four minutes away, and there's a helicopter pad at the resort. Conrad's business maintains a two-bedroom apartment in DC that Conrad and Rikki use when they need to stay there overnight. But they both are on the go a lot, and *Bayside* is a great place to come home to and decompress compared to DC or Norfolk.

The best part of *Bayside* though is the group of people that make the private South Dock their home, at least in the summer. Casey lives there with his fiancée and business partner, Dawn McAlister. They make a great looking couple; at forty-two he's six-feet tall with shaggy sandy-colored hair. Dawn is only an inch shorter, with bright red below-her-shoulder length hair and bright blue eyes that you can spot from across the room. She's much sharper at business than most folks many years older than her thirty years. The two of them live aboard their 110-foot Hargrave yacht, *Lady Dawn*.

Then there's Conrad, who has a Mainship Pilot 34 called *Plan B*. He found this place after meeting Casey, Dawn, and Casey's now soon to be ex-wife Sally (the "ex" part being a story for another day) and being told about their new marina. After seeing it, Conrad turned me on to *Bayside* too.

Rikki, or Rik as her closest friends now call her, and her girlfriend Cindy Crenshaw own an older fifty-two-foot Hatteras motor yacht named *Hibiscus*. The two of them met about the time Rikki was leaving field work, and they clicked the minute they saw each other. Cindy started off as the resort manager but was quickly brought in as a partner by Casey and Dawn, no doubt because they have big plans for her. Looks like she also has a bright future with Rikki.

Conrad and I both like Cindy and the difference in Rikki since they got together has been amazing. Not that she wasn't ever happy before, but just not at this level. She has had a hard time trusting people. Part of it was due to the job, but also due to some rough personal experiences in her past. Casey was much the same way when he and Rikki met, and it initially caused some friction between the two. Now though, other than his fiancée Dawn, Rikki has become his number one "gal pal" and fishing companion. He's at the very top of her friends list.

Speaking of rough starts, Casey's other good buddy has become part of the *Bayside* scene, Eric Clarke. Eric and his daughter, Elaina, or as her close friends and father call her, Missy, are both new to the South Dock. They came to *Bayside* over the Memorial Day holiday and were invited to a "meet the owners" party at Casey's hideaway "clubhouse" nicknamed C3. It turned out that Casey and Eric both hated crowds, and they also had issues with each other when they first met. But both loved fishing, and Dawn pushed them to go (with me and Conrad, too.) Once away from the crowds both relaxed and found out they had a lot in common other than just their ages and they became fast friends. It was funny; Casey knew Eric was a "hitter," his mint condition seventy-five-foot vintage Trumpy yacht "*Miss E*" was a tipoff about that. But at the time he didn't know Eric was the multi-billionaire owner of Clarke Foods, the largest organic food company in the country. To meet the guy, you would pick up on the fact he's a class act and doesn't put on airs. But if he's in his fishing duds you might not figure that he has two nickels to rub together. Now he's building the first house at *Chesapeake Bayside Club*, a high-end, high-service-level development Casey, Dawn, and Cindy are creating. Eric recently bought into *Bayside* too, but they are all tight-lipped about that (I know the details, and I'm not telling either).

Eric met his current girlfriend, Congresswoman Candace "Candi" Ryan, a few months ago when she came over to *Bayside* to spend a weekend with her good friend Janice Colton, Conrad's girlfriend. Candi is retiring from Congress at the end of the year after over a decade, and is landing a few board seats, including one at *Bayside*. Oops, I'm not supposed to say anything about that yet.

Last, but not least, is the most colorful member of the *Bayside* South Dock Bunch, Sanford "Sandy" Morgan. Best-selling author in his latter-60's, owner of the best fishing store in the Florida Keys, and one hell of a great fisherman. Looks the part, too. At 5'-9", he has longish white hair, a scruffy beard, and a gold circle earring in his left ear. But a word of warning about Sandy, he has *no* "filter" when it comes to opinions. He says what he's thinking, all the time. Which is okay with me because he's funny as hell, and you never have a problem trying to figure out where he's coming from.

Sandy lives aboard his fifty-five-foot trawler with his two blond mates/muses, Micah and Carol, who are in their early twenties. They idolize Sandy, and we were all wondering just how far that relationship stretched until we found out they are his nieces. Again, something no one outside our group is supposed to know.

After Sandy's wife died, he sold his house and moved aboard, determined to cruise and write his way up and down the east coast. His two younger sisters worried about the idea until their daughters decided to go to work for him. The young women take care of the trawler and Sandy's flats boat while they watch out for him. He pays them regular mate's pay, plus he's teaching them about the writing business since both are aspiring novelists. All three say it's a great deal, especially when Sandy's fans buy rounds in bars, thinking they really are his girlfriends. He claims the whole "Hefner" facade helps him sell books. The jury is still out on that because he sells millions of each new title, muses or not, but I think it's more to keep unattached widows at bay. Anyway, he was headed to New England, but hit *Bayside* and decided to stay for the summer. I'm glad he did because he's a lot of fun. He and I have had long talks on his back deck after he found out I was a technical consultant for one of his fellow best-selling authors. I'm looking forward to hanging out with him this weekend after I get this business issue out of the way, whatever it is.

Forty-five minutes after leaving *Blitz's* slip on the Occoquan River, I passed the Little Wicomico River's inlet on the Virginia side, at the mouth of the Potomac where it meets the Chesapeake. I set a new more southerly course that would take me below Tangier Island, and straight to *Bayside Marina's* inlet. On this calm day at low cruise with these new engines I can be there in twenty-five minutes. Or I can push it and make it in close to ten. I went to wide-open-throttle for two minutes, thankful for the sturdy curved windscreen that's taking the brunt of the wind at 120 mph. Even so, I'm still getting buffeted, and my eyes are streaming tears behind my wraparound sunglasses. The feeling of exhilaration at this speed is intense. I'm jammed back into the custom Fountain racing-style seats that wrap around my torso and hold me still; grateful for the kill switch lanyard attached to my shirt. Not that I believe I'd survive being ejected at this speed. I slowly pull the throttles back to what I consider a high-speed cruise, about 60 mph. The engine lifespan at this speed is hundreds of hours longer than it is at full throttle. It's not about always running over a hundred, it's just nice to know I can if I need to.

I pulled into *Bayside Marina* twenty minutes later and backed into my new slip next to Sandy's trawler. Climbing onto the new finger pier I secured *Blitz* while letting the engines idle for two minutes before I shut them off. Their four turbochargers don't like being shut down hot, as that's a great way to seize their uber-expensive bearings. It's a good idea to let them cool down with a nice steady flow of oil.

Casey and crew just had four new finger piers installed perpendicular to the main South Dock that created these slips for Sandy, Conrad, and me. They left the rest of the 700-foot-long dock open for larger yachts, though *Hibiscus* is moored on it too. It's more comfortable for Conrad and Rikki that way, with a little room between them. Not that they don't get along, because they do. But space at the dock helps ensure this'll continue.

"I thought you said you were getting quieter engines!" Sandy was at the rail on his aft deck yelling louder than necessary. I forgot to tell you, he's kind of a curmudgeon. Just ignore that part because I do. He doesn't mean it. At least not much.

"I did. These are much quieter, Sandy."

"These still rattle the fillings out of my teeth! Shut those sonofabitches down!"

"In a minute. Have to let them cool."

"Damned noisy Johnson extender. That's all that thing is!"

"I missed you this week too, Sandy. Glad to be back for an EXTENDED weekend, you can buy me a few beers."

Sandy snorted. "You, first." He has gotten too used to people buying him drinks. "Hey, I've got something I want to show you that's weird."

"We aren't talking about a rash or anything medical, right? Nancy isn't here this weekend. Plus, she sees enough of that at Fairfax General."

"Ha, ha. Funny guy. No, I'm serious. This is something you should look into."

"I have to go meet with Conrad, but after that I'll come over."

"Good. Make sure you bring beer though, I'm out."

I doubted that. "It's not even noon yet!"

"It will be by the time you get through jawboning with Conrad. So, I'll show you this first, then we can go to the *Beach Café* and you can buy me a beer AND lunch." He turned from the rail and crossed back to his writing chair and table.

I shook my head, knowing I would indeed be on the hook for lunch, and there would definitely be more than one beer involved. No doubt it wouldn't be the last time this summer, either. I shut down both engines and climbed over the gunwale again onto the finger pier and then down the main dock. The tide was out, and the aluminum ramp that led up to land was at a steep angle, so it slowed me a bit. I lost both legs below the knees over in, well, never mind where or how I lost them, that story is still under wraps. Anyway, I take ramps just a tad slower with my prosthetics. At the top, I went through the new security gate in the fence which now partitions off the South Dock from the public. Casey hired Conrad's company to secure *Bayside*, and this was one of the new changes. With higher-profile customers like Eric Clarke, Congresswoman Ryan, and Sandy Morgan, protecting privacy and providing security around here had become a big concern of the resort's management.

I walked over to Conrad and Rikki's offices, following the marina's asphalt driveway to the brick paver circular drive in front of *Bayside's* boutique hotel. All of the resort's buildings are clad in gray faux cedar shingles and green metal roofs, giving them a real Nantucket-esque feel. They've also installed extensive landscaping with colorful flower beds. Conrad's office is in a long, low, single-story building, partially obscured by some of these new plantings. At the far end next to a glass entrance was a small black sign with gold letters, "McAlister and Shaw." However, the near end had just a simple glass door with no signage. Until now. In gold leaf with black outlines across the glass it now read, "ESVA Security Corporation." That caught me off guard. I'd never heard of ESVA Security before. I walked through the door, and as usual, there was no one behind the reception desk, the place looked deserted.

"Come on back, Colt." Conrad's voice boomed from his office; no doubt he'd seen me on his camera monitor. As I walked back, I noticed a door on the left side of the hallway that hadn't been there a week ago. What the heck is going on with that? On the right Rikki's office was empty, but I saw she was already in Conrad's as I entered and sat in the client chair next to hers. She smiled at me and shrugged her shoulders as if to say, "I don't know what this is about, either."

"Thanks for coming. I know you picked up on the changes as you came in. They were a surprise to Rikki too, she just got back from a two-day new client meeting on the west coast, and I've been busy while she was gone.

"I've been doing a lot of thinking these past few months since you've been out of field work, Rikki. You've come on strong in the office, and you impressed the hell out of Eric Clarke and Casey Shaw, getting us both Eric's business and *Bayside's* business as well as a seat on *Bayside's* board for yourself. In the process, you've bolstered our high end client protection unit and created a whole new division for us, facility security. With that new west coast client Eric just sent our way, this new division is going to get even busier. All this is happening when there have been changes in my life, and I want to make even more.

"Finding Janice has been good for me, and I want to spend more time with her. She makes me happy, and apparently vice versa. But with the business poised to expand, it would mean more time away from here and Janice, and that's not something I want nor am willing to do at this point in my life."

As Conrad paused and leaned back into his chair, I glanced over at Rik and gave her a "Why am I here?" look. The look she shot back said, "We're both about to find out." Conrad named his boat "Plan B" because he always had one. Usually a Plan C, too. So, whatever this is was well thought out.

"Colt, you're no doubt wondering why I asked you to be here."

"Well, so far this seems like a conversation just the two of you should be having, alone."

"Is that what you think, Rikki?"

"I think I might know where you are going with this, so no, I don't. Colt needs to be here."

I saw her wink at Conrad, and he returned a smile.

"Colt, you have been the closest thing to family to both Rikki and me for the past twenty-some years. You've covered our butts and helped me expand this business more than anyone except Rikki. We've built this business by being willing to change and adapt, and it looks like there will be a lot more of that soon, which is why there's a name on the door now. Part of the changes will be that the new side of the business needs to be somewhat more visible. Right at the time when I want to become even less visible. I've decided that I want to offer Rikki an "earn-out" for seventy-five percent of the business, meaning she'll pay me a percentage of profits up to a certain number. Plus, the business will continue to pay me rent on the Norfolk complex, which I'll still own. Rikki does that sound like something you'd be interested in?"

"Absolutely, Dad, thank you. But with you gone, and the business growing, I'm going to need some help. Someone who knows the business. A partner." Again, she winked at Conrad.

"I was hoping you'd say that. You have anyone in mind?" He grinned.

"What do you think, Colt? Are you up for it?" Rik raised an eyebrow at me.

I took my time answering. This was the last thing I expected when I walked in here, and it would change my life. In most ways, it looked on the surface to be good, but I had concerns. As an independent contractor, I chose the jobs I wanted, I worked when I wanted and was my own boss with no employees, just customers. Granted there was no one else that I'd want as a partner other than Rikki, but it might change our personal relationship, and I like things the way they are.

"It's a lot to absorb. Can I give you an answer after I think about it? You and I will need to sit down and chat about a lot of things before I do, Rikki. Is that all right with you?"

Rik smiled at me. "I'd have been disappointed in you if you didn't want time to think this over. How about coming over for drinks on *Hibiscus* about five, and I can answer anything you think of by then. I'm not pushing for an answer today, just creating an opportunity to chat over any concerns you might have with no pressure attached. Then how about dinner at Rooftops with Cindy and me afterward? You and Janice too, Dad?"

I nodded. "That makes good sense. Five it is."

Conrad replied, "I was about to suggest dinner myself. There's more to this, but it has to wait until tonight."

"One more thing, what's that new door in the hallway, Dad?"

"My new smaller office. It'll be finished in a week, then you can have this one. Whoever joins you to help run this will get your old office." My old friend and customer gave me a hopeful look.

2

———

MEDIA FOR SALE

"You know I've been helping Carol and Micah with their writing."

"I do, Sandy. Darned nice of you, considering your busy writing schedule."

"Well, they are both naturals at it, so it doesn't take up a lot of my time. Micah has now finished her first book, I've read it, and we had it edited and proofread. Since it's so tough getting an agent these days and even tougher getting signed by a traditional publisher, she decided on going the independent route. I offered to help her get an agent, but both she and Carol want to do this on their own. I admire them for that, it's difficult to make a go in publishing today, especially via the 'indie' route. You need to provide your own editing, marketing, advertising, basically everything. The big advantage to indie publishing is they accept everything, at least they had up until now. You don't need to build an inventory, it's all sent either electronically, or printed one at a time in a 'just in time' system. Order a book today, it's printed tonight, and in your mailbox the day after tomorrow. There are also no advance dollars to pay back out of sales. So, whatever you make, you get to keep."

"So, what's the weird thing you wanted to show me?"

19

"I'm getting to that dammit, hold your horses. Anyway, the biggest, baddest indie house out there is Big Nile Publishing."

"I know. They have their own line of readers—"

"Are you going to let me tell this story, or you wanna write your own?" Sandy was even more agitated than usual. "So, the three of us go to upload her book, and we get this message, 'Sorry, but we are limiting the number of new authors and books we accept.' Can you believe it?"

"Maybe they are running out of server space?"

Sandy snorted. "I thought you were a computer guy. You should know on their retail sales non-book side they have the biggest Artificial Intelligence research lab of any corporation in the world. If anybody has extra server space, it would be them. They buy and lease servers by the boxcar load. And they are still asking manufacturers to sign up and sell other products across their platform. They don't want to miss a damned sale, it's part of their corporate culture. They want to sell everything that gets sold, anywhere in the world. So, by shutting out new submissions and new authors, they KNOW they're pushing them to the number two eBook seller and they'll end up competing with them. BNP has consistently paid more than any of the others because they want first crack at all the new stuff. They currently have over ten million titles in their catalog. Nine and a half million of them only sell a book or a download or less per month. If they were looking to make server space, wouldn't you ditch those and make room for new product first? Plus, none of that catalog costs them a dime other than server storage, they only pay the authors after something sells."

Sandy paused and looked at me to make sure he had my full attention. He did for now, but so far this wasn't earth-shaking stuff.

"That's just the start, it gets even weirder. The muses and I went to their New Releases list, to see who they were keeping on. None of their top-rated books are by anybody you've ever heard of. In fact, these authors don't exist! The girls found there wasn't any social media nor internet history for any of them, at least at first. Then slowly it started appearing, like somebody was making up their history for them."

I said with as much sarcasm as I could manage, "Yeah, well, if it's on the internet, it must be true."

"You want me to stop talking, or do you want to listen? I haven't gotten to the part that'll blow your mind yet. So, I got my muses the best software I could that digs down into Big Nile to analyze sales data, key search engine words, and title rankings. Don't look at me like that, it's all legal. Anyway, I can see a list of new titles as they are being added. I looked up a few, and they already have almost a hundred reader reviews. In ONE day. I'm lucky to get that in a week, and some unknown writer is getting this in a day? It's not possible. They don't even have time to read the damned things!"

"Don't they have advanced reader copy giveaways? Perhaps they were read over the past week."

"I thought about that, but then I found the part that will blow your mind. It's not possible they could have existed a week ago. They center some of these new political books on things that the president said just hours ago. These are 350+ pages long. It's not possible that a human being wrote these. They are machine written."

Now he had my full attention. "Like AI? Wow. Makes sense. The Japanese have AI-assisted song lyric writers. So, they are bent on replacing humans with machines. It's happening in factories all over the world. So, then they'll keep the book royalties for themselves, and I guess we are talking big bucks here. If they are willing to drop new authors, it would only be for a product with higher margins. Like ones with no royalty payout. And they wouldn't want competition for those."

Sandy nodded. "Exactly. Their Big Nile Book Club where readers pay a fixed monthly fee for unlimited access to books pays out almost a billion dollars in royalties to its authors each year. That doesn't even include the income from regular downloads and printed media. AI product would become almost pure profit to them. Five years ago, they were losing money, and now they are profitable overall. Think what this would do for them."

"Interesting, but hardly illegal. Maybe they'll have to put a disclaimer on there, 'Written by Machine.' I doubt it'll put you out of business, Sandy."

"It won't, but I still haven't gotten to the scary part."

"Trust me, I'm listening."

He handed me a tablet opened to the library page of his e-reader. "Look at those first two books and their author names. Michael Johnson and John Michaelson. These are the two of the books I was talking about that included those hour-old comments from the president. These two books are total opposites and are as raw and rabid politically as they come. One to the left, and the other to the right. Over the same subject, spun in opposing directions. These are designed to foment hate and incite the reader and are full of false and misleading statements. They make the big two cable news outlets that are so politically opposed to each other seem like centrists."

"Not great, I'll agree, but it's likely protected under the First Amendment. Nothing illegal here."

"What if I told you these were ads, offering their services to the highest bidder? Rip one party or the other for a price."

"That would be bad, but again, I see nothing illegal here."

"Check the endorsements on the inside page. You'll see they are the same in both books. They also disappeared an hour after I read them. I downloaded those copies and shut off the WIFI on the tablet, so Big Nile couldn't upload a new copy on it and erase the old one."

I went to the page Sandy was talking about. There written in French, Hebrew, Arabic, Russian, Korean and Chinese was the message, 'As we said, you can control the political narrative for a price. You now see we can deliver what we promised. Books, blogs, news, all of it. The election is in one hundred days.'

"Sandy, I'm going to need this tablet."

"I already ordered a new one. It'll be here tomorrow. Here's the invoice for it for you to give Conrad."

"This tablet is a basic model at least five years old! You want him to replace it with the deluxe one?"

"Yeah, but the information is brand new, and you can't get it anywhere else." He grinned his "you can buy me another beer" grin. "And I'm guessing lunch is gonna be late." I nodded then took the tablet and headed for the office again.

Rik and I sat in the same chairs across from Conrad again as I laid out the scenario to her and Conrad. He looked across his desk at both of us. "There could be some First Amendment entanglements here, but it's definitely intended as information warfare. A mercenary advertising campaign."

Rik shook her head. "I disagree that it might be protected, or at least it shouldn't be. The First Amendment was intended to protect the voices of American citizens, and a free press, regardless of bias. This isn't about either. That offer isn't in either English or Spanish, so it's obvious the intent was to sell some foreign entity influence in the upcoming election by controlling the largest player in the literary market while shutting out any opposition. Plus, I doubt they'll stop there, I bet they go with 'wide distribution' across the major ebook selling platforms. Those all follow Big Nile and its ratings. Don't forget the tens of millions that were spent on investigating a single politically motivated dossier. Imagine what would happen if the book market was flooded with not just one but hundreds or even thousands of books on current events biased in a single direction. Some of them 'over the top' political books, but some not so 'in your face,' yet still with the same message in a subliminal form. Everything from techno-thrillers to children's books. Who needs online leaks when you can print whatever you want in books you can guarantee top ratings for and get everyone talking about? Pure propaganda that you have to pay for."

Conrad nodded thoughtfully. "What about authors? They would need authors for talk shows and interviews."

Rik answered, "Only for the largest sellers. No doubt they'll use actors, well briefed and prepared. And it looks like they also have a plan to flood blogs and news feeds, too. Maybe tap into the newswires with fake bylines? Who knows how far this goes."

I sat back and watched what was happening. Conrad "got" all this, but he wanted to make sure that Rik did, that she was ready to present our case to their company's government connections. Whatever this was, if we got turned loose on it, it was likely to have a huge payday. And ramifications that would be even bigger if we screwed up. Our confidentiality has a big price tag attached, and this one would need to be kept quiet, which meant Sandy, too. I knew who would be assigned that job, and I sure as heck wasn't looking forward to THAT conversation.

Rik looked over at me and I saw it coming. Her ice-blue eyes drilled into me as she smiled, silently conveying what I was afraid of. I said, "I know. How much do I offer him to stay quiet?"

"It's not how much, Colt. You have something much more valuable to him than money. Information. When he heard you were a tech advisor to that other writer, he lit up like a marlin on a live bait."

"That's the thing, Rik, he writes books about fishing, the water and people in marinas."

"Ah, but have you read Carol and Micah's work? Techno-thrillers. He'll do anything for his 'muses.' He's already supplied them with the best software, editors, and proofreaders."

"Okay, done. I'll see if I can sell it."

"My money is on you, which is partly why I'm hoping we end up as partners." She smiled that same smile again.

"So, I was right." Sandy shot me a look as I climbed up his gangway. It said this would cost me more than just lunch.

"Could be."

He snorted again. "Why don't you admit it?"

"Why don't we forget the whole thing happened."

"How about no? This is book material."

"You can't put it in a book, Sandy."

"Colt, I like you. But nobody, not even my late wife, God rest her, has ever been able to tell me what I can or can't do ever since I came of age. Especially not what I can or can't write. That includes you."

I leaned back as I settled into a deck chair as Sandy and I stared at each other. "Yeah, I guess it might make a decent book if there were more to the story. But then there's the whole First Amendment thing, and this is more of a gray area."

"I get the feeling you live in a gray world, and you're comfortable there."

I shrugged. "Life isn't always black and white, but I only work in a gray world, it's not where I live."

Sandy was silent again, which wasn't his normal state. He was usually talking or typing, and this time I knew he was thinking, just not out loud.

"I still say it could make a decent book, and if I were to whip it out in say six weeks, it could be a huge seller right before the election."

"Sandy, do you like what they are doing with this?"

"Of course not, that's why I want to write about it!"

"If you do that, your book could have just as much impact. The result being though that it would tear the country apart. Each side would blame the other, and neither would accept the election results. This might make you some money, but it would also gain you some enemies too. You could even do more damage than whoever is behind this."

"It's wrong, Colt. You know it, and I know it."

"And you want to profit from that?"

"No, but I want it stopped."

"Then just forget about everything we've said today and trust me to do that."

"That will take a lot of pull."

I nodded. "Sure will."

"Colt, I bet you've got a bunch of stories you haven't told your hack of a friend yet."

I smiled. Sandy took it as an answer, but I meant it as a sign of setting the hook. "One or two."

"My muses are into writing techno-thrillers."

"That's what I hear."

"There is nothing I'd love better than to see them succeed at the craft. They are great wordsmiths, but they need great plot material and advising to get their careers launched."

"I like Carol and Micah, and I'd love to help both of them succeed."

"A few books worth of material."

"At least, Sandy."

"Okay. Besides, I write fiction, and nobody would believe this story coming from me anyway. Now, about that first of many lunches you owe me..."

That's when I spied Rik headed down the dock and turning onto Sandy's finger pier. "Colt, is *Blitz* gassed up?"

Sounded like we would make a Norfolk run. "Yeah, climb aboard, I'll get the lines." I turned to Sandy, "Looks like I will owe you that lunch."

"And more. I take it this has to do with what we talked about."

"I don't recall any conversation, Sandy. See you soon."

3

TYLER TOO

s we idled out of the marina Rik told me that there were now alarms going off all over DC because of what we found. They were keeping it compartmentalized at the highest levels but treating it with the same seriousness as a potential full-on cyber-attack, part of information warfare. She and Conrad now had a "carte blanche" contract to investigate it further and take "all appropriate action." That was part of the whole plausible deniability thing. The "Powers That Be" wanted it to go away, and they're willing to pay to make it so without involving agencies that could drag it into the spotlight of the political realm. Now Rik had her business face on. "We need to be at the shop like yesterday."

I shoved the throttles to the firewall, and *Blitz* responded. Further conversation was impossible at over a hundred miles an hour because of the wind and the roar of the engines. But I could see that despite the seriousness of the task ahead, Rik was enjoying the ride. She used to wear her naturally platinum hair long, and it got all tangled riding on *Blitz* unless she secured it. But a few months ago she went with a short look, and it now agreed with speed. She had a big smile as we rocketed across the bay.

A little under half an hour later we pulled into the Elizabeth

River, idling past the fleet at Naval Station Norfolk and over the Midtown Tunnel. This gave us time to discuss our additional thoughts and scenarios. Then we ducked down Scott Creek past a big marina and idled back up a side channel that led to a dilapidated boat shed with four roll-up doors. I hit the button on a fob attached to my port engine key and the nearest door raised. As soon as we were clear, I closed it behind us. The slip next to this one was empty, but the far two held a pair of thirty-two-foot "go fasts" with flat finish paint jobs. Not quite as fast as *Blitz*, but few were. The whole setup here screamed "drug smugglers," which is exactly what we wanted it to. Local law enforcement understood we were "quasi-governmental" and left us alone. Everyone on the water did the same out of fear of the unknown. It all worked.

Rik and I walked across a deserted parking area to a large dilapidated industrial building behind the Portsmouth Marine Terminal. The side door opened into a large enclosed parking area that could hold a few dozen vehicles, and it was already well over half full. This was the complex that Conrad was now keeping and renting back to Rikki, a place we called "The Shop." Despite how it looked outside, it was in perfect condition and partitioned out into offices, conference rooms, armory, communications center, and electronics lab. Not everything we use is available off the shelf, and we have some great electronics gurus.

We headed into the largest conference room where Rik's hand-picked team members were assembled and waiting. Most were ex-military, and those that weren't had various intelligence agency experience. We had the same basic goals, but the pay was better in this part of the private sector. Rik explained the situation and pointed out whoever in the company took part was "running naked," because if they got caught at any point, they would be "DKed by DC." Meaning they 'Don't Know" us, and we'd all be open to criminal prosecution. Uncle Sam would have his legal blinders on even though "he" was our client, in an arm's length kind of way. But this also meant that we would use as much latitude as we needed, legal or not, to avoid getting caught. Being as stealthy as possible would be essential. The fewer electronic and physical footprints we left, the better.

Rikki continued, "You would think this is a clear-cut case of treason or foreign espionage, but it isn't. This is one of those times where the law has not kept up with technology. We are certain an AI program that was given instructions to lean in a certain political direction wrote that. If it libels someone, who then is responsible? And assuming they gave it free rein other than political direction, again who is responsible? The programmer didn't write the books, the computer did. You can't arrest a computer, but you can darned sure pull the power plug. And you can also put pressure on whoever is funding the project. To do that, we need to understand who the players are, and where their vulnerabilities lie.

"We think it's likely David Buxton, the chairman and founder of Big Nile Publishing and their related enterprises, might be the one pulling the strings on this. No doubt his board of directors would have had to approve a project of this size, thinking it was just about replacing human writers and reducing the cost of the publisher's content. We're talking ten figures in annual profit here. However, the way they handled that leads us to conclude there is or will shortly be an auction of some sort, with the winner controlling the direction of the writing in the time leading up to the election as part of their information warfare. As a public company, Big Nile couldn't be the recipient of the proceeds from such a mercenary messaging auction, it would be too damaging if it were discovered. We suspect that they developed this as an afterthought, piggybacking on BNP's AI writing project. They would have kept it to a tight group that stands to benefit, and we suspect someone hand-picked by David Buxton controls this group.

"You all have worked with Colt Toffler, and he will be taking point position on the electronic and research sides of this. Colt?"

"Thanks, Rikki. Okay, here's what we theorize so far. As Rikki said, David Buxton is probably the lead bad actor in this, but he's unlikely to be the one dealing with the auction participants. There is probably some private website for the auction and any communication between them beforehand. It's highly unlikely that it's in any way attached to Big Nile or even on their servers. We need to find it wherever it is.

"The AI brain is likely to be on Big Nile servers somewhere because of its massive size. They lease server farms all over the world, they would likely want to have it here in the US, just for physical security reasons. You wouldn't want this kind of technological breakthrough in a country where it might be seized and isolated if you want to continue to profit from it. And no doubt what we are calling the 'AI Writer Project' would be known throughout various parts of the company. There would be payroll, legal, security, and other departments that would have to be aware of it. There should be a subgroup that controls the political targeting portion that isn't anywhere on Big Nile property, and that would be 'off the books.' They would have to run simulations like the one we just saw and have a backdoor connection to what we'll call the 'AI Writer Brain.' In addition to Big Nile's servers, they would need some hefty computing power themselves and a fast and secure com link, probably fiber. This location might also be where that auction platform is supported. Big Nile's headquarters is in Fairfax, Virginia, so it's not too far of a run for us.

"When you extrapolate it out farther, this AI Writer project had to have been in secret development for a while, under the auspices of their board. Somewhere during its creation, someone got the idea of slanting the finished product, and they hatched this separate plot. My bet is it was someone high in their AI department who would have been close to Buxton. I'd also bet he or she left the company, moving to wherever they created this sub project, and that some of their software engineers would have gone with that person. A project like this could have a payout a lot higher than any Big Nile options they would have hung around for, and this is likely to be in the form of offshore cash for all of them including Buxton. No sharing this with the public stockholders. Even though Buxton is chairman, he owns far less than ten percent of Big Nile."

I could see the wheels turning among the team, and there were side glances among certain members when I mentioned things that would be in their areas. "Okay, so here's where we start. You need to dig down through Big Nile's Annual and Quarterly reports. We are looking for large increases in AI spending. You are also looking for some person or persons high in their AI group that left after the AI Writer project was far along in development who might've also been close to Buxton. We're also looking for communication links between their headquarters and this AI Writer server farm. I want to find where it is. Then I want to find the communication link to that 'off the books' AI lab from the AI Writer server farm. I want to find its location, then I want to know who works there and everything about them including anything we could use as leverage against them. Wherever these servers are will no doubt have the highest security, both physical and cyber. This will be a complex multi-faceted operation. Not only do we have to stop this, but we also need to make sure it can't get started again. Information is our best weapon. Tomorrow being Friday, we need a group to head to Fairfax and find the 'local watering hole' where Big Nile employees go after work and see if we can't find out more about the AI Writer project group. Chat them up and see what we can get out of them.

"We need to identify everyone in the 'off the books' group; all the ones who could put this back together again after we take it apart. Rikki and I have a plan for dealing with them so that never happens. Make no mistake about what they're doing; for lack of a better word, it's treason. Maybe it doesn't fit the legal definition, and they might try to hide behind a warped interpretation of our First Amendment, but they are apparently offering to sell something beyond normal influence to a foreign entity for cash. Here instead of it being direct political influence, it's voter influence. They are trying to sell out America for money, and they're being damned smug about it. We will make sure that doesn't happen. Okay, let's get on it. We'll meet in here again at ten hundred hours tomorrow."

Rik and I idled out on *Blitz* just after four, happy to be on the water instead of the roads. Traffic had already backed up at the tunnels and bridges as was the norm for this time of day late in the workweek. We wouldn't be running as fast on the way back, but we'd still be at *Bayside* around an hour after we hit the Chesapeake, meaning we'd be only a half-hour late for the start of cocktail hour. Rik didn't bring up the stock offer while we idled back out to the Chesapeake. I was glad because I hadn't really thought about it yet, focusing instead on this AI threat. When we reached the bay I hit the gas, bringing *Blitz* up to a fast sixty-plus mph cruise. We could still talk, but we needed to almost yell, and both of us were lost in our own thoughts, anyway. An hour later we slowed down to make the turn into *Bayside Marina's* inlet, but we were behind a vintage twenty-five-foot Bertram Bahia Mar that was idling in ahead of us. It looked like only one person and a dog were aboard. He pulled over to the South Dock behind *Hibiscus* as we slid by and backed into my slip. This time I avoided Sandy's grumbling since he was nowhere in sight, probably over at the *Beach Café* with the muses for happy hour.

Rik hopped off and tied us up, and I joined her on the dock. That's when we noticed Carol was over by the Bertram, helping the young man tie up and connect his shore power. Rik said, "I think he's on the wrong side of the marina." We both knew they normally put smaller craft like that Bertram on the north side.

I replied, "That's strange because Carol would have told him that instead of helping him tie up." We walked up to the boat and gave her questioning looks, as she gave us a down low wave, so the man couldn't see it. He was busy operating a small hydraulic hoist connected to something with two parallel wheels. When he lifted it off the deck, we saw it was a Segway fitted with a folding seat and knobby BMX tires. This is a self-balancing personal transporter that can go up to twelve miles an hour, about the speed a top-ranked marathon runner can average. He moved it out over the dock and lowered it so that the handle hooked over the Bertram's gunwale, then it couldn't roll away once he detached it from the lift. Cindy walked up and handed him a paper just as he did. "Hi, Tyler, we spoke on the phone earlier, I'm Cindy. Here's your gate combination, and you can get signed in at the front desk of the hotel. Did you meet

Carol, Rikki, and Colt? We're all on the South Dock, too. Guys, meet Tyler MacKenzie."

"No, ma'am, I didn't. Nice to meet y'all." He looked to be in his mid-twenties, and I got a kick out of him calling Cindy, "ma'am." Apparently, Rik did too, as she tried to hide a smile. I had caught the light Southern accent he had and figured it had more to do with the culture of wherever he grew up rather than Cindy's age since she was probably less than ten years older than him. "And this is Kaili, my four-pawed helper." He motioned toward a good-looking golden doodle with a sweet face. She was lying down on the cushioned engine cover in the aft part of the cockpit, the same place Rik and I had spotted her on the way in. Her tail wagged at Tyler's mention of her name. Tyler swung his legs over the side as he sat on the covering board. He was in board shorts, so it was easy to see the multiple surgical scars on his misshapen knees and thin legs. Tyler stood up with the help of two walking staffs, then fired up the Segway. His one knee was bent in an outward angle, and his natural stance seemed to be a crouch, so the Segway was a great mobility solution for him. Looking at Carol he said, "After I get all signed in I'd love to buy you a libation to thank you for helping me, if you're so inclined."

"I believe I am so inclined, Tyler, I'd love to have a 'libation' with you. I'll just walk over with you. Oh, well..." She looked embarrassed, as if she said something wrong.

He chuckled. "I'll be the one rolling, you'll be the one walking, so don't worry, you were correct. I need to walk Kaili first and get her dressed." He had a red service dog vest in one hand. "C'mere, Kaili." She got up and jumped over the gunwale onto the dock then stood in front of Tyler and waited expectantly. He hung onto the Segway with one hand for balance as he fastened two straps around her that were attached to what almost looked like a tiny saddle-shaped piece of nylon. It read "Service Dog – Please Ask Before Petting."

"You can pet her. She's friendly, and she loves her job, but some people freak out about a dog being in certain places. The vest minimizes that."

Carol looked interested as she petted Kaili's head. "What does she do for you?"

"She brings things and picks up things I drop. I can't bend over or keep my balance without holding onto something, and I can't go that far on the canes. Here, take one of them down the dock and drop it." Carol took the cane about fifty feet down the dock and placed it in the middle. Kaili watched her and then looked at Tyler. "Kaili, go get my cane." She walked over, picked up the cane, brought it back, and carefully placed the grip in Tyler's outstretched hand then sat in front of him. "Good girl! She's also great company for me."

It impressed all of us, but none more than Carol. And it wasn't just Kaili she was impressed with.

"She's awesome, Tyler! Let's walk her, I'll show you a great grassy area that Casey and Dawn use for Bimini, their golden retriever. Don't worry, I'll fill you in on who's who in the marina population. Bimini is the only other dog in the marina so far. Do you think your machine can make it up the ramp okay?" There was a ramp that connected the floating dock with land, hinged at one end to allow for the rise and fall of the tide.

"It can take a forty-five-degree angle, so that's a piece of cake. C'mon, I'll show you." He looked at the three of us. "Nice to have met y'all."

The three of them "walked" down the dock, and true to what Tyler said, the Segway went up the ramp with ease since it was at a much lower angle than its limit.

Cindy looked at the two of us and said, "I'll tell you the whole story about Tyler when we get cocktails in hand on *Hibiscus*. Well, maybe not the whole story because it looks like Carol might be adding to it. Did you see the way she looked at him? I'd be really surprised if 'libations' don't turn into dinner. He's cute, and they look about the same age."

Rik and I settled into our seats on *Hibiscus*'s aft deck as Cindy passed us our own "libations" which earned her a "Thank you, ma'am!" with a grin from each of us.

"Hey, at least he's polite, even though he's obviously nearsighted, calling me ma'am. Anyway, I've been dealing with Tyler for the last two days on the phone. He's going to put a skydiving operation in on ESVA, and he's negotiating with the county for a 'drop zone' on the west side of the airfield here. He loves the idea of a potential tie-in with *Bayside*, and it would be just another great and unique activity nearby for us."

Rik looked dubious, and I picked up on her concerns right away. "There are a lot of para-skydivers, Rik. Lots more since all the action in the Mideast. Though his didn't look like battle injuries."

Cindy nodded. "He said he has cerebral palsy and has had a lot of leg surgeries. The Segway is why we put him on this dock, so he doesn't have to navigate a skinny finger pier with it when he gets off his boat. This side is more handicapped accessible."

"Well, if he hangs around, I'll have someone to share my latest 'gimp' jokes with."

Cindy looked at me, horrified. "That's terrible!"

"No, it would be terrible if *you* told them. I've earned the right to. It tells something about not just the person telling them, but the people around him or her. So many people make a big deal about being comfortable around people with disabilities, but if they can laugh at a 'gimp joke' you know they really are. A lot of people fake it, but you can't fake a reaction to these. I was recovering in Walter Reed after having lost my second leg when all the operations to save it had failed. A civilian friend with mobility issues called to check on me, and I was still loopy on pain meds. I had the phone on speaker and this wiseass started in with a fake heavy Southern accent: 'Lew-tennant Daaaan!' You know, that guy from Forrest Gump who lost both legs. The guy in the next bed over almost fell out of it he was laughing so hard. I bet Tyler would have too, I got that kind of vibe from him."

Rik winked, "I don't think you were the only one that got a 'vibe' from him this afternoon."

"Nope, he looked like he was doing all right."

"So, did she."

Cindy was still shaking her head over the non-PC jokes. Then she said, "He seems pretty set on the idea. He's very persuasive and determined."

I nodded. "He handled that rig well by himself coming into the dock, and he was here what, a whole five minutes before he had a date for cocktails and I'd wager for dinner, too. Did you see that Segway? It was far from stock. Looks like he's an innovator and a problem solver. If anyone can charm the county into this, my money would be on him."

"Speaking of new businesses, Cindy, I haven't had a chance yet to tell you about what my dad did this morning." She related his offer and her acceptance. She also told Cindy about them offering me the other twenty-five percent of the business. "You know, in our meeting with the team you sounded a lot more like a part-owner than a contractor. Have you given it any more thought?"

I nodded. "I have. It's a great opportunity, one I didn't see coming. But I'm wondering how much it would change what I do, and how I do it."

Rik cocked her head to the side, "You've already changed. You led most of the meeting this morning. Did you see the difference in the team you've worked in concert with for years now? They didn't bat an eye, they accepted you as leading this operation. No grumbling, no questions, or even shared looks between each other. They're ready to follow you, if you want to lead them."

"Meaning I'd be more in operations?"

"Meaning you would be in charge of the operations group."

"I wouldn't have to get involved with the billing and new client hand-holding?"

"Heck no! You've always been an operations guy. I'd never stick you with accounting. As I see it, we'll both be doing government liaison work, though even that would be more me than you. I'll do most of the new private client meetings, oversee accounting and the office, and you'll do what you've always done. Only now the team will be totally under you, doing more of the legwork for you. Catch the pun there?" She grinned, and Cindy swatted her arm.

"It's okay, Cindy. We made her an honorary 'gimp' long ago, so she can tell those jokes too."

Cindy sighed. "You two are so bad."

Rik grinned. "Which is why we work together so well, and why I want to keep it that way. Colt, I can trust you, I know what you are capable of, and I know if I were gone for any length of time, I would be leaving things in great hands. The only question now in my mind is whether you want to do this. I don't really want anyone else for the job, and I wouldn't offer anybody else an equity stake. But at the rate things are growing I can't do it by myself, so I need someone I can count on, and I'd rather have a partner."

Now it was my turn to sigh.

"What?"

"I've always liked being a contractor, and I hate administration and bureaucracy as much as I love my independence. I've always been able to pick the jobs I wanted."

"And you've never turned one down from Dad because he never took a bad one. I bet you can't say that about your other customers. And now you'll get to help choose which jobs we take from now on as a business. If you think one isn't right, you veto it and we walk away. But it's up to you, if you want to be my partner.

"Dad said something about there being more to this that he'd tell us tonight. I'm guessing it has something to do with Janice and spending more time with her. But I know he won't want to do that until I get a good number two person in place."

I nodded. But there was more to it than we had discussed so far. "I guess this would also mean more time over here and in Norfolk."

"You're thinking about Nancy."

I nodded. "Yes, though it isn't like we have been seeing a lot of each other as it is, with her residency at the hospital. She was thinking about needing to get out of NOVA. She likes the coast better, and that might mean Norfolk, Virginia Beach, or even out of state, who knows? It'll be where the job opportunity arises for her." I paused a minute, "Just like it is for me. I thought it would be her job that would put more distance between us. But I don't see her coming over here."

Rik looked somber. "I get it. I'm just lucky that Cindy and I had both gotten anchored to our jobs here before we got serious. When you need to go in different directions for work, that's tough, I'm sorry I don't have a better answer for you, Colt." She looked me straight in the eye. "I can understand you not taking the offer. I don't want to be the person to drive a wedge between you and Nancy; happiness counts so much more than money. Don't worry, I can find someone else to take the number two spot here."

"Stock in the company is a huge enticement for someone."

"Like I said, I'm not offering anyone else stock. I'll start looking for another employee instead of a partner. Hey, look at the time. We were so late coming back; we need to drink up and head over to meet up with my dad and Janice."

I knew she was dodging, wanting to drop a disappointing subject. The truth is, I was torn. I had even thought briefly about following Nancy wherever she ended up, but the truth is that neither of us truly believed there was a grand future ahead for us together.

In this business, I always travel a lot anyway, so it isn't as important where I'm based. But I had been more of an employee of Conrad's, just without the benefits and the structure as well as without gaining equity. Kind of a part-timer. I did well at it, very well, but that would be a fraction of what I knew I'd earn owning a quarter of the business. I had to weigh the cost. One part might or might not be the end of my current relationship. That I was having to weigh everything gave me more insight into my true feelings. I think I had been kidding myself about following Nancy wherever she ended up, the truth was we have really been drifting apart, with neither of us wanting to admit it. I knew if I asked her to follow me here, that wouldn't be happening, she was uber serious about her career. And we don't know for sure what's down the road. Except that I know I'll never get another opportunity like this one. These don't grow on trees in our business. And you rarely get to work with a pal. Plus, there was someone at "The Shop" in Norfolk that I'd been more than a bit interested in for quite some time, even before Nancy, but our timing was always been a little off. One of us was always dating someone when the other was unattached. Maybe that would change if I was around more.

"If you still want me, I'm in."

Rik grinned and raced over to hug me and kissed me on the cheek. "If I still want you? I can't do it without you! I only trust Dad more than you. He's going to be so pleased."

"No, he won't. Because knowing Conrad, he never doubted for a second that I'd take it."

Rik gave me a bashful look. "I didn't either, but I thought it would take you longer. I've known you for over half of my life, Colt. And I've trusted my life to you on more occasions than I'd like to remember. I know you better than anybody except Cindy."

Cindy looked indignant, "Hey, I'd like to think I can surprise you from time to time."

"You do."

"Which? Surprise you or think I can?"

"Yes!"

"Funny gal."

"I have my moments. Speaking of which, we need to get going. Dad said there was more to what he brought up in our meeting this morning. I guess he has another surprise to spring on us."

4

COMMODORE COLT

Rooftops Bar & Grille is one of the two latest restaurants at *Bayside* to open. It's on the second floor on the south side of the resort's boutique hotel, perched on top of the other new venue, the *Bayside Dining Room*, which was more elegant and much more dressy. *Rooftops'* atmosphere is casual; it's screened on three sides and overlooks both the marina and the Chesapeake. It's a great place to watch a sunset and have some of their house aged beef. In the corner toward the front of the hotel is an open charcoal grill with a giant exhaust hood manned by a grill chef. The food at *Bayside* is one of the big draws. Casey and Dawn brought a fantastic Cuban chef up with them from Florida, Carlos Ramirez. Self-taught, he has an incredible talent, which they recognized early on and encouraged him to develop. He now oversees their four restaurants, which are soon to be six, and from what I've heard, possibly seven.

It was already getting crowded as we walked in, but Conrad had snagged a table on the marina side with Janice. We greeted each other as we sat down.

Rik was eager to tell Conrad her news. "Dad, Colt agreed to come in with me, so we need to get all the figures together and complete the deal." She had a huge smile that made me feel great as Conrad broke out one of his own.

"That's fantastic! We have news of our own too, but let's get you all drinks and put our orders in first."

This must be the news he hinted at earlier, but Conrad loved suspense, and nobody could rush his announcement. From the look on Rik's face, I knew what she was now thinking, that she might get a stepmom. My money was on it being something like that, but not quite a march down the aisle. We would hear soon enough. I knew Conrad, just like I knew he would be in chinos and the only vintage, loud Hawaiian shirt in the restaurant. He stood out in the middle of a sea of Polo's, oxfords, Patagonia's and open-air casting shirts. He was as constant as the Gulfstream current.

After the drinks arrived, Janice took a large manila envelope out of her purse and handed it to Conrad, who smiled. "Now we've figured out what you two will do when you grow up, it's time to see what I'm going to do for my second childhood."

Janice spoke up, "He means what WE are going to do for his second childhood." She also broke into a big grin. There was a lot of that going around right now.

Conrad pulled out several pictures of a boat along with a specification sheet. "This is a fifty-five-foot Ocean Alexander Flybridge Motor yacht. Janice and I bought it today. I give you *Plan J*. We are now officially snowbirds! Although this time when I go to Florida in the winter it won't be on business, it'll be R&R only."

Rik looked amused. "So, you two are moving in together?" They had been spending a lot of weekends together on *Plan B*.

Now it was Conrad's turn to be amused. "Did you miss the part about us buying the boat together? Naming her *Plan J*, as in for Janice? I knew a few weeks after meeting her she was who I wanted to be with for the last chapters of my life. I've been working toward this since we pulled you out of the field. You were ready to take over the business, and I didn't need to worry about that anymore. We've both now found two wonderful people to spend our lives with." He glanced over at Cindy, who smiled appreciatively at him.

"Are you okay with this, Rikki?" Janice had a concerned edge to her voice.

"I am, Janice. I'm happy for you both, I guess I hadn't realized how far along your relationship had progressed. While I knew you two were spending a lot of time together, Dad has never been this serious about anyone since my mom died so many years ago. I guess it is kind of catching me off guard. I'm happy for you guys, and so glad you're with him." She reached over and patted Janice's hand and smiled after Janice took her hand and squeezed it.

"Thank you, Rikki. It worried me about how you might react. I know your father hasn't been one for serious long-term relationships. We've been casual friends for so many years, and we kept bumping into each other at functions in DC. It kind of came as a surprise when he first asked me out. Then I surprised myself when I accepted. I wasn't sure how long things might last. Don't look at me like that, Conrad, you had a well-earned reputation. But I enjoy his company so much it was worth the uncertainty. It floored me when he proposed this idea, but I didn't need much more than a minute to think it over."

"After Janice said she was up for moving aboard with me, we came up with a list of what we both wanted in a boat. This Ocean Alexander has it all. It feels a lot larger than fifty-five feet, but we can still handle her easily with just the two of us. She's a tad faster than *Plan B*, but has a lot more room, and room for you and Cindy to visit when we're down south for the winter. Her kids, too."

I could read on Rik's face she hadn't thought that far ahead and didn't even know Janice had kids of her own. Her family had grown a lot in the past ten minutes, so it was a shock to her. It was a side of Rikki I rarely saw. In the business, it seemed like nothing ever phased her; she was ready for just about anything. Her personal side was a different story altogether. I saw Cindy looking at her, and then she glanced at me, and I nodded back at her. I'm so glad she's with Rik, this is a lot for her to absorb in a single day, but Cindy was there for her as a sounding board.

The three of us pored over the photos, admiring their new home, and appreciating the craftsmanship, especially the woodwork in her interior.

I had an idea. "Conrad, what are you going to do with *Plan B* now that you have this new boat?"

"She's going on the market, why?"

"I'd be interested in buying her. *Blitz* is great for a night or two, but she gets kind of cramped for long stretches. The cabin was almost an afterthought; they built her for speed. The engines and cockpit take up most of her usable space. *Plan B* is just the opposite, designed around her living spaces, and I can stand up everywhere but in the stateroom. *Blitz* doesn't have her kind of headroom. Since I'm going to be spending a lot more time over here, she would be the perfect home base for me. I'll still use *Blitz* to get from point to point in the bay and for overnight trips to other locations."

"Without a broker in the middle, I can make you a great deal, Colt. And I think you're right, she would make a great home base for you here."

Conrad threw me a number I couldn't refuse, and then I was a two-boat owner. I thought of a line from that big pirate movie and chuckled to myself. Rik looked over at me with an amused face.

"What?"

"Just call me Commodore Colt."

She roared, "I'll get you a really big hat!" I didn't know she'd even seen the movie, much less that she knew one of the best lines.

Cindy rolled her eyes and looked at me.

"What?"

"You two. You're like brother and sister."

"Uncle and niece." Rik swatted my shoulder as I continued, "At times. Great times. Like now. But you knew we were a package deal; that you got me along with her. Now we'll even be neighbors."

She shook her head. "There goes the neighborhood."

Conrad had sat back in his chair, watching this exchange. I knew what he was thinking, our interaction just validated that he had made a good decision. I know he likes that Cindy and I get along so well, too. The deal could have turned into a disaster if we didn't. This business keeps odd hours and is built on personal relationships. If there was friction between the partners, or friction at home because of a partner, the business could suffer for it.

The truth is I like Cindy. She's smart, pretty, has a great figure, blond shoulder-length hair, and beautiful blue-gray eyes. At thirty-five-years old and five-feet-eight-inches tall, she's almost five years older and an inch shorter than Rik. Cindy is settled and knows what she wants in life, just as Rikki does. When Rik got shot here, Cindy only knew that she had been injured in a boating accident, which was also true. When Rikki finally told her the whole story and what she did for a living, Cindy didn't run, back away, or even get angry like so many people would have. She weighed the risks and figured that Rik was worth the worry that came with her job. That told me a lot about her, that she was very level-headed and a good judge of character.

Working in this business can be tough on relationships. We often have to leave with little or no notice, not always knowing how long we'll be away. Plus, our risk factor is a lot higher than most typical security jobs. In the past, we've gone up against some rough, very smart operators. That increases the risk factor, and the pay rate goes up along with it. Yet Conrad has an instinct for knowing which ones to avoid. Even though Rik and I will now be in the office more, we'll still be taking risks. I have a feeling this new AI investigation might end up in that high-risk category. If there's one thing I've learned in this business, it's trusting my feelings. That has saved my life more than once.

But tonight, this was less about risks and more about celebrating new beginnings for all of us. Not celebrating too hard, because Rik and I had to be back at Norfolk for that 10 a.m. briefing. Conrad and Janice were headed to Annapolis in the morning to pick up *Plan J*, and Cindy was knee-deep in the resort business. As I said, she's now a partner in that company. So, with a busy day ahead we all left soon after dinner, agreeing to reconvene on *Plan J* for a tour and cocktails tomorrow night.

On the way out we spotted Tyler, Carol, and Kaili ahead of us, also headed back to the South Dock. Our instincts had been right, "libations" had morphed into dinner at the *Beach Café*. They went through the security gate and took Kaili to the grassy area for a walk. I spotted Casey Shaw and his fiancée Dawn McAlister already walking Bimini there. Rik, Cindy, and I walked over to join them after parting company with Conrad and Janice who went back to Plan B. By the time we caught up with Tyler and Carol, they had already reached Casey, Dawn, and Bimini. Tyler told Kaili, "Go play." With that, she made an exaggerated "play bow" toward Bimini, who gave her a "chuff" and a feigned lunge and run. They went tearing up and down the lawn as Carol introduced Tyler to Casey and Dawn.

"So, is that your Bertram over at the dock?"

"Yes, ma'am. Kaili's and mine."

"Quite a classic, and in beautiful shape."

"It had been my parents' boat years ago. I tracked it down and bought it after I lost them both in an accident. They had gone out for dates fishing and diving in it when they were my age, and they used it to run to Walker's Cay in the Bahamas when they got married there. They even honeymooned on it cruising down through the Abacos. It made me kind of feel closer to them in it if that makes sense."

Dawn's voice had softened when she answered. "It does. That's a sweet story."

Tyler shrugged. "I guess I'm kind of funny that way." He looked over as Carol put a hand on his arm, also moved by the story. He looked back up. "I hope y'all don't mind me walking Kaili over here."

Casey answered, "Not at all, Tyler. That's what this area is for. And it looks like those two are enjoying themselves." Bimini and Kaili had slowed to a jog, bumping into each other like a pair of NASCAR divers and playing. "In fact, a little canine company is just what Bim needs, and they're having a ball. Can Kaili swim?"

"Yes, sir, she can. She loves the water. Gets up on the dive platform and back into the boat all by herself."

"We've got a private pool over here that Bim loves. I can fix everyone a cocktail and we can let the dogs swim."

"That would be great, Mr. Shaw, thanks."

"On one condition, you call us Casey and Dawn."

"Yes si... er... Casey."

Rik jumped in. "Lots to tell you, Case."

"Then let's go to C3 and you can tell me all about it. Oh and, Carol, these are for you, Micah, and Sandy, I've been meaning to give them to you." He handed her three cards with magnetic strips.

"Thanks, Casey."

"This way you can use C3 whenever you want, without having to find one of us to let you in. Tyler, C3 is what we call our little private hideaway over here."

We passed through another security gate off a brick paver path through the grass strip. There was another security fence hidden in the middle of a thick wall of evergreens. Once through the gate, we followed the winding path several yards through the green forest until it opened out onto a brick paver patio. To the right was an outdoor kitchen, circular brick fire pit with benches, an infinity-edged hot tub and pool combination with several chaises and chairs. This patio looked out over the pool to an inhospitable rocky shore and then the Chesapeake Bay. To the left was the "Clubhouse" with a glass wall facing the pool and the bay. Inside was a bar, sauna, steam room, changing rooms, a buffet set up, pool table, widescreen TV and overstuffed sofas.

It bowled Tyler over. "This place is wild!"

Casey nodded. "Thanks. We like it. I designed it as a place for us all to get away from everyone. When you live where you work, sometimes you need somewhere to go blow off steam. Originally, we didn't fence off the South Dock, but now that we have, this second gate isn't as important as it was. Though it comes in handy when the ladies work on removing their tan lines." He chuckled. "So, can Kaili swim with that vest, or do you want to take it off of her?"

"Best to take it off. Here, Kaili." She came up to the lounge where he was sitting. Once free of the vest, again he told her, "Go play." Bimini heard that and led her over to the steps of the pool, then they took a lap around it. They stopped in an area where there are integrally sculpted chaises underwater, and Bimini showed her how they could lay there with their heads still above the surface. They started "fake snapping" at each other; pretending they were biting and pawing playfully.

Casey bartended for all of us while Rik brought Dawn and him up to speed on the day's events. Carol brought over two beers for herself and Tyler, taking the chair next to him. We all pulled up chairs, watching the dogs play while keeping an eye on the sun as it approached the horizon. *Bayside* was becoming known for some of the best sunsets. Even though the days had now started to get shorter, it was still light beyond 8:30, though not for much longer.

Casey and Dawn sat down. "Congratulations, Colt. That's great news about you and Rik buying Conrad's business."

"Thanks, Dawn. It hasn't sunk in yet though."

"So, *Plan B* is here to stay on South Dock?"

"If you'll have me, Casey. I'll probably be bouncing from Norfolk to DC to here, but mostly here now, I guess. We'll see how it plays out."

"What did Nancy think of it?"

"I haven't talked to her about it yet. Been a kind of eventful day. Figured I'd call her tonight." Casey and I are fishing friends. Not as tight as he and Rik are, but still good friends, so I didn't mind sharing this info. He nodded.

We hung out until after the sun disappeared and twilight set in, then I went over to *Blitz* to call Nancy. Rikki and I are going to leave for Norfolk around 8 a.m. I wanted to have breakfast at the *Beach Café* first, so I planned on turning in early.

~

The next day Tyler rolled into the cafe with Kaili, right after I sat down. I pointed at the chair across the table from me if he wanted it. He did.

"Thanks, Colt. Nice not to have to eat alone. Nothing personal,

Kaili." She looked up, cocked her head, and then lay down next to him.

"Looked like you weren't hard up for company last night at dinner."

"Yeah, appetizers kind of led into dinner. I like Carol, she's good company, and fun to talk to."

"I'm glad you think so, because you are too." She had walked up behind him without his knowledge and had a big smile. "Can I sit with you guys?" We both nodded. "Last night was fun, thank you, Tyler."

"No, thank you. I had a good time, and I appreciated you bringing me up to speed on who's who around here. Saved me a ton of time."

"My pleasure. It's an interesting place, for sure."

"Colt, Carol tells me you and Rikki are in the security business and have some former military employees. Any that might be interested in skydiving?"

"Quite a few, I think. As soon as you get set up, I can point them your way."

"That would be great, Colt, thanks! Yeah, I have a meeting with some county supervisors this morning. Hopefully, I can talk them into putting me on their agenda on Monday's meeting, and we can make a deal. This would be a perfect place. The views from 14,000 feet here would be unreal, and there's a nice wide field on the west side of the runway for the drop zone landing area, and an abandoned hanger I can refurbish. With the airport being not that busy, this could work well."

He and Carol then launched into a conversation about skydiving. She hadn't done it but wanted to try. I kind of tuned out after that, as I had a lot on my mind, and they seemed content just talking with each other. Truthfully, I was a million miles away. I finished breakfast before they were halfway through theirs, still engrossed in their conversation. They hardly noticed when I left and headed to the boat. Rik was already aboard and waiting for me. As we idled out she asked if I had any additional thoughts or reservations about us buying out her dad.

"Nope. Seems like a logical deal for all of us."

"Did you have time to talk about it with Nancy?"

"Yeah. That didn't go well. Especially the part about buying *Plan B* and spending more time here." I sighed before I realized I was going to. "When she calms down, she should see it was an opportunity I couldn't pass up. I hope. Maybe." With that, I advanced the throttles a little early, before we were out from between *Bayside's* rock jetties. The engine and wind noise discouraged any further conversation. I didn't want to think about relationship stuff, I needed to focus on the case in front of us. I knew Rik would understand and not be offended. She's good with things like that.

In plenty of back rooms, alarms were now sounding in DC. Maybe Congress could get in gear and pass legislation to criminalize what the Big Nile splinter group was doing. Even if it was fast-tracked though, since most in Congress are now focused on trying to get reelected, nothing would get done before next year at the absolute soonest. Meanwhile, the AI system will be free to make up whatever stories it wanted to, wreaking havoc on the election if we can't stop it. Even if it libeled someone, with no human telling it what to do beyond giving it a political direction, it was like a rabid dog that nobody owned, running wild. It was up to us to discover all its tentacles, cut them off, pull the plug on this whole operation, and make sure it didn't get started again. All while being stealthy about it, because the computer part wasn't illegal. Yet. I doubted that Big Nile would want to be publicly connected with this, so our liability exposure wasn't high. No doubt we would still have our hands full with this one though.

5

TEZORC

We walked into the briefing room hoping for some headway, but not expecting much this early into the investigation portion of this case. The team had other ideas though and must have been burning some midnight oil last night.

"Jim, you've got that look that says, 'I've got something big.' Let's have it." Jim Bannister was our research head, and he earned that spot by being the craftiest at what he does. Where others find brick walls, he finds open doors.

"We've got a good lead. Three years ago, Big Nile significantly increased spending in their AI department. I mean by like 300 percent, and it was already a staggering part of their budget. A year and a half later, the executive vice president and head of that department, Lloyd Heatherton, left to create a 'startup' autonomous car system company in Crozet, Virginia. It's a small town about ten miles west of Charlottesville. Hopefully tonight we can find answers at happy hour up by their headquarters as to who might have gone with him. It's a longshot, but worth taking."

"Why do you think he's our guy?"

"Several reasons. One, you don't throw away a job like he had at Big Nile without a big reason. His department was expanding not shrinking, so we assume things were going well, and there were rumors he was in their succession line. That's a lot to leave. Plus, there's the fact he's still pals with David Buxton, the founder of Big Nile. It's well known that one of Buxton's rules is if anyone leaves the company, they are dead to him and are from that point on his sworn enemy. It's one of his quirks. Yet I found pictures of the two watching polo together at a winery in Crozet on several occasions since he left. Heatherton does own the farm next to it, but they didn't just happen to run into each other, they were obviously meeting there."

I was skeptical. "Maybe this guy is the exception that proves the rule about leaving the company."

"I'd be with you on that except there's more. Heatherton's company, Contour Auto Tech, rents its property from Tezorc, LLC. Tezorc owns one other property in Virginia, a huge nine-building server farm in NOVA. Guess who their biggest customer is."

"Big Nile."

"You've got it. Their lease started right after that increase in Big Nile's AI budget."

"And Tezorc is Crozet spelled backward."

"Dang, Colt, you're right! How'd I miss that?"

"So, we have a server farm in NOVA large enough to support the AI Writer system, and—"

"Wait, there's more. Guess what runs right down the road almost within sight of Contour?"

"Fiber?"

"Not just your generic fiber bundle, either. A huge armored line that heads west to some government facility buried in Afton Mountain that even I can't find out more about. To get into that line you have to use a proprietary tool with a diamond blade. If you breach the outer shell, sensors in the line set off alarms. In a nanosecond, they can pinpoint the location of the breach. Contour has a spur in that line, so someone had to have some big friends in high places to get it. Normally it would take proof of a matter of national security to get a spur. The line runs east to Charlottesville and up to a vault at the National Ground Intelligence Center north of there, and on through to DC, right alongside Tezorc NOVA where they also have a spur. Almost a direct shot."

"So, Contour may be a cover for the AI Programming system."

"Looks like it, Colt. Awful lot of coincidences."

"We all know there are no such things as coincidences in this business. Any way to get into that spur?"

"Not without wearing signs on our backs saying, 'We're Hacking You.' The lines run alongside each properties' driveway."

"Tony?"

"Yeah, Colt?" Tony Becker was the tactical leader of the team.

"We'll need a full recon on Contour's perimeter tonight. But be extra careful, if these guys are who we think they are, that place is likely to be booby-trapped six ways from Sunday. Don't get to close to the perimeter, we don't want them to get hinky. We need to do a scan of any defenses. Infrared, video, thermal, lidar, radar, laser, anything they may be using. Expect the unexpected and don't get caught."

"Got it."

Jim spoke up again, "Tony, this isn't only an autonomous car system. They are also creating an autonomous system for earth-movers. That's the 'contour' part of their name. Load in the current contour plat of a property along with the desired changes, and it goes to work. Which means anything there with tracks or wheels could be alive."

"Got it, Jim, thanks."

I looked at Kelly Edwards, our best computer and software specialist, and the one whom I've had the bad timing with personally over the past couple of years. We've been 'flirt friends' almost since the day she was hired. "Kelly, any ideas on how to shut this thing down?"

She smiled. "Ohhh, yeah. We've been working on a new program I call Lestat, because it's got fangs and will suck the life out of any system. What makes this one work so well is that it is tough to find, it's timed and will piggyback itself onto any backup. Once it reaches the detonation time it not only wipes the memory clean, but it damages the drives, either flash drives or motorized hard drives. Think of it as case-contained electromagnetic resonance crossed with acoustic resonance. What it can't zap, it'll shatter. If the backup system is timed to download and go dormant, once it gets past Lestat's detonation time things get interesting. Whenever it goes live again for either another timed backup, or if it's activated to do a reboot or restore, it wipes out the backup and anything it is attached to after a short delay. So, if they switch to a redundant server set, it'll upload and run before it wipes it out, too."

"Wouldn't they figure the backup is corrupt?"

"I sure would. We wrote this one to hide itself well within the code though, which is why it should slip past any firewalls. Since they are so AI-focused, I'm counting on an automated repopulation of the backup system only after a system test and code scan. Then on the stealth program, a timed 'fuse' allows the replacement system to get up and running. If anyone gets in after that and looks through the code, they will lose their system as well during the second 'detonation.' Think of it as the gift that just keeps on giving." There were chuckles among the team. "From listening to how this is set up though, it sounds like a closed fiber circuit between the Writer System and Program System. So, I'm going to need to be inside at the Program System location to upload Lestat."

I said, "That could be a problem if that place is as well defended as I think it should be. They're using armored fiber; I mean who goes to that extreme except the military?"

"One way or another I'll need physical access to their system or circuit. With Contour being the suspected programming center for the targeting, it's possible there are disks or drives which are separate from the system. They need to go away."

"Right. We'll incorporate that into the plan."

"Wouldn't hurt to get a look at that server farm, too. See if there are any vulnerabilities there." Kelly looked hopeful, and I knew she meant she wanted to do the recon. Not usually her "thing" since she hardly ever got out of her computer lab, but I figured it couldn't hurt for the two of us to take a trip and get out of the office together. She's pretty, exceptionally bright, and good company. The trip to NOVA might be a nice opportunity for the two of us to chat.

"Okay, come up with a cover story, and you and I will go check it out after the meeting."

She grinned, and I could see the excitement in her eyes. "I already have. We keep a few corporate profiles for dummy companies, and I've got the perfect one. A shadowy defense contractor established years ago in Richmond. Just enough out there about it to see it exists, but nothing beyond that just as you would expect. Tezorc NOVA offers tours by appointment, and they are up in Lorton."

Lorton wasn't too far away from my slip in Woodbridge. "See if you can set something up for after lunch today."

"Shouldn't be a problem."

"Okay, good work, people. Keep digging and see if we can find out more. Meet here tomorrow at the same time. But before we break, Rikki needs to tell you something."

"Thanks, Colt. I know it has concerned you all that Conrad is around retirement age and you were wondering what would happen when he left. You don't have to worry about that anymore because he's decided. As of yesterday, Colt and I have agreed to buy him out. Colt will oversee operations from now on, so you'll be seeing more of him. But more here, and less in the field. I'll be concentrating on new and existing client relations as we continue growing.

"What does this mean for each of you? Well, things will be pretty much how they've been, though with us adding more business there will be new opportunities created within the company, and we'll be adding people as well. But I wanted to assure all of you that continuity is our focus. We've got a good thing going, Colt and I understand that and we want to build on it. So, I hope this removes any uncertainty that any of you might have been feeling.

"Now let's go get these bastards that want to sell out the future of our country. I want to make sure that doesn't happen, and that we hurt them. Badly."

The applause started in the back of the room, and then everyone stood up as they clapped. Rik and I realized this wasn't about the job at hand, it was for us. Everyone filed by, congratulating us, and shaking our hands as they did. I saw relief on a lot of faces and that's when it hit me how many of the company's employees had worried about the future, maybe wondering if Conrad would sell to some big corporation. I also saw their confidence in Rik and me, and that was humbling. It just reinforced to me that I had made the right decision to throw in with her.

After the room cleared out, Rik and I stayed to talk. "That went well."

She nodded. "I hadn't realized how concerned everyone was about what would happen with the company."

"Me either. That was quite a reaction."

"It's humbling."

"Exactly how I'd describe it too. You were right, there was no hesitation from any of them about us leading the company."

"What's the game plan for today?"

"If Kelly can get us an early afternoon appointment at Tezorc in Lorton, she and I will take *Blitz* to Woodbridge and my car from there. Looks like it's only about ten minutes away from my slip via the backroads."

"She knows her stuff and will have them thinking you want to lease half their servers." Rik laughed.

Kelly handled it perfectly. She came back to the briefing room five minutes later. "We have a 1:00 pm appointment."

"Let's move."

"Your car or mine?"

"Neither. We'd never get there by then. You like going fast?"

Her eyes twinkled. "Depends on what you have in mind... oops, I'm sorry Colt, I have to get used to you being my boss and not the contractor guy I used to kid around with." She was blushing. Kelly was a pretty, thirty-seven-year-old short-haired brunette around five-feet-eight-inches tall with emerald green eyes you could spot from across the room. The blush in her cheeks made her look that much prettier. There was, and definitely had been an attraction between us for quite a while.

I caught Rik's semi-amused look out of the corner of my eye. "No worries, Kelly. We didn't close on the deal yet, so I'm still a lowly contractor." I smiled, and I could see the relief on her face. "And what I have in mind is a fast boat ride across the bay and up the Potomac. I want to be back here before 4:30. Saddle up." She went back out, and I looked at Rik. "Pick you up in a few hours."

"Meanwhile I'll get HR to get your paperwork in order, so we can change that 'contractor' status and keep you out of trouble."

"Take your time, spoilsport."

"What? You don't even know if you are single again."

"Trust me, I am. I got this text on our ride in this morning." I handed over my phone. "She put me on waivers, permanently."

She handed it back. "Wow. Sorry. By text too, that's rough."

"Part of living in this electronic age, I guess."

"Maybe it's not such a bad thing that you're still a contractor then. You two have always had a vibe." She winked at me.

I walked with Kelly to the boathouse. It wasn't her normal realm within the company, and I wasn't sure she had been in there before. I knew she hadn't seen *Blitz*.

"Wow, that's quite a boat, Colt."

"It does the job. We'll cruise at almost full speed across the bay if it isn't too rough. That'll get us to Lorton just in time. You'll want to adjust your seat sides so it's a snug fit."

We idled out down the river as Kelly filled me in on our cover company's story. Since it was a stealthy defense contractor, they should expect us to be short on answers and long on attitude, and that's exactly what we would give them. I loved working with Kelly. She was one of the smartest people in the company, in both book smarts as well as common sense.

I hit the throttle and saw the bay had a short two-foot chop, which Blitz didn't even feel. We rocketed along at just over a hundred mph and made the turn into the Potomac half an hour later. Kelly had a huge smile and looked like she enjoyed herself from the time I cracked the throttle. Most people would have been hanging on for dear life, at least for a while until they got used to that speed, but not her. I didn't slow down until the 301 bridge, and even then, I kept *Blitz* at sixty mph.

Kelly looked over and yelled, "How fast were we going?"

"About a hundred and five." Her eyes widened. "Why? How fast did you think we were going?"

"Sixty!"

"That's what we're doing now." I saw she shook her head in amazement, the smile back again. I like running *Blitz* at this speed because you can converse if you do so loudly. Plus, the wind wasn't as buffeting so your eyes don't water as much. Kelly was now enjoying looking at the scenery along the shoreline at this pace. A few minutes after we passed Quantico I slowed again as we made our turn toward the Occoquan River and Blitz's regular slip.

We hopped in my black Escalade and were at the Tezorc gate in ten minutes. From what we could see, the entire eighty-acre campus was ringed with an anti-climbing security fencing, and there was a raised anti-crash barrier just beyond the guard shack. I pulled up to the window, the guard checked both our ID's and made a phone call. He handed the ID's back and told me to proceed to the parking area of building 1. The barrier lowered, and I drove in. Our guide was waiting for us at the visitor's parking area. She introduced herself and led us to the front entrance.

I recognized the revolving doors as bulletproof "mantraps" that security could activate to detain an intruder. The whole glass front was bulletproof and protected by huge concrete planters designed as anti-ramming barriers. Once inside we were asked to leave our cell phones, watches, and any other electronics we might have in small lockers. She then led us through a slightly inclined narrow hall that opened out into an elevated glass viewing platform overlooking the 200,000-square-foot building. In front of us lay a sea of electronic racks with more servers than I had ever seen. Our guide rattled on down a memorized list of highlights. Redundant power feeds from multiple substations, dedicated vaults, 20 MW IT loads, armored fiber connectivity between buildings, all network manhole accesses locked and camera monitored, redundant power with 40 MW backup, and waterless cooling. All nine buildings were actually double buildings, each formed out of reinforced concrete, with the inner buildings created to act as Faraday cages. Kelly asked enough questions to make our guide believe we were for real, then took some printed literature which was also available online. We collected our electronics from the lockers and headed back to *Blitz*. We would leave just in time to make my 4:30 target.

"That visit confirmed what I thought. The only way to load Lestat is going to be from the Program System. Taking away all our electronics just to get a peek at the farm from a glass room? And that narrow hall she took us through was a scanner. They had auto lock doors at each end."

I glanced over at her. "Why don't we have you doing more fieldwork?"

"Because the company has a contractor named Colt who's been doing most of it for years."

"Yeah, well, that's changing soon. I know the guy who will be heading up operations, and I can put in a good word for you if you like this kind of gig."

"I love this kind of gig, but I like the lab work, too."

"There's no reason you shouldn't do a mixture of both."

"I like the way you think. And speaking of that, you are still a contractor, right?"

"Correct."

"So, I could ask you anything without getting either of us in trouble."

"Unless it involves robbery or murder, yes."

"Neither. It's more like wanting to know why you've never asked me out. We've sure flirted enough these last few years, and I've dropped enough hints."

"A case of bad timing in the past on both our parts."

"That was then, this is now, and I'm not involved. How about you?"

"Not presently."

"That's a change from what I've heard, and why it always pays to check. Mind if I ask how long?"

"What time is it?"

"Ouch, sorry."

"Hey, at least our timing has gotten a little better, and we're both free agents now. And it's not like I haven't wanted to ask you out."

She shook her head. "Sorry, but rebounds are dangerous and rarely turn out well, Colt. Especially ones that are only hours old."

I sighed. "True." Although this didn't have that kind of feel. Nancy's and my relationship had lacked intensity and depth, and I don't think either of us realized it at the time. The fifteen-year difference in our ages hadn't been an issue, but it was the difference in the ages of our careers that was. And over the past few years, Kelly and my flirting had increased in intensity. It had been enough though to make it clear to both of us that we liked each other's company. Apparently, there wasn't enough now on her part to go beyond that, and I had misjudged the situation. Suddenly I didn't feel like talking anymore, and I was glad we were pulling up to the marina. Soon the noise from *Blitz's* engines would hamper our conversation ability and make a nice excuse to keep to ourselves.

I was now in a hurry to get back to Norfolk, so I wouldn't be sparing any horsepower on this ride. We idled out to the Potomac, and I caught Kelly staring at me. "All set?"

"I'm not sure."

"What's the matter?"

"If I knew, I'd be sure."

"I'm talking about being ready to go."

"I know. Evidently, you don't recognize stalling when you see it."

"Stalling for what?"

"Time. I think I want to say something, and I'm trying to work up the nerve."

Putting *Blitz's* gears in neutral I turned my full attention to Kelly, crossing my arms.

"I wish you had been free for a while, I really do, Colt. I just don't want to mess up right out of the gate when I feel there could have been something great between us."

"I have been free for a while, Kelly, but I just didn't realize it. Neither she nor I did while we just went through the motions. Can I ask you a personal question?"

"Sure, I guess."

"You ever buy stock in the market?"

She looked confused. "Yes?"

"Ever lose money on a stock?"

She nodded, "Once or twice."

"Okay, this is a bad analogy, but think about it. Sometimes you lose money on a stock, but you hang in there, hoping that it'll change, but it doesn't. You really lost the money a while back, but you only realize and admit that loss when you finally get out. You took your licks a while ago." I saw her face soften. "Ready to go home?" She nodded, and I hit the throttle. I was right, I was glad for all the noise.

I slowed to the requisite six knots only after I hit the Elizabeth River.

"Looks like we'll be back before you needed to be. How fast were we going then?"

"About 120 for the last half hour. I rarely do that for too long because it takes a toll on the engines."

She nodded. "I hope I didn't push you to do that."

"I think better at a higher speed sometimes."

"Seems that I do too. I thought about what you said, and you're right."

I hoped I knew about what, but I wasn't sure this was a conversation I wanted to have, at least not right now, if ever again. Really, I don't know what the hell I had been thinking about before. With this AI case and buying into Conrad's company, I had a lot on my plate already. Plus, I'm not sure she hadn't been right about rebounds. I nodded, knowing she was expecting me to say something, but I stayed silent, not knowing exactly what to say. I liked Kelly and didn't want to hurt her if I was in a rebound situation, even though it didn't feel like I was. It felt like once again our timing was off, and some things just aren't meant to be. We rode back in an uncomfortable silence.

We pulled into the boathouse, and Rik was waiting on the floating dock. Kelly looked over and said, "Thanks for the ride, and the conversation, Colt. I guess I'll see you tomorrow at the meeting."

"Yeah. Have a nice night, Kelly."

"I'll try." She got onto the dock, started to walk away but turned. "I'm sorry that I guess I said the wrong thing at the wrong time, Colt. We've always had such crappy timing. I wish we hadn't." She turned and rushed past a confused looking Rikki on her way out the door.

"What did you do?"

"I told her the truth, that I had only just broken up with Nancy. Then I tried to explain that I realized it wasn't just then, but it actually had been a while ago. I was just recognizing the fact now, but she shut me down."

"You know, coming from any other guy but you that would be the biggest load of crap I've ever heard. But since it's you, I believe it."

"No, she was right, Rik. It was all I thought about on the way back, and I'm too busy now to get involved with anyone. Plus, I wouldn't want to take a chance on hurting her. She's a terrific woman, and I care a lot about her. She deserves much better than that."

Rik looked at her briefcase she had put on the seat. "Hang on, I left my tablet in the shop. I'll be right back."

"Double time it, would you? I want to make the gas dock next door before they close." She waved as she ran out the door.

Five minutes later she came back through the door, empty-handed.

"Where's your tablet?"

"I must have put it in my briefcase after all." She opened it, "Here it is! Sorry to hold you up. Let's go see my dad's new home."

6

PLAN J

We fueled, and then I told Rik about what Kelly and I saw up in Lorton as we idled toward the bay. Once there, I set *Blitz* at a low cruise, giving my new engines a break. We pulled into *Bayside* a little over an hour later. *Plan J* was already on the South Dock, and she was a beauty. I backed into my slip as Sandy's predictable barrage erupted from his aft deck.

"Don't mind me! I'm just back here trying to be quiet, so I don't disturb your cocktail hour, Colt!" He took a swig of his beer.

"Hi, Sandy! Glad you missed me, and sure, I'll take a beer, thanks!"

"Sorry, this is my last one, so you'll need to give me one of yours."

I had expected this. I went to *Blitz's* refrigerator and took out a bottle with a white label that said simply, "Beer." A team member found it for me at a convenience store up in Maryland. Rik had read the look on my face and realized something was up, so she had stayed to watch the show. I showed her the bottle then covered the label with the palm of my hand as I got on the finger pier and handed it up to him.

"What the hell is this crap, Colt? I said give me a beer! This is just water that was dragged through the parking lot of a brewery."

"I bought that especially for you, Sandy! Free beer. What, you don't like it?"

"Ohhh, ho ho hoh. I'm not even going to taste this stuff. Game on, fella!"

"Bring it, big guy!"

Sandy wore the largest grin I'd ever seen on him before. He loved a challenge. I hoped I hadn't bitten off more than I could chew.

Rik left to go to *Hibiscus* to find Cindy, still chuckling over my beer gag. I puttered around in my cabin and heard Rik on the dock a few minutes later. By then I had been rerunning my conversation with Kelly in my mind. Again. It didn't turn out any different or better this time, either. I had told her the truth, and it was the right thing to do. When you know you wouldn't go back and change anything, you did things right the first time.

"Hey! You coming, or not?" Rik stuck her head through the hatchway.

"Go on over I'll be there in a bit, I'm just tidying up."

"And brooding. I know you, Colt, better than you know yourself. I know you said the right things and were honest because, well, you are you. That's what you do. I also know Kelly was one sad lady when she left the boathouse, no doubt from second thoughts that came too little, too late. I get that. But I can't believe you blew it. Been there, done that. Picked myself up, dusted my butt off, and now you need to do the same. You said, 'she deserves better,' well, pal, newsflash for you, I know there is no guy better for her than you, and apparently she had figured that out, too. So, you aren't protecting her from getting hurt, instead you hurt her. But what's done is done.

"So, get off your duff, quit being such a 'Dougie downer,' and let's go see this new rig. Dad needs to know we're happy for him. That all of us are."

"You know something, Rik? At this point in time I should be more upset about Nancy. But instead, I'm more upset about having hurt Kelly."

"You've known Kelly longer, and you may even know her better. If you compare hour for hour, you've spent more time with her than Nancy, right?"

I nodded. "Sure. A lot more."

"Then what you are feeling is correct, if you ask me. Though nobody asked me. Now get off your butt and let's get moving. I have several surprises planned for my favorite people."

I looked at her questioningly, but she had her "I'm not telling" face on, and I sighed while I followed her outside. Cindy had already gone onboard *Plan J*. We walked over to where she was tied up parallel to the main dock, in between *Hibiscus* and *TyMac*, Tyler's Bertram. Some people don't like anyone naming a boat after themselves, but I think in his case it's a cool thing. He said his parents had named some of their other boats that, after him, and he liked the reminder.

Conrad and Janice's pictures of *Plan J* hadn't done her justice. The boat was nothing short of incredible. I could see my old friend was happier than I had ever seen him in the past twenty years. Back then someone killed his wife while she was on a case. He had gone through hell afterward, only pulling himself together to raise his then ten-year-old only child, Rikki. Conrad deserved to be happy, he had been through a lot over the years. After his wife died he had immersed himself in raising Rik as a single father while also building his business. He had been extremely successful at both, and I was so glad I had been there to see it.

The cocktail party was going on in the large salon, which is the nautical term for the living room. Or in this case, it was the great room, since this was a "galley up" model, with the kitchen on the same deck level. Half an hour later I snuck out and sat with my drink on the aft deck's sofa. Through the glass bulkhead I saw Rik and Conrad look my way from inside, and Rik put a hand on her dad's arm and said something as her dad smiled and nodded. She came out and sat next to me.

"I'm happy for my dad. Both Janice and him."

"Me, too. But I think I will finish up this drink and head out. Not feeling 'party like' tonight."

"Remember I said I had surprises planned? One is a full-on spread by Chef Carlos over at C3 in Janice and Dad's honor. So, don't go home, please? There's more than just that. Wait, what's that boat over on the north side?"

I turned to look, but the dock was full for the weekend. "Which one?"

She stood up and pointed at the middle of the pack. "That one." I still didn't know which one she meant.

She put her arm across my shoulder. "It doesn't matter. Just remember, there is little in this world that's done, which can't be undone, my friend." She pulled her arm back.

"What?" I turned back around, and a tentative looking Kelly was standing at the top of the gangway. You could have knocked me over with a feather.

"Oh, yeah, I forgot to tell you, I invited Kelly up to be a guest on *Hibiscus* for the weekend, and she accepted. That's another of those surprises. But here's the thing, you two, word of this does not get back to work. You both have had the whole 'puppy dog eyes' thing going on for years, and you need to get it out of your systems, one way or another. The way it went this afternoon was not it, and you both know that. You've had a little time to feel sorry for yourselves, so now maybe you'll both be in a better frame of mind to figure things out. If you don't, neither of you will be worth a damn on this case, and I need you two to be focused by Monday. But by Kelly being my guest, there's no pressure on either of you, if you know what I mean. Except for the whole Monday thing. It will be a fun weekend, except for that one meeting which I'll drive us all down for in the morning. And that Monday deadline looming. But no pressure, kids!"

I saw Kelly mouth a "thank you" to Rik before she slipped back inside. "Can I sit down?"

I was sitting on the couch and motioned to the spot next to me. "Please."

"Don't be mad at Rikki, Colt, I didn't want to leave things like they were, and I guess she saw that at the boathouse. I was glad when she invited me up."

I nodded. "To tell the truth, I didn't want to leave it that way either, and I'm not mad at Rik, she's looking out for me. And you. But to tell another truth, Kelly, I've been running what we both said back through my head, and I wouldn't change a word, I'd still tell you everything I did."

"You told me the truth."

I nodded. "I did."

"She said you did, that you are a straight shooter. You've always been that way at work. I guess in relationships, too."

I nodded, and she smiled.

"I'm glad, though I'm sorry I didn't think things through as fast as I probably should have."

"I have a friend who has always said that you should never be sorry for being cautious, nor for being upfront. So, I don't think either of us have anything to be sorry about."

"I'd have been really sorry if she hadn't invited me up here."

"In keeping with being upfront, I would have, too."

She smiled for the first time since getting here, and it felt like neither of us knew what to say next. Maybe we were hesitant to, but I figured that at least seeing her smile was a good start.

"Well, I guess I need to say hello to my soon-to-be ex-boss since I'm hanging out on his yacht and he can see me sitting here."

"That would be a good idea. And it's more than a boat, it's his home, with his new partner. Mind if I go in with you?"

"I'd appreciate it. I've never socialized with either him or Rikki outside of work, and I'm nervous."

"Yet you were calm at Lorton, scoping out the enemy."

"That was easy."

"So is this, they're all great people." I saw her staring through the glass.

"Is that Eric Clarke? The billionaire from Fairfax?"

"No, that's Eric Clarke, my fishing partner and friend from Fairfax. That's the best thing about this place, it's an equalizer. Everyone is here because they can relax. That's also the thing about the South

Dock, everyone here is judged by who they are as a person. Not by their bank account, the size of their boat, their title, or what they do for a living. Here it's about how we all get along. We also help each other; Eric put some friends in touch with Rik, and now we earned their business. His too, all because we met at *Bayside*, and because of Casey Shaw, and Dawn McAlister. They both started the place and introduced everyone. Have you met Cindy Crenshaw yet?"

"No. Who is she?"

"She's Rik's other half and your co-hostess for the weekend." I was watching Kelly for any "tells" of disapproval or discomfort. I saw none.

"No, I haven't. I'd appreciate your introducing us though. And if you were looking for a reaction from that, you won't get one. I don't judge anyone by who they are with or even who they want to be with. That's a good way to miss out on some good people."

"Sorry, it's just that I'm kind of protective of Rik."

"Colt, knowing Rikki as I do, I'm sure she would say you don't need to be."

I grinned. "She would. And she has. I still can't help it though. She's been my 'little sister/niece' for almost two decades, and now my business partner for a day and a half. She looks out for me, too. And you'll love Cindy, everyone does."

"I found out how much Rikki looks after you and me today and I'm grateful that she does, or I wouldn't be here."

"True. But enough chitchat for now, we'll have plenty of time for it this weekend. First, we need to get you a drink after fighting all that Norfolk traffic and facing the Bridge Tunnel."

"I won't argue with you on that point."

I led Kelly inside, got her a drink, and introduced her around. After about the third introduction, I saw her relax. This can be an overwhelming crowd when you first meet them, but there's a reason they all have the South Dock gate combination; they are good, unpretentious people. Soon Rikki herded everyone over to C3 for more drinks and dinner.

Kelly had quickly gotten over her shyness and was now enjoying herself, making the rounds and dragging me along. Everyone seemed to enjoy her, and they saw her the way I always have, as both funny and extremely intelligent. While I'm always quiet at these things, it turned out she's outgoing and engaging at cocktail parties. If we did end up dating, her personality would be a big plus. Nobody enjoys a couple who are both quiet all the time. It's not that I don't enjoy a good conversation, it's more about liking a good one-on-one chat. In crowded party situations, I tend to listen because I learn a lot more that way.

I quickly found I liked watching Kelly interact with people. And I liked the occasional sideways glances she gave me when she did. Those said I was really her focus, no matter who she was talking with. That was a good feeling. At the risk of doing a comparison (and getting back into the whole "rebound" debate), Nancy had also known how to work a crowd, but I quickly became lost to her when she did, even if I was standing beside her. I should have read that sign a long time ago, but I guess there were a lot of things I should have caught onto a while ago, too.

I grabbed a fresh drink and headed for the curved benches around the fire pit, wanting to get off my prosthetics for a bit. They can be tiring after standing for long periods. As I sat down, Bimini came over to visit and get his chin scratched, one of his favorite things. He's one of the funniest and smartest dogs I've ever met, with a lot of human traits. The sun had gone down a few minutes before, and I think he just wanted to hang by the fire. Even though it was late summer, it was getting chilly at night and the fire felt good, apparently to Bim, too. I loved this place and enjoyed the new friends I had made here, both two and four-footed.

A few minutes after I sat down, Dawn came over and sat next to me. "Your new friend is nice."

"Old friend, actually. She has worked for Conrad for a few years, and we've worked on several projects together."

"In any case, I like her. Think she'll be around often?"

"I don't know, that's up to her."

"The better answer is, 'I hope she will,' because she hopes she will, too."

Kelly had again walked up behind me without my noticing. Either the drinks they were pouring tonight were very strong, or I was losing my touch.

"Sorry, I didn't mean to eavesdrop on you two."

Dawn smiled and patted a spot on the bench next to her. "You didn't overhear anything that either of us wouldn't have wanted you to. Right, Colt?"

"Pretty much." That was one of Dawn's favorite sayings, and most of us liked kidding her about it.

Dawn chuckled. "Touché."

As Kelly sat down next to her, Bimini came over and lay down on her feet. Dawn looked over at me, raised her eyebrows, and cocked her head. Bimini has a real sense about people, and this was about his highest compliment, meaning that Kelly was "good in his book." He had only been wrong once that I was aware of, about someone who also fooled a bunch of us humans, as well. But I think he's back on track now. Dawn did too, and so this wasn't lost on her.

"Are you two here Sunday morning?" When we both nodded, Dawn asked, "Do you fish, Kelly?"

She smiled. "A favorite pastime of mine, but I don't get to go as often as I'd like."

"Sunday is supposed to be flat calm, so Casey and I are planning on taking the kayaks out in the morning for some flounder fishing. We have two spares if you guys want to join us."

Kelly looked over, apparently wanting me to answer for both of us. "That would be a lot of fun, thanks."

"Good! I'll tell Casey you are both in. How about dinner on *Lady Dawn* tomorrow night, or do you have plans?"

This time I looked at Kelly, who took the hint. "We would love to, thanks. What can we bring?"

"Just yourselves, and a good appetite. I'll get it set up. Oh, and cocktails start around five." She wandered back over to the now thinning crowd.

"Looks like we now get invited places together. I hope you don't mind." Kelly smiled at me.

"Yeah, 'we.' First weekend I've had a full dance card in a while. My friends like you, as do I, so of course I don't mind."

"I like everyone I've met so far; they all seem nice."

"Life's too short to hang with anyone who isn't."

"I agree." She scooted over to the spot Dawn vacated. Bim followed her. "Conrad's new yacht is gorgeous."

"A smart choice for them. They can be mobile, comfortable, and have no grass to mow. And it's way less expensive to buy than a waterfront home. You don't like the neighbors? Change slips or marinas."

Kelly laughed; I always liked her laugh. "Where did he live before?"

"On the boat two slips down from *Blitz* called *Plan B*. I bought it from him yesterday since I'm going to be spending more time working out of here. It's a step up from *Blitz* in comfort, but a step down in speed. He's moving the rest of his stuff over to *Plan J* in the morning. I had planned on getting settled in tomorrow afternoon, but I can do it next week."

She jumped in. "I'd love to help you tomorrow if you want."

"Sure, I'd like that."

Rikki walked over. "Hey, I hate to be a spoilsport, but Cindy and I are headed back to *Hibiscus*, and I still need to show you which is your stateroom."

I said, "I need to get going, too."

Kelly put a hand on my arm, "Please don't. I'll run over and put my bag aboard and come back, if that works for you. We've got a great fire going, and I'm enjoying talking about things other than work with you."

"Sure." In the light of the fire, I saw Rik smile.

"You don't mind if I don't crash right now, do you, Rikki? I don't want to be a bad guest."

"I don't mind at all. Only a bad host sets a guest curfew." She winked at the two of us. "We'll leave a quarter after eight tomorrow."

"Buy you guys breakfast at the *Beach Café* first? Cindy, too?" I loved having breakfast on the beach.

"Sounds like a plan. Seven fifteen?"

"Meet you there. Kelly, you'll need this to get back in here." I handed her my C3 gate card.

"I felt a bit like a jerk, you know." Kelly handed back my C3 card ten minutes later.

Damn, she had snuck up on me again. "What was Congresswoman Ryan wearing?"

"Peach-colored casting shirt with a one-inch American flag above her left breast pocket, and white Sportif shorts with white canvas deck shoes. You want her waist and bra sizes, too? And why do you want to know?"

"Only someone practiced in tradecraft would remember all that detail, do that security scan of everyone you did when we got here, and be able to sneak up on me. How long have you been learning, and from whom?"

"Someone pre-you, way back in the wake of my life. Well over the aft horizon."

"He was good."

"If he was that good, I wouldn't be here, now would I?" Even in the firelight her emerald green eyes twinkled.

"You snuck up on me twice tonight."

"Three times, but I didn't let you know about the other one. They pour a stiff drink here, and we're supposed to be off the clock, so don't beat yourself up too badly."

I still wasn't happy about it. I was never "off the clock." "Okay, you were saying, before I interrupted you?"

"You just want me to repeat it. Okay, I felt like a jerk this afternoon."

"About...?"

"Putting you on the spot about why you never asked me out, and if you were still involved. Could have led to a long ride back."

"It led to a long ride back for me, but I'm glad you're a jerk. Otherwise, I'd be down on *Blitz* by myself right now. Thanks for that."

"You still haven't asked me out."

"You believe I'm on a rebound. So, I'm not going to ask you out. Worrying about a rebound is a recipe for a disaster. I like you too much and have liked you for a while, enough so I'm not going to do anything to screw things up down the road, if there might ever be a 'down the road.'"

"You'll be part of the company soon, and there are rules against employees dating."

"If I come into the company already dating an employee, that's not against the rules. No one is supposed to *start* an employee relationship while employed there."

"So, when are you going to ask me out?"

"Like I said, I've decided I'm not going to."

"What? Why not?"

"Because I'm not the one worried about a rebound. I'm the one worried about getting shot down or rushing into things and messing up what otherwise might have been great."

"And we'll never know what it might or might not turn into if we don't go out."

"Correct."

"But you aren't going to ask me out on a date."

"Correct again."

"You are frustrating as hell, you know that?"

"I'm really not. You're just the one who hasn't thought this all the way through."

"I haven't... *really*? Who drove through rush hour traffic busting her butt to get here? Think about this, we've been friends for several years now."

"Right."

"And good work pals."

"I agree."

"We've been 'flirt friends' for a few years."

"Again, I'm still not disagreeing with you."

"So, we've been attracted to each other, but our timing with relationships has always been off."

"So far off that we could never have even double dated."

"You would have wanted to go on a double date with me, Colt?"

"Never in a million years would I have wanted to sit at dinner watching my 'flirt friend' out on a date with someone else. I'm usually armed, and things could have ended up badly. What if the guy had burped in front of you? Justifiable grounds for the use of lethal force." Kelly scooted over closer, and leaned against me, putting her head on my shoulder. I said, "That's very distracting, you know."

"Deal with it, *friend*. I'm comfortable. Where were we?"

"You were listing all the reasons why we should never go out."

"I was not! I was pointing out all the reasons why we should."

"You haven't touched on that whole 'rebound' landmine."

"Because several of your friends talked to me about that tonight."

"You can't believe a word they say. They're all pathological liars."

"To a one they said all summer they've only met Nancy once, and yet you hardly missed a weekend and even spent parts of weeks here, always alone. They said in their view it was more a relationship in name only and she was always too busy at the hospital. That she was nice the one time she was here, but she kind of ignored you too, more interested in talking with everyone else. That it looked more like a 'friends with occasional benefits' friendship than an actual committed relationship."

"None of those folks have ever told a lie in their entire lives. Who were they? I need to move them up higher on my Christmas gift list."

"Just people who said they were glad you finally moved on, though there wasn't much to move on from. Why didn't you tell me all this, Colt?"

I shrugged.

"Pride?"

"Maybe."

"Screw pride. Just level with me."

"Okay, can I be serious for a second?"

"I wish you would."

"On the way back here tonight, I told Rik that I was more upset by how badly my talk went with you than over my breakup with Nancy. She pointed out I've spent more time with you than I ever have with Nancy, so that made sense. And I haven't been as happy in months as I was when I saw you standing at Conrad's gangway tonight."

"Rikki just moved up higher on *my* Christmas gift list."

I laughed. I really liked Kelly, and it was true; in the few short hours since she arrived I felt happier than I had in a long time. I knew it took a lot for her to come here, not knowing what lay ahead.

"Okay, so here's my jerk question again. When are you going to ask me out?"

"Asked and answered, counselor."

"You're not."

"Nope."

"What if I ask you out?"

"What if."

"Okay, stubborn one. How about going out with me?"

"I'd have to check my schedule. I might be washing my hair."

"Your head is shaved, Colt."

"You got me; I have no excuse then. Okay, where and when?"

"Right now. I want to go over to the far side of the deck and lay back on a chaise with you and look at the stars. Even with the fire-light blocking some of it right here, I'm seeing more stars than I've ever seen in Norfolk. It's incredible. And by the way, this is the cheapest date we will ever have, so don't get used to it. I'm a barbecue dinner date kind of girl, and I like coleslaw on my sandwich, not the side. And if we go out for burritos, I'll want the guacamole, even if it costs an extra buck. You'll just have to spring for it."

"Noted and agreed. Fix you another drink while we move?"

"Absolutely."

Besides the drinks, I brought out a blanket. Casey and Dawn love the sunsets across the bay and always have plenty of blankets for themselves and guests for the cooler months. I lay back on the chaise with my legs off each side while Kelly lay back against me and covered us with the blanket. Each of us held a drink in one hand while we found each other's empty hand with the other. We talked until past midnight, about where we grew up, Kelly in Wisconsin, me in Texas, about family, friends, and what we each wanted out of life. We found out we had so much more in common than we had realized.

7

———————

FIBER TAP

The next morning on *Hibiscus*, Kelly bounded out of her stateroom at a quarter to seven, dressed and ready for the day. A surprised Rikki was in her robe, making coffee in the galley.

"Coffee?"

"Got a 'to go' cup?"

"Sure."

Kelly said, "Hey, one business note?"

"Geeze, you start early, but okay."

"Just to officially inform you in case this person becomes an employee of your company at some point, I'm dating Colt Toffler, who is *not* currently employed by you."

Rik put the pot down, came over and hugged her. "I'm so happy for the two of you. You guys had me worried." She poured Kelly's cup and handed it to her.

"Rikki, thank you so much. I owe you."

"If you two are happy together for a long time, we'll call it even. You look eager to get going. Gee, I wonder why. I'll catch up with you two over there, Cindy's going to sleep in."

I slept soundly, from 1 a.m. until 6. That was all she wrote. I

76

dressed, made coffee, and headed over to the *Beach Café* with my tablet, getting there shortly after they opened. I grabbed the best table in the corner by the pool and the beach, and took the chair with my back to both, leaving the best views for Kelly, Rik, and Cindy if she was joining us too. Several emails into my list, I felt rather than heard Kelly sneaking up behind me in the pool area. Without taking my eyes off the screen I said, "Not today you don't."

"How did you know? I was ultra-quiet!"

"Screen reflection."

"Really?"

I turned and smiled. "No. Two cups of coffee. Caffeine voodoo." I put my tablet down. Email could wait.

Kelly came around the pool fence and up to the table, then kissed me. That caught me off guard. True, we shared an extended good-night kiss when I walked her back to *Hibiscus* last night, but I hadn't expected this one. She sat down next to me, taking in the beach view. I motioned to our waitress for a cup of coffee for her.

"This is the most romantic and beautiful place for breakfast I've been in a long time. What a view! And last night was amazing. The stars were incredible, and the conversation was even better."

"The view this morning is pretty incredible."

"You aren't even looking at the bay."

"I know, that's the good part."

"Flattery will get you… everywhere. It is so good to flirt with you again, and this time have it be for real. Years of flirting while kind of meaning it, more than not. Lots of pent-up emotions."

I nodded. "Same here. I just don't want to screw anything up."

"We won't, Colt. Again, last night was amazing. That was the best…"

Someone coughed, and we looked up at a very surprised Rikki. She sat down with an amused look on her face.

Kelly blushed. "No, you didn't hear all of what I was saying, Rikki, I didn't finish!"

"Blame that on Colt, not me."

Just when I thought Kelly couldn't blush more…

"No! I was talking about our *conversation* last night. The stars were amazing, and our talk was the best I've had in a long time, if not *of* all time."

"Sure. Okay, I'll buy that." Rik put her hand up at an angle in front of her mouth as if whispering but instead saying loudly, "She's swooning, Colt. Way to go!"

"I'm not swooning!"

"If you say so."

"Rikki, I'm here because you set us up!"

"Did not. I'll deny it in court."

This was hilarious. Kelly was seeing a side of Rik that I'm sure she hadn't seen before. She reserved it for her close friends. I said, "Kelly, you're getting sucked into the 'Dead Parrot' routine."

"Wait, what?"

"Monty Python? The guy trying to return the dead parrot, but the shopkeeper claims it's just sleeping? You know that one?"

I saw the realization dawn on her as Rikki burst out laughing. Kelly joined in. Any concern that either Kelly or I might have ever had about her fitting in around here was long gone. When Rik picks on you, you're in. And just wait until she discovers that mild-mannered Cindy is an even bigger jokester. But the most important part of this was we found we could compartmentalize work and keep time spent here separate.

❧

We pulled into the parking area fifteen minutes before the meeting was slated to start. Coming by car early on a Saturday with little traffic took only a little longer than *Blitz* at regular cruise but used a fraction of the amount of gas. Plus, I had two stops to make on the way back.

We walked into the briefing room a few minutes apart from each other, not that Kelly and I would fool anyone for long. These folks all worked here for a reason, they were the very best at what each of them did.

"Tony, what did you find in Crozet?"

"You were right, that place is booby-trapped like you wouldn't believe, but not like you might think. It was the wildest thing I've seen. Let me show you." He started a video on the big screen, shot after dark in infrared. He panned across the property from outside the fence, and it was easy to see the lidar coming from the old pickup under the pole barn. "I'm certain this old truck is just for detection, purposes. That's not a charge cord leading to it, that's an armored data cable. I looked it over closely and there doesn't appear to be any weaponry attached, but in a minute, you'll see why." The video zoomed in on a bush next to the building that shook. They watched as it panned out and one of the Teslas's lidar became active as it rolled out of the garage and headed for the bush. Then the front-end loader combination moved toward it. Suddenly a raccoon shot out of the bush and headed toward the property edge. The combination reversed itself and shut down while the Tesla returned to the covered area and shut down. "Here's the thing, while this was happening several deer were moving around in the field. The truck lidar was painting them the whole time, but the AI brain recognized they weren't a threat. It didn't know what was causing the bush to move, so it sent mechanical defenders, who quickly recognized the raccoon for what it was. No humans showed up, AI was guarding the property on its own. It might call someone if there was a verified incident, but apparently not until that point. But that truck makes this whole property a killing field. No way to outrun a fleet of autonomous Teslas."

"Kelly? What's your take on what you just saw?"

"Tony is right, AI is defending that building. With what we know and suspect about their system, I'm certain now that it's the Program System, tied to the Writer System in NOVA. It would have the computing power and capability we witnessed, and with that armored data cable it's got to be there, probably underground. Tony, did you see any way we could get in there other than taking that truck out?"

"Not likely, Kelly. It covers everything."

"If we take it out by blowing it up, all hell might break loose, the AI would see the attack."

"Count on it."

"Colt and I surveilled what I'm certain is the Writer System in NOVA. There's no way to get into it to upload Lestat. They built the place like Fort Knox. Even the manhole covers to the fiber vaults are locked and camera monitored. Probably the same at the Programing Center. No way to get in there and still leave it up and operating, they are likely to have a detection and isolation system in NOVA if it thinks something is hinky." She stopped and looked thoughtful.

Rikki looked at her. "What?"

Kelly was smiling now. "We know that the vaults in NOVA are protected, and it's reasonable to assume that the ones in Crozet are the same way. Where is the only other place between Crozet and NOVA where their fiber would be out of that armored casing? A place where we can easily access it even though it's also secured? A place they could count on having that same kind of security even though it's out of their control?"

Rikki's face lit up. "NGIC! The National Ground Intelligence Center."

Kelly nodded, smiling. "NGIC. If we can get access to their vaults, we just need to sort through the fiber that's passing through it. When we find the right lines and we can access not just their programming feed, but hopefully their auction connection as well. We can direct a tap feed from NGIC's vault to here using our network. We'll watch them in real time from the comfort of our own offices. What do you think, Mark, can you sort it out and send it this way?"

"Needle in a haystack with the fiber, Kelly, but yes I can, once I locate it. How much traffic could there be from Crozet to NOVA, anyway?"

Jim Bannister weighed in. "There are 9,500 people in Crozet. Most work at the University of Virginia or related or dependent businesses. Second largest employment sector out there is the government, mostly in the intelligence sector. There are over 3,000 homes and businesses. Maybe a third of those are on fiber, at the most. Say maybe ten with constant data flow to NOVA, if even that many."

"I'll find it. Once I do, you'll even be able to upload Lestat from here, Kelly. I've got a new fiber tap 'toy' I built that will be perfect for this."

Colt spoke up again. "Okay, Jim, did you find a Big Nile watering hole?"

"No, I found the Big Nile info gold mine. Lots of resentment within the company from when the AI budget tripled. Plenty of other projects got back-burnered with plenty of unhappy campers. I got the names of a half dozen of their brightest engineers who quit about the same time as Lloyd Heatherton. Guess where they all relocated. Crozet."

"Great. We need a full workup on all of them. Banks, Passport numbers, houses, mortgages, credit cards, cars, the works."

"Got it, Colt."

"Anybody else? Okay, let's meet back here Monday at fourteen hundred for an update. Great work, people, thank you! We'll put these mothers out of business."

Jim and Mike's departments had the leads in the next steps, so after Rikki made a few phone calls smoothing their way into NGIC, we were out of the shop.

I had two stops to make on the way back, starting with a good wine store in Virginia Beach. I hopped out and picked up two bottles from Casey and Dawn's favorite winery. Next, we went to see my friend Mark, at what the South Dock Bunch had nicknamed 'the jewelry store' because we were always lucky to get out of there without spending a fortune, and it didn't happen often. It was the best independent tackle store in Virginia, and they had everything.

Mark came out from behind the counter when he saw us. "Rikki, Colt, great to see you guys again! What are you up to today?"

"Flailing at flounder, Mark. And this is Kelly."

"Nice to meet you, Kelly."

"Mark, I've been depending on Casey's tackle too long, it's time to get my own. Two rods, some lures, leader, the works. And can you order me two of those same kayaks that Casey has? But in camo instead of tan."

"Will do."

"We're going to browse a bit." Rik had already waded into the clothing section, which is where I dragged an amused looking Kelly. I looked at her, judged her sizes, and picked out three casting shirts holding them up on her checking the colors. I added two pairs of fishing shorts, two pairs of long khaki fishing pants, and a pair of canvas deck shoes.

"All this is for me?"

"Yep."

"I own clothes and can do my own shopping you know."

"Yes, but none of your clothes live on my boat."

"I don't live on your boat."

"Did you, or did you not tell Dawn last night you hoped to be around *Bayside* often and hoped I wanted you to be there as well?"

"I guess I did."

"Here's your answer. Or I can put all this back if you'd rather. It's up to you. But you can have the starboard hanging locker. Again, it's up to you. I guess you have a decision to make. I'm not asking you to move in permanently, but if you come up on the spur of the moment, wouldn't it be nice to have some clothes waiting for you? If you are 'going to be around' doesn't this make sense, especially if we are fishing a lot together?"

"You know, for a guy I had to ask out because you refused to ask me, you move pretty fast."

"Give me a hand putting it back then."

"No! You're right, it makes sense. And yes, I want to spend more time there with you. And I can't keep imposing on Rikki and Cindy."

"Problem solved."

"I love these, thank you."

"Thanks for wanting to spend time with me and my friends. Oops, we forgot a belt."

I rode in the back on the driver's side, and Kelly was up front with Rik. She had gotten quiet, and I hoped it wasn't because of the clothes and what she might think went with them. It wasn't. She had been scheming, and I loved the way she thought. She turned to face Rik and me.

"Have you guys figured a way to make sure these engineers don't just rebuild this system after we destroy it?"

Rik answered, "I'm still working that one out, but I can see the gears spinning with you."

Kelly smiled. "First, I have a question. What if there were a way to grab the auction payment? I guess we hand that over to the government since they are the client. But would they give us a 'finder's fee' percentage?"

Rikki smiled. "I like where you are headed with this. I believe I can work that out after I remind them we brought this to them, not the reverse. And I'll also remind them that if there isn't, then there's no incentive for us to go beyond just getting this shut down. It could be found money or lost opportunity, their choice."

"Exactly."

I asked, "What's that got to do with making sure they don't re-start it?"

She replied, "What if the money gets divided up and flows into their personal accounts? Accounts we set up offshore for them they don't even know about. Once it hits there, we drain it, leaving only the trail leading back to them. What do you think will happen when they don't deliver, and we make sure the buyer can follow it back to all of them?"

Rik was smiling wider now. "If we let them know what happened, they will run for their lives. The last thing they'll want to do is see any of their old cronies or get involved in computers again, where they are sure to be found! I like it. You think you can do this without leaving a trail back to our company?"

"I know I can."

I knew right then I could easily fall for Kelly; she was the "whole package." She was without a doubt the smartest lady I had ever dated; she shares the same sense of justice I do, is fun to be around, likes boats and fishing, my friends like her and she's pretty. Scratch that, she's beautiful. I guess the look on my face told her the story, and she winked at me. And I winked right back. I had known how smart she was from our times working together, but I never fully realized the rest of it until the last twenty-four hours.

Rik and I needed to talk. Kelly was an asset the company couldn't afford to ever lose.

8

EAGLE EYES

"She's beautiful, Colt!"

Kelly and I had just boarded *Plan B*, and she was getting her first look around the cockpit and bridge. I opened the hatch, and we descended the three steps. On the left was a head with a wand shower, beyond that was a full galley. On the right was "U" shaped booth seating and a dining table that dropped down and became a double bunk. The bulkhead had a twenty-five-inch flat screen TV. Beyond that was a stateroom with two hanging lockers, a large vee berth with center filler board and cushion, making it almost as wide as a queen at the end. Conrad had custom drawers added under each side of the bunks. Teak and holly strip flooring ran throughout.

"She's comfortable for one or two people for a few days at a time, and four in a pinch." We had come to assess how much cleaning would need to be done before we could move most of my things over from Blitz. The answer was as I expected, none. Conrad had left her in immaculate shape. She didn't even show the signs of wear you would expect to find from all the time he spent aboard, which is another reason I had wanted to buy her. I knew how well she had been maintained. I leaned back against the galley's Corian countertop as Kelly checked everything out. She came over with a very serious look on her face.

"Did you mean it about leaving clothes onboard, and spending weekends here?"

"Having second thoughts already?"

"Just wondering what sort of strings are attached to all of it."

"I told you I don't want to blow this. We've known each other too long, I like you too much, and last night confirmed that we are incredibly comfortable with each other. I'd like to think we might have a future together, but time will tell, I guess. I don't play games, Kelly, and I don't do strings. That's where and who I am."

Kelly came over and put her arms around my neck, drawing me to her, and kissed me.

"We're in the same place, so no, I'm not having second thoughts. What I'm having is one of the best weekends ever, with you. I don't want to blow it either. I hope we have a future together, Colt, more than you know. You're right though, time will tell. But I have one string."

"Which is?"

"I'd rather have the port locker and the port side of the berth." She smiled.

"Agreed." This time I kissed her. "Okay, we've got things to move over from *Blitz*. What about *Hibiscus*?"

"You sure move fast, fella."

"Not fast enough. We have to make a grocery run, too, and be aboard *Lady Dawn* by five. But as far as moving over here, do whatever you want. If you move over today, I promise you can trust me."

I could see her weighing things again, then she gave a small, sly smile. "I'll go get my gear from *Hibiscus*. By the way. who said you can trust me?" She winked. She was kidding. I think.

The grocery run was easier than I thought it would be, since we ended up with the same taste in food, too. Kelly turned a mundane grocery run into a fun outing. We became that annoying couple that enjoys grocery shopping, playing catch with meat and produce, earning us some stares and glares. She wasn't the only one having the best weekend, I was having a ball.

By 4:30 we had the galley stocked, clothes and bathroom gear put away, and Kelly was in the "head" getting ready. I had been expecting an awkward moment when it was time to get changed, but the head had ample room for Kelly, and I could change up by the vee berth. I had just finished putting on chinos and a light blue short-sleeve casting shirt when I was hugged from behind and heard chuckling.

"So, *this* is how it will be, eh?"

Kelly loosened her hug just enough so I could turn to face her. We had picked out identical outfits.

"Oh, crap, I'll change shirts."

"No, don't, Colt! I think it's a riot. We've been thinking alike, and I don't mind if people see proof of that. You're a lot of fun, do you know that?"

"Takes one to know one, lady. But if we are going to keep having fun, we need to get a move on or we'll miss the boat."

"What do you mean, 'miss the boat'? It's at the end of the dock."

"Not for long. Surprise! It's a cocktail and dinner cruise."

"No way! On that huge yacht?" She had an ear to ear grin.

"Yes, way. Now move your..." I swatted her on the butt and she yelped in surprise, still grinning.

We went up the gangway and were greeted by the steward, Andrea, who was waiting inside the watertight side door. "Eagle Eyes Colt! Great to have you back aboard, and thanks again!"

"It was my pleasure, believe me. Andrea, this is Kelly, someone who I'm hoping becomes a fixture around here."

"Kelly, it's great to meet you. Welcome aboard! We'll be leaving as soon as a few more guests arrive."

"Andrea, why 'Eagle Eyes'? What's the story behind that?"

"I better let Colt tell you. If he doesn't, come find me later. He is so humble. He bought me a new car." She smiled. "Casey and Dawn are on the flybridge deck, and Marcie is tending bar. We'll be leaving shortly."

"Thanks, Andrea." I had fast talking to do now. I led a very cool-faced Kelly up the stairway to the lower enclosed bridge where we had some privacy.

"You bought that young girl a car? I guess I should have held out for more than just clothes."

"It's not what you're thinking."

"Oh, you can't even begin to know what I'm thinking right now, buster."

"I fished a tournament up north with Casey and Dawn. I figured out that the so-called tournament leader cheated after I saw his photos. It disqualified him, and we won a prize purse of over a million dollars. We had all decided beforehand to cut the crew of *Lady Dawn* in for a share if we were to win anything, which they split four ways. They ended up with $37,000 each. So, in a way I *helped* buy her a car, I didn't *actually* buy her one. But the crew on *Lady Dawn* worked eighteen-hour days that week, putting up with us when we were behind in points and in terrible moods. Because I spotted the cheating part, they decided to call me Eagle Eyes."

"Tradecraft?"

"Exactly."

"Did you know you keep getting better as the weekend goes on?" She kissed me again. "Let's go find Casey and Dawn."

We went up a flight of four stairs, and onto the flying bridge deck. Lady Dawn was a 110-foot Hargrave, built for family liveaboards or entertaining. This deck was covered by a retractable canvas center hardtop, which was open tonight. Moving aft, there were seats to our left and then to our right, behind the helm and its four large LCD multi-panel screens. Beyond them on the left was a bar with four seats where Marcie, the First Mate, was bartending. Across the deck was a large 'U' shaped booth around a table that could seat ten. Aft of that was a huge hot tub with a cushioned sunning platform around half of it. Across from that was a large stainless propane grill. There were various teak chairs and chaises on the oiled teak deck, and all the way aft was a hydraulic davit next to where Casey's eighteen-foot Maverick flats boat sat in a custom cradle. Casey and Dawn were standing in front of Cindy and Rik, who were perched on two of the barstools. Rik looked over and smirked.

"The Bobbsey twins!"

"We got dressed at opposite ends of the cabin, Rik."

"Where's the fun in that, you smooth talker?"

Dawn looked amused. "Smooth talker, Colt? I don't think I've heard you say two sentences unless you've had a few cocktails!"

I shook Casey's hand as Kelly hugged Dawn. "He's a talker when he's drunk, Dawn?"

"I'm never drunk, Kelly, I'm merely operationally incapacitated at times."

"He's a riot, Kelly! You should have seen him the night he earned the 'Eagle Eyes' moniker. Couldn't shut him up."

I grumbled, "There's only partial truth in that, and you should have seen Dawn."

Kelly looked amused. She held two bottles out for Dawn. "Thank you so much for the invitation. I really enjoyed meeting you both last night."

Casey spied the label. "Crozet Vineyards, my favorite winery! Thank you, Kelly."

I could see she was about to include me in a comment, and I shook my head. I wanted her to get all the credit.

Dawn drilled back in. "Rik, what's this 'smooth talker' bit?"

"I invited Kelly up as a weekend guest. Next thing I know, that silver-tongued devil had packed her up, and carted her down to his new boat." She was trying to hold back in a laugh.

I was staring daggers at Rik.

"Get over it, Colt, there are no secrets on South Dock, and you know it. Okay, before I give Colt too much credit, I've watched these two kids make 'goo-goo' eyes at each other for a few years. But this is the first time both have been unattached at the same time though I guess they aren't any longer. It took all of one evening for them to realize what most of our team has known for years. They even staggered their arrival time at a briefing this morning as if some of the best intelligence operatives on the east coast were oblivious as to what was happening between the two of them. But before you get the wrong idea, I've been hoping this would happen for a long time. You two numbskulls are some of my favorite people, and even though you are just now realizing it, this was long overdue." Rik, Cindy, Casey, and Dawn clapped for us, as Kelly put an arm around me, and for the umpteenth time today, she blushed. Bim came over and chuffed, holding up a paw for Kelly to shake, which she did.

"Hi, Bimini. I haven't seen you all day." He leaned on her legs in reply. He looked at everyone.

Dawn said, "Got it, Bim, she's a good person. We like her, too."

"Chuff!" *You'd better*!

Marcie fixed us both up with cocktails, and over her shoulder on the security camera feed, I saw four people coming up the gangway. Up at the helm, Captain Frank Cunningham was now at the controls, warming up the huge diesels in preparation for departure, since the last guests had arrived.

The four people came up the bridge companionway and turned out to be Eric Clarke, his fourteen-year-old daughter Elaina, Eric's girlfriend, Congresswoman "Candi" Ryan, and a weekend guest of theirs, Christina Farmington, who rather forcefully stated she was to be called Chris. She looked to be in her mid-40's and had "Virginia horse country" written all over her. Despite that, she was more than a tad pushy, and I noticed that Bimini had slunk behind Dawn, eyeing Chris. As soon as she turned her back, he shot over to the companionway, hiding out of sight while keeping an eye on her. I'd never seen him do *that* before.

I said, "Honey, let's go watch Frank take us out. Excuse us for a minute?"

Casey nodded and smiled. We walked up behind the helm seats, watching as the LCD screens now were showing the engine information system, and navigation screens, plus a split video screen with bow and stern station cameras. Frank had on a boom headset talking to the crew members handling the dock lines. We watched, and I also glanced over at the companionway where Bim looked up at me with a worried face, then went back to observing Chris. I pretended to nuzzle Kelly's ear. "Do you see Bimini?"

She whispered in my ear, "Yeah, that's so weird."

"I've never seen him do that before. Eyes on that woman tonight, and this weekend. I trust that dog a hell of a lot more than I trust someone I don't know."

"Got it. And 'honey?' Really?"

"I was at a loss and needed an endearment term."

"I like 'Kel' next time you get stuck."

"Gotcha."

"I know, but what are you going to do with me now that you do?"

I leaned back and looked into a pair of eyes I could fall into. They were smiling as was she, and now me, too.

We turned and watched Frank as he choreographed our dock departure. "He'll kick the starboard gear in reverse as he hits the bow thruster. When she comes off the dock, he'll kick her forward, then hit the port gear in reverse, and we'll spin in place until we're headed out the inlet."

So as not to distract Frank I waited until we were in the inlet before we went around the seats to the helm and I introduced Kelly to him.

"Oh, you're Eagle Eyes's new friend I've heard so much about!"

I stared at him with a questioning look.

"Sorry, Colt, the South Dock telegraph you know..."

I shook my head.

"Have you been aboard other yachts before, Kelly?"

"First time on a yacht. Before this, the largest boat I had been out on was one of the Virginia Beach drift fishing boats. Colt's *Fountain* held the record for me for private boats before this."

"We got this one a few months ago, and she's a sweetheart."

"More like incredible."

"I agree. Hey, I hope you both enjoy the trip tonight, it's great to have you aboard."

"Thanks, Frank, great to meet you."

We walked back to the bar area, and we both caught Rik's eye. We gave slight nods. She was watching, too, having seen Bim act so weird. We had *Bayside's* contract for their new high-end development, and we do consulting work for Eric's company. We also watch over Casey, Dawn, and Eric, but that had less to do with business; it was more because they were our friends. Maybe Bimini's reaction was a coincidence, but as I said, I'm not big on believing in those. As a precaution, Rik, Kelly, and I switched to club soda with lime for the rest of the evening.

Chris surveyed the surroundings and spied the two wine bottles on the bar. "Crozet Vineyards! They are two farms over from me in Crozet, and three from Candi, who is my neighbor to the west. I go over to the winery and watch polo on Sundays with my other neighbor, Lloyd Heatherton. You all should meet him, he's an amazing tech genius. He could put you onto some fantastic investments, just as he has with me."

We all three smiled as you would when having to listen to any other self-important jerkwater. She must have twisted Candi's arm to bring her along this weekend, so she could meet Eric, Casey, and Dawn. But why? Because they were neighbors? She no more seemed to be Candi's type of friend than the man in the moon. Candi must have owed her a favor, or just wanted to shut her up.

Alarm bells were now ringing on full volume for the three of us. The mention of Crozet started it off, then Lloyd Heatherton's name kicked it into overdrive.

"You all must come and watch polo at the vineyards with us, people come from as far away as DC and North Carolina. It's the main attraction in Crozet on the weekends. We go almost every Sunday, and Lloyd has a huge tent put up with a catered spread next to the field. I insist that you all come. I've been trying to get Candi over there for years, but she's always so busy. What about a week from tomorrow? Eric, you can bring your helicopter, and Casey, there's a grass runway at the vineyard I can get permission for you to use. I know the owners very well."

Of course, she did. She would be a tough one to get away from, so they probably wouldn't have had a chance to get away with her living so close. I spoke up, "You know, Casey and Dawn, your old pal Henry Stefano goes on occasion, and he has been raving about how much fun it is watching polo over there. We might bump into him." I was passing a message to Casey and Dawn by saying this. Henry Stefano was dead and had been an enemy of Casey's.

Casey smiled and said, "Colt, why don't you, Kelly, Rik, Cindy, Dawn, and I plan on going next Sunday? Maybe we'll run into old Henry. He's such an interesting guy. Sounds like you think maybe Chris and he should meet."

"They would get along great, Casey!" Now both of their defenses were on alert. Eric glanced over at me, looking casual overall, but I read "full-on alarm" in his eyes. He knew the story behind Stefano and now wondered what the hell was going on. I pointed at my eyes and then at Chris while she faced away from us. I held a finger to my lips as his eyes widened, but he nodded and played it cool. We were all on the same page now.

Rik watched as Chris was busy with Casey and Dawn. I was able to sneak away and text Jim Bannister, asking him to do a background check on Chris Farmington. Fifteen minutes later he sent a text that I forwarded to Rik and Kelly. If Lloyd Heatherton had put Chris Farmington onto some "fantastic investments" as she claimed, Jim hadn't found them. In fact, she was up to her eyeballs in debt. She wasn't "old Virginia money" as she so desperately wanted people to believe. The farm, and the money she used to have had all come from her late husband, who had died on a horse trail ride with her. The coroner's finding on the death was "inconclusive." What the hell did that mean? You fall off a horse and die, it should be an easy determination of an accidental death. Clearly not so in this case. We now had more reasons to watch Chris Farmington if she might have been involved in her husband's death. Especially if the motive was his money. Kelly and Rik would read that text on the sly when they could.

Normally in a situation like this, we would brief the "protectees" and then let them make the call on whether we remove the person of concern, or if they shut off contact and we enforce that separation. Here, however, she would still live next to Eric's girlfriend, and now knew the ins and outs of Casey and Dawn's boat and property. Not a good situation, but one we could still deal with. If she was as deep in debt as it appeared, she wouldn't have the farm much longer, anyway. Once the dominos begin to fall, she won't be able to afford to stay around *Bayside*, either. And there was no way in hell I would let Eric, Candi, Elaina, Casey, or Dawn go anywhere near Crozet next weekend. But Rik, Kelly, and I were going, because I wanted to get a good up-close look at Lloyd Heatherton. And now I had a personal invitation to do so.

We all moved down to the main deck level and had dinner at the large aft deck dining table, watching as the sun set and lights came on along the shore. It would have been such a relaxing and romantic time if we hadn't switched into "work mode." Dawn had arranged the table seating so that Chris was at the far end in between both Rik and me. Casey and Eric were at the opposite end on either side of Dawn with Elaina, Candi, Cindy, and Kelly in the middle. Casey must have gotten word to Dawn, and so the two largest targets were now somewhat isolated from Chris during dinner. Bimini's reaction still nagged at me, especially since he had now rejoined the group and taken up a protective stance between Casey and Dawn. Normally he would lie down at their feet. Instead he was in alert mode and staring in Chris's general direction. He never moved throughout dinner.

Andrea had cleared the table when I told Casey, "Hey, I forgot to ask you to show me that new fish finder on your flats boat. Would you mind? And, Eric, you've got to see this thing, it does everything except make coffee."

"Sure, let's go. We'll be right back, ladies."

Once up on the flybridge deck we moved away from the stairwell so as not to be overheard. Eric faced me. "Colt, what the hell is going on?"

I related what we had found out about Chris Farmington, and said I couldn't go into much detail, but her polo friend was in the center of an investigation that was a matter of national security. "So, I don't want either of you two going near Crozet or that woman alone until we get things wrapped up." I don't think there are too many people Eric would take that kind of direction from, but I'm one of them.

"You don't have to worry about that, I can't stand her. She had leaned hard on Candi to bring her along to meet both you and me, Casey. She had been a big campaign donation bundler, so Candi felt she owed her a return favor. Turns out she twisted a lot of arms around Crozet and Charlottesville for donations but gave very little of her own money. Chances are most of those people wrote the checks just so she would go away."

"I need to go to that polo match next Sunday. Make it sound like you are all eager to go and let her set up the use of the runway. Then I'll charter your Aerostar, Casey, and Kelly, Rikki, and I will go. I want the chance to get a close look at that Heatherton guy."

Casey nodded. "Done. But what about her, do you think she's dangerous?"

"Probably only if you are married to her. There's no advantage to her to pull something right now. I think she's on the hunt for a new bankroll, and neither of you two are married. She probably sees both of you as potential marks."

Eric shook his head. "I want her out of here ASAP. Tonight, I'll say there's an issue with one of my businesses, and I've got to go to the west coast first thing in the morning. I'm bringing Candi and Elaina with me and will get the jet to pick us up here. I'll apologize and get the helicopter to pick her up after breakfast and take her back to her farm. She'll eat that up. Then I'll get it to come back here and pick us up on Monday morning as usual."

I nodded. "Perfect."

Casey asked, "How dangerous is her friend?"

"Put it this way, I wouldn't turn my back on him if I was wearing full body armor."

By the time we were back at the dock, Eric had communicated stealthily to Candi that they needed to cut the evening short, so she feigned a headache. Chris could see her options for extending the evening were dwindling here, so she said she was heading to the

Beach Café for a nightcap. She left out on the hunt soon after we docked. The rest of us acted like we were all turning in but hung on the aft deck.

Dawn was disgusted. "That woman was so obnoxious! Casey said she might be involved in something with national security consequences?"

Kelly nodded. "Not so sure yet how involved she may be if at all, but her friend is hip-deep in it. That's all we can say about that for now."

"Well, she wrecked a nice evening. I saw something was up when I saw you three switch over to drinking soda water. You didn't even get to relax and enjoy yourselves like we wanted you to, instead you got tied up in protecting us and our guests. We owe you a raincheck and a huge thank you."

Kelly replied, "That's not necessary, I had a great time, Dawn, thank you, the dinner was fantastic. And your yacht is so beautiful."

"Kelly, you're sweet to put on such a good face, but you are getting a raincheck, anyway. Since that woman is by now someone else's problem over at the café, let me at least make you a real drink and give you the nickel tour."

"I'd like that, thanks."

Dawn made drinks for everyone, then led Kelly away on the tour.

Rik looked at me. "She's good, and I hate to say it, but we may waste her talents by keeping her only in the lab."

I knew where this was going, it was a flashback to what happened to Rik's mom, and it worried her. "I already figured that and planned to expand her responsibilities into fieldwork. Her idea involving the money may make us a fortune, depending on how this goes."

"I agree. We need to keep our options open with her, we don't want her leaving."

"Agreed."

"The business either. I have ideas about that, but the other part is up to you, stud."

"You're a riot."

"Just saying..."

"Rik! I've been going out with her for a grand total of twenty-four hours. Give it a rest."

"At what point did you get her to move in with you, hour eighteen? I meant what I said, I'm glad you two numbskulls finally saw what had been so obvious to the rest of us for so long."

Cindy and Casey had been listening to and watching our exchange, with occasional knowing glances at each other. They were partners in *Bayside* with Dawn and now Eric, so they understood the dynamic all too well that Rik and I shared. But they were enjoying this way too much.

Kelly and Dawn came back out ten minutes later. "Casey, *Lady Dawn* is gorgeous."

"You know, Kelly, you're right no matter if you are talking about our boat, or my wife to be, so thank you. I'm a very lucky man in both respects."

"Hear, hear!" I raised my glass in a toast that everyone joined, except Dawn. True redheads like her blush in almost fluorescent color, and right now she was glowing.

"Thank you, Colt. But I'm the lucky one, and part of that's because I have friends like all of you. That includes you, Kelly, because I think we'll be great friends from now on, and I'm looking forward to you being here a lot."

I was one happy man right then. Happier than I had been since coming to *Bayside*. So much had happened in just a few days, and a lot of it revolved around Kelly. I was so glad my friends accepted her; we are all a really different bunch.

"Are we still on for flounder fishing in the morning?" Casey asked.

Kelly and I nodded. "Looking forward to it."

"Mind if we invite Eric, Candi, and Elaina?"

"Sounds like a plan."

Casey texted Eric. "They're in! 8:30 at the boathouse?"

"We'll be there." With that, Cindy, Rik, Kelly, and I got up and said goodnight to Casey and Dawn. Rik and Cindy said goodnight to the two of us at the bottom of the gangway as they headed back to *Hibiscus*.

"Well," I said.

"Well," Kelly replied.

"It's early. Want to go back over to C3 and star gaze again?"

She looked up, then back at me. "You know, last night is a special memory for me. I think trying to repeat it or improve on it might be disappointing. And I feel you might be trying to avoid having to go back to the boat with me."

I thought about that a minute before answering. "You're right, I am."

"Wow. Honesty, what a freaking concept."

"I told you, I don't do games. I don't attach strings."

"Yes, you did. You meant it too, and that's rare."

I shrugged. I mean, what do you say to something like that? Then she slipped her hand in mine.

"Here's what I suggest we do. We go back to the boat, build a pair of cocktails, and sit on the cockpit bench behind the helm seat and talk. About whatever each of us wants to talk about. Then we get into our pajamas, um, you do wear pajamas of some sort, right?" I nodded. "Then we get into the bunk and continue our talk and fall asleep whenever. We get up early, go to the *Beach Café* around 6:30, and I will buy you whatever you would like for breakfast. A nice, long, leisurely breakfast in that romantic beachfront café. Then we go kayak fishing. Do you think we could swim at C3 afterward?" I nodded again. "Then I'm buying you dinner at *Rooftops* to cap that day off. It will end the most unbelievable weekend I've had in a very long time."

9

RIK'S WRECK

I woke up on a new boat, in a new bunk, and with my arm across a new woman. It was early, sometime well before dawn. With only pre-dawn light showing through the portholes, I suspected it was around four-something o'clock. We had drifted off around midnight after once again talking about whatever came to mind, and we had run the gamut of subjects.

I carefully lifted my arm and started to extract myself from the bunk trying not to wake Kelly.

"You know, this only works when you are at the girl's place and you leave a note on the pillow or counter. But you own this place, so I should be the one sneaking out."

"You feel like you want to sneak out?"

"I don't know what I feel like, Colt. It's strange though."

"Good strange, or bad strange?"

"I don't know what kind of strange. Maybe like a one-night stand without the sex kind of strange. Which is a new one on me. Not that I've had that many one-night stands, mind you."

"So, you aren't staying over tonight? Are you heading back down to VB today?" I was lost here, not knowing what to think or do.

She was quiet for a minute. "I'd still like to stay if that's okay."

99

That she needed to think it over first worried me. "Yes, it's okay. I'm a little confused. I thought... I guess I don't know what I thought. Maybe I took too much for granted."

"That's it! That's how I feel. I'm a little confused, too."

"By the way, I wasn't sneaking out, I was just restless."

I slid back down under the covers and put my arm across her again, only this time I tucked her in close. "Go back to sleep, Kel. We'll wake up whenever we wake up, and we can talk about it then."

A little after six o'clock I woke when she shifted a little. I said to the back of her head, "Good morning."

"Good morning backatcha."

"Better?"

"Better. Do you always know what to say and do?"

"Absolutely not."

"You did this morning. Made me feel secure again."

"That makes one of us."

"You're insecure?"

"To be honest, I am."

"About...?"

"This morning, I feel bad you woke up feeling like you did. I pushed you into moving over from *Hibiscus*, and that wasn't fair. That's what I woke up thinking and what made me so restless. I'm sorry, I don't mean to push you into anything."

She rolled over with a serious and concerned look. "Colt, I'm thirty-seven-years old, I'm not some teenager with her first crush. I wouldn't be here if I didn't want to be. Don't think over the years when we've been flirting and kidding around I haven't thought about ending up right here. Or, that I didn't want to end up here, with you, even when I was lying next to someone else? I know that sounds terrible, and it probably is. No, it definitely is. But we've been honest with each other, and I don't want that to stop. So, you didn't push me into anything; I do what I want.

"Last night I had a moment of insecurity. I was like the dog that always chased the car, but this time the car stopped, and I caught it. Does that make sense? And where the car stopped was a place I hadn't counted on. All those times I wondered about being with you it was only about you, not where you were or the people around you. It turned out there were a lot of gaps in what I knew about Colt Toffler's life. I knew you had a boat you ran back and forth in, but figured it was a little outboard. I heard you lived up in NOVA, and you and Rikki were tight, but I didn't know what that meant. On more than one occasion I was jealous of her, wondering if you two were together. I figured that she might eventually own the company, but I never dreamed you would have part of it too. My perception of your reality has changed completely in the last few days, and it's taking some getting used to."

"My reality has changed a lot in the last few days. I can tell you this, it wouldn't be as good if you weren't here in it with me, Kelly."

"Colt, I don't want you thinking it's about the boats, buying the business, your wealthy friends, living part-time at a resort, and all of this. I had no idea about it, I swear."

"If I for a nanosecond believed it was, you wouldn't be here. Yes, I thought about waking up next to you on more than one occasion, but when I woke up it was never you. Most of the time that side of the bed was empty. And yes, I'm like that dog with the car, too. But I know what I want to do, and that's sink my teeth into the car's bumper and not let it take off even if the light changes." We both moved closer and kissed, recoiling quickly.

Kelly exclaimed, "Ew, 'last night's rum' breath!"

"Both of us. So, you hit the head first, I have to put on my legs."

"I'm sorry but that sounds... strange."

"Another part of my reality you're finding out about."

"I know, but the wording caught me off guard. I'll get used to it."

"I hope that means you're still planning on being around."

She slid out of the bunk. "Kind of hard to leave with your teeth sunk into my butt."

The Chesapeake was as flat as a sheet of glass, and there wasn't a breath of air stirring. We sat at that same corner table in the café since we were the first ones in the place. Sunday had a much later crowd for breakfast.

"Colt, look at the water, it's beautiful."

"I know, I love it here. It blew me away when I first saw it. The hotel and the cottages weren't open yet, and this was the only restaurant that was operating. Soon after, Conrad started using their air charter service and put the office here. It has worked well since the airport isn't that busy, and we have no travel delays."

"Oh, look." She was pointing over my shoulder. I turned and spotted Rik and Cindy headed out on their paddleboards.

"Great day for it. You ever use one?"

"I've tried it. Kind of fun exercise. I'd do it again."

"Want to get one for the boat?"

"Seriously? Can you use one?"

"I can, but it might not be comfortable for extended periods. I'll stick with my sit-on-top kayak."

"Then why get one?"

"So you aren't stuck with a kayak on days you would rather do that." I could tell what she was thinking, that I was in the "we" mode, not the "me" mode. "Kelly, if we don't plan on being together, we won't be, so I'd rather make plans like we will. If you think I'm pushing you, or if I'm making you uncomfortable say so, and I'll back off."

Kelly was quiet again, and I could see the gears turning. I was so used to this from our time working together, and I appreciated how she thought things through. I wanted her to do the same in our relationship, but it was unnerving not knowing what conclusions she would draw.

"It kind of struck me when you said 'the boat' instead of 'my boat' but I didn't want to read too much into it. After finding out the paddleboard would be for me; my initial reaction was that it was too much. I don't want you to feel obligated to buy me anything, and I don't want to feel obligated if you do."

"It's not like that."

"Wait, I didn't finish. But I get it's part of the whole 'planning on being together' thing, and with you it's not a bribe. I get that about you, Colt, but I'm not used to it yet. And yes, I mean 'yet' as in I plan on us being together, staying together, on 'the boat,' if that's what you want to call it instead of 'your boat.' I get it, I'm okay with it, but be patient with me because it's going to take some time." She took a deep breath, something was coming, and I hoped it would be a good something.

"I will be totally upfront like you were with your stock analogy, and I hope it comes out right. You know my favorite part of the weekend so far? I mean other than finding out you were happy that I showed up? It was when I was so confused and insecure last night, not knowing if this was the right thing to do, if this was the right place to be, if we were right together, or if it was the worst idea ever and I should get in my car and race back to my condo. You told me to go back to sleep, and you called me 'Kel.' I don't know if it was the way you said it or what, but in that instant with that one word all my insecurity about us evaporated. I realized I was with my longtime friend and 'flirt buddy,' and I was experiencing all the emotions that had been hinted at by both of us over those years. While I've been called 'Kel' a few times in my life, by a few different people, that was the single best time ever. The way it felt right then was like you wanted it to express all those emotions at once. I know, it sounds dumb now I've said it and makes me look like a hopeless romantic sap."

God, her eyes were incredible. Not only the color, but the way they expressed emotion, and right now they were at full volume. "The last thing you are is a helpless romantic sap. You want 'totally upfront,' here it is: you are one of the smartest people I know. I felt all that when I called you 'Kel' last night. I meant it then and I still do now. You are the 'complete package,' as in everything I could ever want in a partner. You are smart, perceptive, sexy, and a great conversationalist who impressed the hell out of a room full of my friends while still making me feel like I was the only one there. And to top it off, you're beautiful. Your eyes have a language all their own, and I'm glad I'm learning how to understand what they say. I hope I'm reading them correctly right now and you aren't about to jump up and run out of here."

She leaned forward, put a hand behind my neck, and drew me into a kiss. "If that was a question, I hope that answered it. I guess my eyes say more than I realized, and we had both been building up larger feelings over those past few years than I had been wanting to admit."

"Me, too. I don't know why I wasted time with some of the others I dated. I should have waited for you."

"Because you weren't sure if we would ever get 'our shot' the same way I wasn't sure. What if you or I had stayed in a relationship with someone else? We weren't ready for each other yet. Sounds corny, but that's how I feel."

"And we are ready now?"

"It looks that way, but it'll take time. The attraction is there, the trust and the figuring each other out parts will come when they're ready. We haven't talked about this yet, and I don't know if we ever will or need to, but I'm sure we've both been hurt in the past. Heck, we already hurt each other a little on Friday, but that's all part of it. That's what makes time together like this so damned special. It's the contrasts. What I'm trying to tell you is that I'm willing to risk getting hurt by you, because I believe the reward could be so much bigger than the risk. You're worth it. The only thing I can promise you right now though is that I'll be honest with you and try like hell never to hurt you."

I was pretty much at a loss for words, so I said, "Ditto."

"Ditto? I pour my heart out and get back 'ditto', Colt?"

"Ever see someone make a speech so eloquent that the next person rips their notes up and says, 'How the hell do you follow something like that?' That's how I feel right now. So, yes, ditto. I am so glad you said all that, and I can't equal or top it with anything I could say, no one could. Thanks for putting your heart in my hands, and here's mine for yours, Kel."

She sighed happily. "You topped it."

"Oh, one thing you should know, if you order food that looks better than mine, I'm going to steal some." I smiled at her and was only half kidding.

"What are you having?"

"Crab Benedict. It's unbelievable."

"Three guesses then about what I'm having, and the first three don't count. But I still reserve the right to steal from your plate, too."

The Crab Benedict was amazing as always, the company was awesome, and I had three leisurely cups of coffee with the most beautiful woman on ESVA. I couldn't recall a better breakfast. Then a Sikorsky S-76 helicopter came overhead, landing behind the office. It took off headed west ten minutes later.

"Eric's?"

I nodded. "Beautiful brand-new machine. He lives on the top floor of his five-story office building in Fairfax and has a helipad there. They put one in here for him because he's driving so much business this way, and they wanted to make it as easy as possible for him to go back and forth. Takes him a half-hour."

She shook her head. "He seemed so normal."

"Because he *is* normal. He's just great at business, and he's now a friend of yours. Call his office tomorrow and they'll put you right through. Some US Senators wish they had that ability. Welcome to *Bayside's* South Dock Bunch, you are now a member."

"What does that mean?"

"You'll see later." The glare she gave me changed that schedule. "Oh, what the heck, I'll tell you now." I held up my phone. "They took a text vote of all the C3 members. It was unanimous. Dawn did the polling this morning, she nominated you, so you must have impressed the hell out of her last night. Bim even gets a vote, and we all know he was for you."

"Okay? What was the vote for?"

"C3. You get your own card to the security gate now. If I'm not here and you come up for the weekend and stay on the boat, you can use the private pool, hot tub, the clubhouse, all of it."

"I wouldn't come up here if you weren't here."

"Why not? You have friends here now. Dawn was quite taken by you, and you know Rik's a friend, she and Cindy would love to have you go paddleboarding and hang out with them. If you don't want to, it's okay, but at least you know it's all available to you, and they're all here for you."

"I'm still trying to absorb us."

"That's the first time you've referred to 'us.' That sounded nice. But it's a package deal. You even get Sandy Morgan, but you have to bring your own beer."

"The author?"

"Yeah, he's our neighbor in the next slip over. Better to show you the beer part rather than tell the story, it's much funnier that way. Plus, it's inevitable." Kelly gave me a questioning look, then trusted me on that.

"Being with you is so different from what I expected."

"Bad?"

"No. Better, but still different. I didn't know you were friends with all these people. That's the different part."

"They're just people, Kel. Good people. You'll find that out."

"You're a lot more confident now than you were this morning. I'm glad. And I like all your friends I've met."

I smiled. The day was off to a great start.

The seven of us filed out of the boathouse in Casey and Eric's fleet of kayaks. Kelly and I brought our new rods, eager to break them in. As we passed Sandy Morgan's trawler, he greeted us with the usual verbal barrage.

"Oh, joy, the recycled milk jug fleet sails again. So, where are you headed this time?"

Casey smiled. "Rik's Wreck."

"Ohhh, big flounder! Hey, remember your old pal Sandy when you come back!"

"Somebody new in here named Sandy?" I loved 'exchanging verbal fire' with Sandy.

"Colt, you just remember to bring me some beer, and not that generic crap! And who might you be?"

"I'm Kelly, Sandy. I was going to stop by and introduce myself."

"Drop on by, darlin', and we'll have a beer or two!"

"Thank you so much, Sandy, but I don't drink beer. You can share those with my boyfriend though. Colt loves beer, so we'll stop by!"

Sandy didn't know what to do because Kelly's smile had him captivated. He sputtered as we passed, and she looked over and winked at me. No matter what happened with the beer later, it made my day since she called me her boyfriend. I know, I know, it's almost kind of 'high school.' But it gave me a thrill.

Rik's Wreck was a story in itself. The Russian mobster owner of a ninety-foot yacht came up against our team during an attempt to kidnap Dawn. While she was protecting her, Rik ended up getting that bullet in the arm in the process. So, now we have our own secret ninety-foot-long flounder reef a mile away that the locals don't even know exists yet.

A little over three hours later we returned to the marina, showing Sandy our limit of fourteen flounder between eighteen and twenty-four inches. I pulled up to his swim platform and dropped off my two for his nieces and him.

"What? Aren't you even going to clean them?"

"I'll meet you down at the fish cleaning table. And I even brought beer!" I reached into my cooler and took out a generic labeled bottle. "Want one?"

"Not more of that crap! Forget it! I'll drink my own."

"Aren't you out?"

"I lied."

"Suit yourself." I passed one to Kelly.

"You said you didn't drink beer!"

Kelly smiled as she peeled off the fake label revealing it was a bottle of Red Stripe, Sandy's favorite. "I lied."

"No wonder he's your damned boyfriend, you two are meant for each other. And you," He pointed at me, "It is SO on, fella! Just you wait."

"Thanks for the compliment, Sandy, and bring it! Score's two to zip."

"Score, my butt. It's on, just you remember that!"

Eric, Casey, and I cleaned the fish, including Sandy's. I left the whole ones with him on purpose, so he'd have to take a break from his writing and bring them down to the cleaning table at the end of the dock and chat with us while we worked. He knew that when I dropped them off, and I handed him a Red Stripe as he walked up. Sandy assumed that would happen, too. He'd probably use this as a scene in his next book. Then I took two nice filets over to the hotel's kitchen for them to cook for Kelly and me tonight. I grabbed my suit from the boat and we headed to the C3 clubhouse to change. I fixed her up with one of the guest suits Casey and Dawn keep there. My prostheses I was using today are waterproof, and while not the most technologically advanced, they were functional in a pool setting. I was already in the water when Kelly came out in a bikini. I said before that she was beautiful, but now I have to change that description to stunning. Breathtaking. Or just "wow." Take your pick, they all fit. Almost as well as that bikini fits. I couldn't take my eyes off her.

"What? You look like you've never seen a woman in a bikini before."

"I've never seen *you* in a bikini before, just in office clothes or 'Chesapeake Casual.' This is quite a departure from those."

"I guess I'll take that as a compliment."

"Uhhh, yeah!"

She chuckled as she walked down the steps into the pool, then took a lap before swimming up to the reclining area where I was already situated. She tucked in next to me on her side, facing me. "That was so much fun this morning. I've never fished from a kayak before, only paddled around in one. I'm glad you ordered a couple."

"For us."

"Okay, for us. I want to do more of that. With you."

"Casey's letting us keep them and your new paddleboard in the extra racks in the boathouse. He's putting in a freezer in there as well for the fish we all catch."

"*Our* new paddleboard."

"Okay, our new paddleboard. You know, this place is feeling more like home."

"I bet the new boat helps."

"So, do you. Thanks for not calling it *my* new boat."

"You'd only correct me if I did." She punched my shoulder. "Speaking of home, now you will be more involved at the shop, so where do you stay in Norfolk?"

"On *Blitz*, except in January and February, then I get a hotel room. Too cold to run around in her open cockpit, so I put her up for the winter."

"You stay in that dark old boat shed?"

"It's not that bad and it keeps the rain off."

"No."

"No what?"

"I mean no, not anymore. We have a perfectly good condo down by Rudee Inlet."

"We? Now, who's moving fast?"

"Well, we've already got the 'friends without benefits' part down, and you don't snore, so what the heck." She rolled over on her back beside me and found my hand with hers. I was a happy guy.

"When you go to DC, you stay in Woodbridge?"

"I have a condo there. But the company has a two-bedroom condo in Alexandria, so I'll use that one now with Rik. I'm putting mine up for sale this week, furnished. I'll go get my SUV and bring it down. Rik and I'll use a car service when we're in DC. Beats trying to park there."

"So, you need to go up and get your clothes and vehicle."

"That's all there is to get."

"I could drive you up and help you pack."

"I was hoping you would offer."

"Done deal."

Bimini appeared, walking down the steps of the pool and swimming over and lying down next to Kelly, putting his chin on her chest. Lucky dog.

"If he's bothering you, just tell him to go away." Dawn was pulling two chaises together.

"I like Bimini, and I hear he voted for me."

"I was talking about Colt." They both laughed.

I pretended to glare. "Gee, thanks, Dawn, I like you, too." She laughed again as Casey came up.

Kelly looked over at them, "Thank you both for the vote of confidence this morning. That was flattering, considering you've only known me for two days."

Dawn smiled. "We've known *about* you for over a month. In Colt's 'Operationally Incapacitated' moment at the Delaware tournament, he mentioned you. Yammered on and on about you in fact. He was the most inebriated I'd ever seen him that night. You know that Latin saying? 'In vino, veritas' meaning; In wine, there is truth. Babbled incessantly about you the more he drank."

"I did?"

"You did, and you were. Then Rikki filled us all in about you two the next day and told us how she hoped that the two of you would get it together because you were perfect for each other."

"She did?" I didn't know this part. Then again, I recalled very little of talking about Kelly that night.

"I did." Rik was walking up and heading for the pool. "Because you were, and you still are." She took two laps around the pool and lay down on the vacant side next to me.

Dawn walked over. "I'm opening some wine. Any takers?"

Rik and I held up our hands while Kelly hopped out to help, leaving a very disgruntled Bimini. He looked at me, sighed, and swam over to Rik's side, using her as a new chin rest.

"What am I, pal, chopped liver?" Bim grinned at me. Yes, dogs smile, and this one is smart as a whip and has one heck of a good sense of humor.

"I have something I want to run by you before Kelly gets back."

I was curious. "Okay?"

"If this banking idea of Kelly's works out, I'd like to do bonuses throughout the company with half."

"I had the same idea."

"We were talking about making sure she stays put in the business, and giving her a bonus, albeit a large one, is not a great way to assure that."

"True. We could be talking about a retirement sized sum if we do it in proportion to the value of her idea. But I want to do something that's fair."

"Colt, what would you think about us making her a ten percent partner, and then she gets ten percent of the profit, which would be even higher than her bonus? Then the partner shares would be her anchor, and a big part of our talent pool will stay with the company. In fact, I'd like to make her a partner even if the money scheme doesn't work. You and I would each have to give up some of our equity, but that would sure be a great incentive to stick around, so it would be a great tradeoff."

"I would have a tough time being objective because between you and me I'm pretty sure I'm falling for her."

She laughed. "You fell for her a while ago, but you had your shields up so far that it has taken you this long to realize it. Babbling on like you did at the tournament? Nancy was just a placeholder, dude. That's why it didn't hurt as bad when she left, and why you didn't see much of her all summer. And, I'll take your answer as a 'yes.' So, tell her before you sleep with her. Yes, I know you slept in the same bed, but I'm talking about before you do the whole 'horizontal bop' thing."

"How do you know we haven't already?"

"Because I know you, and I know her. Which is part of why I want you both as partners. Tell her now while 'things' are already inevitable, and not afterward, so it is clear it wasn't either a bribe or a payoff. Which was why I needed to talk to you now before you have that romantic dinner tonight." She smiled. "One more thing, I'm thrilled for you, pal."

Kelly came over with three glasses of wine, having seen Rik and I huddled together, but she didn't mention it. The five of us hung out the rest of the afternoon while Cindy bounced in and out, making her rounds of the hotel, marina, and the restaurants on one of their busier days of the week. She also dropped off Kelly's gate card for C3, making her official now.

We walked back to the boat a little after 6:00 to get ready. I planned cocktails in the cockpit chairs for the two of us and Kelly had us going over to *Rooftops* at 8:00.

I sat on the edge of the vee berth. "Kel, can we talk for a second?" I patted the mattress next to me. She came over with a questioning look. "I need to discuss some business with you."

"Is this what you and Rikki were being so secretive about this afternoon?"

I nodded. "She suggested I bring it up before we go to dinner tonight."

"Ah. Before the romantic 'seal the deal' dinner." She crossed her arms and then leaned back against the hull. "Then this ought to be good, whatever it is."

"The 'seal the deal' dinner?"

"I kind of figured on making it that, but you don't sound so sure."

"She must have figured that out. But I don't have an agenda."

"You don't, do you?"

"I'm flying by the seat of my pants right at the moment."

"No seduction plans?"

"I go by plans at work. I go hand in hand with you, wherever we go, whatever we do. Damn, that sounded corny."

"Then we are even for my cornball comment this morning. So, what's so important that you have to tell me before we have dinner?"

"I wish she was here, but she wanted me to tell you, to ask you. We were both so impressed with your idea of snatching the auction money. If it works, we plan to hand out bonuses to everyone but me, Rik, and you."

She looked amused, but I'd have been pissed. "Okay, I'll bite, why don't I get a bonus, too?"

"Because it was your idea. And partners don't get bonuses, they get percentages. Whether this works or not, we want to make you a ten percent partner and ask you to join us in buying out Conrad. We're each willing to give up some of our equity to make that happen, that's how much we want you as a partner. If you want the deal."

I'd never seen her stunned before, probably because she's so smart not much catches her off guard. But this stunned her at first until the gears kicked in.

"Just for the record, whose idea was this?

"We each thought of it independently. I had planned to pitch it to her tomorrow, but she brought it up today in the pool. I think she might have waited, except for the whole dinner thing. She thought the timing was important."

"So, it wouldn't appear to be a carnal bribe or a carnal payoff."

"I hadn't thought about it like that until she brought it up."

"That's because you are a good man, Colt, and you wouldn't think of it in those terms. But you are forgetting something that Rikki didn't know, I asked you to dinner, and it's my buy. And yes, I had planned on making it a 'seal the deal' dinner. Yes, I had an agenda, but that got all blown to hell a minute ago with your offer and that whole 'hand in hand' comment. I love the way you think, and I'd love to be your partner." She smiled, and those eyes were talking again, "Your business partner, too." Then she kissed me. "I guess we'll just have to wing it from this point on. Since it's my dinner, I'll call Rikki and invite her and Cindy over for cocktails in the cockpit at 7:30. Then I'll push our *Rooftops* reservation back to 8:30 and add them to it because I want to have dinner with all my new partners." She smiled again. "Don't look so disappointed, I'm moving everything back for a reason. Cocktails and dinner will give us a nice breather afterward before round two." She winked, although it was seductively this time. We ended up pushing cocktails back even another fifteen minutes.

Dinner was one of the best in my life, with the food and drinks that were "spot on" as always. We brought two additional filets with us, and then all four were stuffed and baked with crabmeat and topped with mornay sauce. Chef Carlos was nothing if not amazing.

But what made dinner so special for me is that I was now at the most exciting and successful point of my life so far. While that was nice, for the first time I had someone in my life I could share it all with who understood my job and everything that came with it; the hours, the danger, and the excitement. Someone who enjoyed so many of the same things I did. Someone who kept looking my way and smiling throughout dinner, and I'm sure I was doing the same. I couldn't help myself, that was the best part. I even carried my end of the dinner conversation.

Rik and Cindy were happy for me, for *us*. Falling in love with a stranger can be so tough because you don't know what to expect. Falling in love with a friend can be much easier because you know most of what to expect from them. Sure, we had both surprised each other with a few things, but overall, we were comfortable. Being together at work might throw a few hurdles at us, but we'll work through whatever comes our way. While it wasn't quite love, at least not yet but it was well on its way to becoming that. Her partner comment earlier didn't shake me up, in fact, it had the opposite effect.

We said goodnight to Rik and Cindy at *Plan B* as they headed back to *Hibiscus*. We looked at each other as we stepped into the cockpit. Those eyes were at it again. I now had the name to replace *Plan B*.

"What!"

I was grinning. "It's a surprise."

"Un huh. What kind of surprise?"

"Show you on Friday. Assuming you want to come back here on Friday."

"Twist my arm. Meanwhile, you sit on the bench up here, and I'll make us drinks."

"Then I suspect we will talk."

She zippered shut the canvas and isinglass windowed drop that separated the bridge, which had A/C, from the cockpit which did not.

"If we went to the stateroom I wouldn't be in a talking mood. Sit. Stay."

"Now I'm Bimini."

"He minds better. I'll be right back." Two minutes later she reappeared with drinks in hand. "You know, I said I was buying you dinner to top off one of the most unbelievable weekends I've ever had, and that was even before I made partner."

"Was it? I hope we aren't talking about the business now. You said you had this whole agenda thing going on."

"It was, I wasn't, and believe me I do."

"I was hoping you meant something by what you said about being a partner before dinner."

She lay down on the 'L' shaped bench with her head across my chest, looking up at me. "What if I did? Colt, I know this is crazy. Seventy-two hours ago, I asked you why you never asked me out, and you answered by saying you never would. If we didn't have over two years of history working and yes, flirting like hell together, I'd never be about to say what I think I'm about to now. Then again, this is my umpteenth and last rum drink of the night, and we need to be out of here by 7 a.m. to avoid the worst of the traffic. I'm fixing us breakfast, by the way."

"And avoiding what you were so close to saying before you chickened out."

"Thought you weren't going to hurt me."

"Not trying to hurt you, I'm trying to encourage you."

"To make a fool of myself?"

"You know you can't do that with me, right? You can say whatever is on your mind, and I mean whatever. It stays with me, and only me."

"Okay, it was already on track to be one of my best weekends ever, and that was even before I went kayak fishing, insulted a best-selling author, made love with a new best friend who I only realized was a best friend about the same time I realized I was falling for him. Oh crap, I can't believe I said all that now." She closed her eyes.

I put my arms around her and held her. "Would you answer one question before I tell you something?"

She nodded. "Yes."

"Are you happy?"

She sucked in a deep breath. "More than I've been at any point in my adult life."

"Do you regret saying any of that?"

"I thought this was one question."

"Humor me. And I mean about being my partner, too."

"Regret it? No more than I've ever regretted telling the truth, which is what that was. Does it scare me? It scares me I've put my heart out on my sleeve. But if I hadn't, you couldn't be sure of where I was coming from. I'm scared of what you are thinking, what we are doing, and where I go from here if we aren't on the same path, and if I've made a fool of myself."

"You haven't made a fool of yourself at all. I told Rik when we were talking at the pool about the partnership I would have a tough time being objective because I think I'm falling for you. She said, and I quote, 'You fell for her a while ago, but you had your shields up so far that it has taken you this long to realize it.' That's where I'm coming from, Kelly. So, here goes. Rik wanted us to get 'this' figured out by Monday, so we have less than two hours left until midnight. I am in record territory here, and yet I'm kind of not. We've been friends for a while. Good friends, and friends that thought a lot about each other, and still do."

Kelly nodded; her eyes now fixed on mine.

"Here's what I've figured out. I want a relationship with you, just you, no more 'flirt buddies.' Call it partners, call it what you want, but I want just you. I told you upfront I don't do games, and I meant what I said. I think we have a great future together, and I'm not talking about work. Though we do there, too. I said 'the boat' because I want to share it with you. I want to share everything with you and build a future with you. Talk about putting your heart out on your sleeve. So, that's where I am, Kel."

"Ditto."

"Ditto? Ditto? I pour my heart out and get back 'ditto,' Kelly?" I was grinning again.

"Paybacks are a bitch, aren't they, Colt!"

"Better now?

"Much. We're on the same path, and I can't even tell you how I feel right now. You're amazing. We're amazing. This place is magical, and I owe Rikki Jenkins so much at this point. At the shop, I almost got in my car and went home, but she wouldn't take 'no' for an answer. She literally stood behind my car and refused to move until I got out and talked to her. Rikki told me she knew how you felt, that she knew you better than anyone, and I'd be making a big mistake if I didn't listen to her. I didn't believe her at first, but she convinced me to come here, and you have no idea how many times I almost turned around and went back. I didn't know how you would react, what you would say, and what we would say together. She knows you so well."

"She knows us both so well. Which is why we three are such a great team together. And she's right. I fell for you way back then; I know that now."

"Remember when I said if we went to our stateroom I wouldn't be in a talking mood anymore? I'm through talking."

"I love hearing you call it 'our stateroom.' Maybe we can work toward 'our boat.' Kind of a goal of mine."

"It's our stateroom because if I ever catch another woman in there, we won't need to buy any chum for a year! Follow me, partner." She sighed. "I love our boat."

I smiled.

10

EMERALD IZ

Traffic was getting heavy as we turned into the shop property. We talked it over on the way down and decided Rik was right. The people we worked with were way too bright to be hoodwinked, and we didn't want to be dishonest about it. Many of them had already seen what Kelly and I hadn't even recognized, and they had expected this would happen. Even long before I ever thought about joining the company, much less thought about buying into it. We agreed however to keep Kelly's partner news under wraps until we saw if there would be a windfall from this case. It would seem much more logical and acceptable to everyone when they were all holding big checks in their hands made possible by the newest partner. This should erase any doubts about how Kelly got her promotion.

Kelly went to her lab group, and I made rounds. Mark Foster had already been in the vault up at NGIC for two hours, sorting through the thousands of fiber threads, using one of his "toys." We couldn't reach him in there, but even if we could, there was no way we would; he needed to be able to focus.

Tony Becker was already in the planning stages with the rest of his team, getting ready for the building breach in Crozet. The only thing we would lack by the end of the day would be the actual timing, which would be dictated by many so far as yet unknown factors. One of the largest would be the ending date and time of the auction.

We would need to simultaneously hijack the auction and detonate Kelly's team's Lestat program. Once we had control of the auction platform, we could change the payment information, directing it to the offshore account that would split it and deposit it into the individual offshore accounts. Then one by one we would drain those over the next day, sending the funds in different directions, through different secretive banking organizations in multiple countries. Then it would make its way stealthily back into one account in the US, minus our predetermined 'finder's fee' percentage. If it all worked that is. A lot of this depended on some of Mark's new inventions, and everything was riding on Lestat.

At 2 p.m., we all convened in the briefing room, and we brought in Rikki via teleconference from the ESVA office. Mark had texted saying he was still digging through the thousands of fibers in the armored bundles that converged there. At the rate he was going, he should be able to find it by midnight at the latest. But you never knew if it might be the next line he tested.

Everything now was on hold until we tapped that line and accessed the auction. No doubt the bidders had all been issued invitations, and even if we stumbled onto the site from outside that feed, we wouldn't be able to access it. We needed to see in it to determine who was bidding, how much time was left before the end, and how to hijack it. Without that timetable, nothing could move forward. We were now as prepared as we could get. With the information Jim had already found about who was involved, Kelly and her team set up all the offshore accounts and prepared the obvious and the stealthy transfer routes.

Tony's team's action plan was in place and ready to go once the defenses were down. They would grab any backups and blow the Program System.

But for now, we were on hold and would be until at least tomorrow morning. Since we had no idea what the timing would be after that, I suggested that everyone leave and get some rest, because once things were rolling, there was no telling how long we would work at a stretch. We would meet back here at 8 a.m.

"Want to take a trip to NOVA?"

Kelly nodded. "As good a time as any. At least we'll miss the traffic here."

My phone app said with current traffic, we would be there in three hours and twenty-five minutes, but I didn't expect that to hold. Surprisingly, especially for the I-95 leg of the trip at that hour, it did.

I guess my place was a shock to Kelly. White walls, generic pictures that had been there when I moved in, not a lot of kitchen utensils because I rarely cooked when I was here. There wasn't any food in the refrigerator because it had been over a week since I'd been there. I didn't even have a desktop computer. I used a laptop, a tablet, and a cell phone. Until now, I had kept on the move, out of town during the week, and for the past several months I had been at *Bayside* on most weekends. I hadn't spent five nights here in the last month.

"You weren't kidding about not having much to pick up other than clothes and bathroom gear. We only need a couple of the cardboard boxes I picked up."

"I was never here much."

"Okay, you surprised me again. I thought there would be pictures and things."

"I've got a good memory, and there are photos on the laptop. Disappointed?"

"At least there isn't a gallery of photos of old girlfriends. But none of your family?"

"Conrad and Rik are my family. Nobody else left. I was an only child, and as I told you the other night, my parents are gone."

"I know, Colt, I'm sorry."

"Why? I've got Conrad, Rik, and you, who else do I need? Plus, Bimini likes me. At least he does when you and Rik aren't around."

"That was so funny yesterday."

"He did that on purpose you know."

"You think so?"

"I know so. He's one very smart dog, and he plays tricks on people he likes. Yesterday was a case in point,"

"He sure pegged Chris Farmington."

"Yes, he did. I need to pick up one of those huge cow leg bones for him from the grocery store. He loves those."

Ten minutes later we were headed out. I told Kelly to follow me as I had a surprise. I pulled into a handicapped space in front of Chalupa's, the best Mexican food around. She had to hunt for a space. "See? A bonus when you ride with me, I get better parking!"

"Funny guy."

Not only did we get guacamole in our burritos, I got a bowl with freshly made tortilla chips. "That bowl's more than a buck, and it's terrific." She was smiling.

"You are now going out with a big spender. I got it to impress you."

"It worked. I'm so impressed that you might get lucky when we get home."

I so loved watching her eyes. "In that case, Costco is right up the road. I think they have a five-gallon bucket of this stuff and a fifty-pound bag of chips. I want to be sure we don't run out." Watching her eyes was still the best but listening to her laugh was a close second.

We pulled into her two assigned parking spaces and unloaded. Her place was a true home. The second I walked through the door I knew it felt like her. In a living room bookcase there were pictures of Kelly with her sister growing up in Wisconsin, and some pictures of an older couple that looked like they were taken in Florida, probably her parents. The kitchen had electric gadgets on the countertops, and the refrigerator had post-it notes and more photos of her sister and kids held in place by funny magnets. Suddenly, I had that same feeling Kelly had on Sunday morning. Insecurity. This place was all Kelly. I didn't know if I'd fit in. Where I'd fit in. How I'd fit in. We were both old enough to be set in our ways, and I was afraid that she might start to trip over me and resent me for it. This suddenly seemed like a terrible idea.

"Colt? Colt? What's the matter?"

I didn't know what to say. I didn't want to say anything because whatever I said might be taken the wrong way. Then again, it was Kelly. I needed to be honest. "Remember Sunday morning, at 4 a.m.? That's how I feel right now. It's your place. I'll be underfoot. You're used to things a certain way, and I don't want you to resent me for invading your space."

"Is that how you felt about me on your boat?"

I sighed. I'd blown it. *Plan B* was back to being "your boat" again.

She saw the disappointment on my face. "I meant, the boat. Sorry, this is catching me off guard."

"I didn't, and don't feel that way about us on the boat."

"I thought you'd be happy here with me, and I don't get the difference between here and the boat."

"I am, but I foresee you being unhappy here with me being in your way, and that scares me."

"What, are you a fortune teller now? In the way of what?"

"Your routines. We didn't have any routines because I had just bought the boat. We were forming new routines together."

The gears were turning again. She grabbed my hand and led me over to the couch. Her surprised face had turned to one of concern. "Colt, we both said we hoped we had a future together. Do you still mean that?"

"I do."

"Well, part of that future is being here with me, or somewhere with me, but I love this place. Yes, I have routines, and so do you. Yes, they will clash. And yes, we'll compromise and find a way of doing things. Our own way of doing things; yours and mine together. And before it comes up, no, there's been no one else who has ever lived or stayed here with me before, so I'm not talking from experience. I've never wanted anyone to live here with me before. Does that sound like someone who will resent you, or someone who wants to find a path with you, who wants a future with you?"

Her face was clouded with concern. I hadn't even thought about the possibility of someone else having lived here before. We both had people in our pasts, and that's where those ghosts should stay. But I hadn't realized I was the first person she was willing to let live with her in this place she loved, and I damned sure wanted to be the last. "Thanks, Kelly. I'll love living here with you."

"Darned right you will. Just stay out of my way."

"What?"

"Just kidding! You are easily riled when you're nervous, you know that? Let's put your stuff away tomorrow and go work off that guacamole now."

The next morning Kelly was up and fixing herself an English muffin as I walked out of her bedroom. Okay, *the* bedroom. "Got yogurt?"

"Yep. The same brand that's on *Plan B.* You comfortable?" She passed a cup and a spoon across the counter and poured me a coffee.

"Yep, thanks, I am. Newsflash, it's not *Plan B* anymore."

"What?"

"Remember I said I had a surprise for Friday? Name change."

"What is it?"

"If I tell you, it won't be a surprise."

"That's not fair!"

"Life's not fair."

"Make it fair!"

"I'll give you a hint. I named her after you."

"You did? Really? Kelly?"

"Not exactly."

"KE?"

"Nope."

"WHAT?"

"You'll see on Friday. That way you can't kick me to the curb before then when you keep tripping over me."

We got to the shop a little after 7 a.m., and Mark was already hooking up the tap to our system. It had been almost 10 o'clock last night before he found the right line. He couldn't have slept more than a few hours, but he was moving fast and happy this morning, excited to show off his latest gizmo. He and Kelly got right to work. She quickly accessed the auction site, then Rikki called.

"How's it going?"

"Mark got the tap hooked up, and Kelly's found the auction platform."

"Outstanding! And... I made a deal."

"Okay, Monty Hall, what's behind door number three?"

"I started at twenty-five hoping to end up around ten."

"And?"

"Twelve percent."

"Get out!"

"Nope."

"Sweet!"

"Any idea where the bidding is?"

I gulped as I read the screen over Kel's shoulder. "$280 million."

"Be serious."

"Doesn't get much more serious than that."

"When does the auction end?"

I read again, figuring the countdown clock.

"Sunday at 7 p.m. Eastern time zone."

"It could go up higher?"

"Just did. $290 now."

"Get Kelly to ship me a feed here."

"Will do."

"Call me later."

"Kelly, can you get Rikk—"

"Already have a feed set up over there. She can pull it up and watch it in real time. Oh. Uh, oh."

"What?"

"They have their own private message board with auto-translation software."

"So?"

"So, there's a conversation on it from last night. A bidder was challenging them, saying that putting two books out means nothing. The bidder gave the names of two congressmen, a conservative, and a liberal, and challenged them to show what they could do to each. They responded by saying 'watch the morning news.' This isn't good."

We turned the two displays in the briefing room on to opposing cable news channels. There was breaking news about each of those two congressmen, and newswire reports said one was linked to a decade-old case about a woman who disappeared who had worked on the congressman's campaign a few years ago. It hinted that they had been romantically connected before she disappeared. The story about the other congressman quoted anonymous sources saying he had an affair with an exotic dancer and had paid her a hefty sum in hush money. They even had publicity photos of the woman, with video of her refusing to comment about the alleged affair, but with a smug and knowing look on her face. Both congressmen denied that any of it was true.

Kelly was shocked. "This is all machine fabricated! It probably searched for old news and cross-referenced things about these people. All they had to be was in the same area."

I nodded. "But it's out there now, and there's no pulling it back. They'll investigate the disappearance again, and they have to question the congressman now. They'll have video of him with his lawyer, walking out of the police station. It doesn't matter that they'll eventually clear him, what matters is the voters will remember that video.

"The other story the congressman will deny, but you can bet that dancer drops hints she might have been involved with him, and the media will report that. Sex sells. She can't buy the publicity she'll get from this; she'll no doubt get magazine photoshoots and go on a strip club publicity tour around their state and make a bundle."

"And he'll be ruined!"

I said, "This close to the election, it'll finish both politicians. Which is why we have to stop this bunch before this happens to more people. This is just a taste of what can happen when AI gets unleashed."

Kelly and I pulled Mark and Tony into the briefing room, bringing them up to speed on these latest developments. We explained how we had gotten an invitation to watch a polo match with our lead suspect on Sunday, and how the timing could be perfect. Kelly's team was now cloning the auction site address on our server, and we will swap them right before Lestat detonates, a little before 3 p.m. If it all worked well, none of the bidders would notice any difference. Heatherton's group would be dealing with the loss of their server farm and the Programming Center. They should assume that the auction site died with the server farm and have no clue it continued. Even if they discovered it was still viable, their passwords and backdoors would all be missing from the new site, and our new payment instructions would be in place. I was still worried about any potential discovery by Heatherton and crew before Tony and his team had time to get out and away. Just in case there was a shot at a cell signal sent to Heatherton's phone, I wanted to take it out.

"Mark, are you still playing with directional EMP grenades?"

"I'm not playing, Colt, I have one that's deadly serious."

"Can it take out a phone?"

"Within twenty yards it can turn it into trash."

"I need it. How about some trackers? Might be nice to bug his car and any of his close associates."

"You'll have whatever you need."

"Tony, you have a plan ready?"

"Colt, I don't go to the head without a plan. After Lestat takes out the NOVA farm and the Programming Center, we'll breach the building and locate the access to the Center. Judging from the roof vent stacks, I'm certain it's underneath the building, which makes it that much easier to cave the whole place in on itself. We'll sweep the place with IR and lidar detectors, just in case there's an independent backup. If there is, Mark has a new toy."

Mark grinned and put a cardboard box on the table. He pulled out a taxidermist quality stuffed rabbit, setting it on the floor. Using a remote control, he directed the rabbit as it hopped around the floor. "With the AI's ability to discern animals versus humans, I figured this guy could get in close enough to do some damage."

I shook my head. "What is this, the 'killer rabbit' from Monty Python?"

He grinned wider. "Yes. He's an EMP grenade, strong enough to fry those Teslas and any detection gear they might have."

"Nice!"

"I know, I know…"

I shook my head. Mark is such a warped genius; I'm glad he works with us. He has a great sense of humor, too.

"Okay, any of you guys have concerns or questions?"

They all shook their heads.

"So, we monitor this for the next few days, test the crap out of Lestat, and pray everything works on Sunday when Rik, Kelly, and I are standing next to this bastard when his world gets rocked. As soon as the money gets transferred, then we take that site down, leaving digital tracks to Heatherton and his group for the winner after we've pulled the plug." I made the nose signal from the movie, "The Sting." Mark did it back, but Kelly and Tony gave us blank stares.

"Helllllooo? 'The Sting,' one of the greatest movies of all time?" They shrugged. Mark roared. I made a mental note to look for it on cable and watch it with Kelly.

By the end of the day, the number was up to $300 million. Kelly and I headed to the condo to put away the rest of my things. I told her on the ride I was taking her out to dinner at a great seafood place a block away from her condo. The condo. Whatever. I got a good look at my new home in daylight and saw it was on a canal that connected with Rudee Inlet. She said she had a slip that came with the condo but had never used it. I planned on changing that, but not with *Blitz*, whose exhaust would rattle the windows of all the condos lining each side of the canal. That wouldn't make us any friends here and draw more attention than we wanted. I'd tell Kelly later what I had in mind if all our plans worked this weekend.

We put away all the rest of my gear, in comfortable silence. Then Kel built two rum drinks, and we sat on the couch. I knew she had something she wanted to say.

"Colt, did Rikki get an answer about the finder's fee?"

"She did, and you need to get all your stuff ready and turned over to your team by Thursday night. We'll head up after work because we need to be there Friday for a partner's meeting to discuss it all. We'll work up there Friday, relax on Saturday, then take Shaw Air's Piper Aerostar over to Crozet at noon on Sunday. Polo starts at 1:30 p.m. We'll come back around 3:15, after everyone has beat feet out of there, and the Programming Center is a hole in the ground."

"Sooo, how much was it?"

"Twelve percent."

For the second time in a week, I had stunned her. "Hold on though, this is why we need to meet. First, there's corporate tax, then we want to hold some back for the company for expansion and a big pay down to Conrad. I'm thinking twenty percent, but that still depends on what you two think. Then maybe half split among the rank and file at the company. Of the rest, seventy percent goes to Rik, twenty percent to me, and ten percent to you."

She was trying to do the math in her head, so I smiled and jumped in. "As of now, your share would still be over a million, pretax."

She shook her head. "I'm a department head, and that's still way more than several years' worth of my salary."

"You don't work for a salary anymore, Kel, and this is just one case. A huge case, but a single case, nonetheless. Welcome to being a partner. Conrad will be pissed he didn't wait a little longer to sell!" I chuckled.

It stunned her as the numbers sunk in.

"That's if the auction doesn't go higher. And it will. Let's hope all your electronic voodoo works."

"I'll make sure it does."

Dinner wasn't a Carlos dinner, but the company and the waterfront location were excellent, and the meal was still great. It was the first time I'd relaxed today. This case was my first as operations manager, and success or failure was on me. The lives of our team depended on my being able to coordinate the efforts of all the departments. I was glad to have the downtime now with Kel.

We went back to the condo, okay, *our* condo, and I found The Sting on a pay channel. At the end, Kelly was smiling. "I can see what you guys were talking about. This almost has the same feeling as what we are doing."

"Don't expect me to say; 'I'm not sticking around for my share,' that 'I'd only blow it' though!"

Kelly laughed; "Me, either! This will be amazing, not just for us, but for everyone in the company." She stopped and looked at me. "Did you guys make me a partner rather than paying me a bonus because you knew this might come up?"

"We did. You deserve more because it was your idea, you are facilitating it, and most of all we didn't want to lose you. We make a great team, and you are important to Rik and me. Very important. Especially to me."

Kelly leaned against me and held my hand. "Are you nervous, Colt?"

"I'm nervous about the field part in Crozet. Us with Heatherton, and the team with the Program System site. I'll be glad when we're all home safe, and this is over." I looked in those eyes again. "I don't want anything to happen to you. No amount of money's worth that, Kel."

She smiled. "Nothing will happen to me unless I get hit with an errant polo ball. But thanks, I'm worried about you, too."

We spent the next two days going over the plan, testing the software, and watching the numbers climb to over a half-billion dollars. Bidders in Germany, France, Russia, and Saudi Arabia had now dropped out. The active bidders that were left were now in Iran and

China. But it was the last second of the last day that counted. It was still any bidder's game.

Kelly turned over the software control to her number two in the department. I met with Tony one more time, and we headed north in my SUV on Thursday night. We could see and do what they could at the shop from the office in ESVA, and we could check in with them on the video conference setup. Another reason we were headed out was so they wouldn't have us breathing down their necks. It would be good for the team to feel that independent responsibility.

We got to the boat a little before dark. It was easy to see Plan B was no more. In its place was *EMERALD IZ*. Kelly was speechless. Again. I liked it when something I did brought that on.

"In our business, it's not a great idea to put our names on anything, Kel. But anyone that knows you will know that this name is all about you."

"Emerald eyes, I don't know what to say, Colt. I've never had a boat named for me."

"You don't need to say anything, so long as you understand why I did it."

"I do, Colt, I do."

"Dinner at the *Beach Café*? We can make the sunset if we hurry."

"I hope they have something with guacamole." She gave me that seductive wink again. I wondered what else I could name after her.

11

———

BEER GAG

Rather than head to a restaurant in the morning, we opted for more rack time. I could say that we slept in, but you probably wouldn't buy it. I don't blame you. So, English muffins and yogurt were the breakfast of champions today, and we headed to the office. Rik had already beaten us there.

It was our first partners' meeting, and we had a lot to cover. We started by checking the auction figure, which was the same as last night, stuck at $510 million from a Chinese bidder, no doubt a consortium, or a front for the government. It sounded steep, but if they were successful in swaying the election to someone who was less of a hardliner because of it, they might even make that back in increased trade imbalances in mere months, not years. With as razor-thin as the voting numbers between the political parties were, the AI Writer project would easily turn the election. It might even steer the politics of Congress and the courts. It would be a free and "honest" election, but they will have fed the participants a diet of manipulated facts and outright lies. The bidders understood all this, and to accomplish this for half a billion dollars was a bargain.

Rikki smiled across the conference room table. "Good morning, kids!"

We smiled back, and I answered. "Good morning, Mom!"

"We have a lot to cover this week, and yes, I'm suggesting we hold these weekly, on Friday mornings so we get all our administrative stuff over by the weekends. It won't always work out like that, but it's what we'll shoot for."

"Sounds good." Kelly was excited. She had always been happy to give an opinion if asked; her intelligence and skills had made her a great department head. But since we made her a partner, she had blossomed and there was no question she was a natural leader. Where she might have hesitated to volunteer something before, that hesitation was now gone. By becoming a partner, it had spoken volumes to her about what we believed her value to be to our team, and she was eager to contribute. This was what Rikki and I had hoped would happen. She was as qualified as either of us to run this company, and she was now feeling the full weight of our confidence in her.

We ran over the numbers of our purchase from Conrad with Kelly, and at what we had been doing before the AI case, it looked like a seven-year payback. If this case went well, we could cut that by more than half.

Kelly was getting her first look at the overall company numbers; they surprised her and she liked what she saw. Conrad had built a heck of a business over the years. The relationships he formed were now paying off. I think the one thing that Kelly was most surprised by was the growth of the private protective services portion of the company. This was due to Rikki and had been her part of the business. Since those employees didn't come into contact much if at all with the team that worked out of the shop, Kelly hadn't realized how large it was. That group was handled here as part of the ESVA Security Corporation. We were upgrading *Bayside's* security, and we would handle that aspect of the design of their new high-end development and club, already under construction here. It was a new but logical departure for us.

Rik brought out the purchase and partnership agreements that our company attorney had drawn up. Each was straightforward. We all signed and were done since Conrad had already signed. It was now our company.

The three of us looked over the potential numbers from the AI case again. We wanted to have a bonus framework in place and ready to go so we could distribute the money when and if we received it. We decided to go along the lines of what I discussed with Kelly, but with department heads and the members of the tactical group that would breach the Program System site receiving fifty percent more than everyone else. The tac group was in harm's way with their butts on the line, and the department heads had worked their way up the ladder and the responsibility for the success or failure of their departments rested with them.

We were comfortable with what we had decided; this would be a game-changer for many of our team, ensuring college for many of their kids, or taking years off mortgages. It was a great feeling for all of us, especially Kelly since it had been her idea to grab the funds and take a finder's fee. We would make sure everyone knew that fact when the bonuses were passed out, and at that point we would announce her becoming a partner. While I doubted if anyone who knew Kelly would think someone promoted her because of our growing relationship, this would reinforce that.

There was a sound like a gunshot, and another. Kelly and I each jumped up, reaching for our concealed pistols. Rikki laughed.

"Relax, that's the crew building Kelly's new office in the front. It was a surprise."

I frowned. "Giving us a heads up would have been nice."

She smiled, "It wouldn't have been a surprise if I had. Anyway, I figured you would need a place to work out of when you are here, Kelly, even though you two will be mostly down at the shop. So, I squared off our footprint in the unfinished part of the building. Casey was happy to rent us more of the unfinished space."

"Thanks, I'm looking forward to Fridays here. An office is a nice surprise, and it'll be good to concentrate and do some planning out away from all of the confusion at the shop."

Rikki nodded. "Plus, we'll keep all the financials confidential, here in this office. Not to mention, it's good for the team to have a day without us hanging over them. Kind of our version of a 'Casual Friday.' Everyone can use one of those."

Rik walked back to her new office, then Kelly and I went into mine. We pulled up aerials of the polo area, Heatherton's farm, Chris's farm, and Candi's. We studied them carefully because we wanted to be prepared in case anything was to "go south." The worst thing you could be in a situation like that was unfamiliar with where you are, and where you need to go. While we were studying the satellite pictures, I heard rain on the window. It was a late summer cool front, signifying that fall wasn't too far off. They expected the line to stretch up and down the Eastern Shore, stalling over us this afternoon and tonight as it did. I was glad it had already passed through Crozet. The runway was grass, and heavy rain could make it too soft for landing for a day or two. Plus, in reading about the polo field, we discovered that if they get half an inch of rain within the twenty-four hours before a match, they cancel. The turf becomes too slick and soft to play without risk of injury to the horse, rider, the field, or all of the above. But with the line having come through there earlier this morning, the match should still be "good to go" on Sunday, especially with the cooler, drier air on the backside. We needed that match to stay on schedule because we wanted the distraction for Heatherton, so there would be no chance he would be at the Program System site. We assumed he might head there after the match.

With everything checked and now double-checked, the three of us took umbrellas to walk over to the *Beach Café* for lunch. Just as we were walking out, Casey, Cindy, and Dawn pulled up in Casey's six-seat ATV.

Casey said, "We're going to the café for lunch."

"So, are we."

"Hop in."

Riding in the covered ATV beat the heck out of walking through this weather. He parked by the marina showers at the south end of the building, so we could take the beach side's covered walkway. I loved looking out over the wet sand. There was something about an empty beach in the rain that tranquilly influenced me. I mentioned it to Kelly and found it was yet another thing we had in common.

Unfortunately for *Bayside*, there wasn't much of a lunch crowd out here today, although they would make up for it tomorrow. But it was so relaxing, listening to the rain on the awning. If it weren't for the rain, the bay would be almost a sheet of glass, with only occasional minuscule boat wakes rolling in tiny "tubes" down along the shore. Instead, the light rain gave the surface a matte finish out as far as you could see until it merged with the gray sky, erasing the horizon. No doubt the rain would later give way to that light but dense mist which is so common in Virginia. You couldn't call it either rain, or fog; it was somewhere in between, and I loved it.

Casey, Cindy, and Rik were engrossed in conversation at one end of the table, while Dawn and Kelly were laughing and leaning forward, talking in low conspiratorial voices. I caught Kelly sneaking one of her side glances at me with a sly smile. She and Dawn had hit it off, and I was so happy that she was making more friends up here than just Rik and me.

I was now in my pre-op zone where I'd try to clear my mind and relax the rest of today, tonight, and tomorrow. Sunday would be all business from well before daylight on. After 7 p.m. we would know just how successful this operation had been. Taking out the Program System and the Writer System server farm in NOVA would be good, but it would only set them back temporarily. To be a complete success, we had to scatter the engineers to the four winds, fleeing for their lives. This would only happen if we could hijack that payment.

"Earth to Colt?" Rik looked amused.

"Hmmm?"

"Got your whole 'downtime Zen' pre-op thing already kicked in, eh?"

She knew me well. I nodded.

"Casey was just saying that Mark had your new 'yaks and paddle-board delivered. Cindy and I are taking an early morning paddle if you guys want to join us."

I looked down the table, but Kel and Dawn were still engrossed in conversation. "We would, thanks. It should be a beautiful morning. I had forgotten about the board and kayaks."

"Gee, I wonder why."

Rikki was smiling, but to tell the truth, I didn't know myself if it was about the upcoming op or Kelly. Wait, that was a "duh" moment. Kelly. Rik knew what I was thinking and was still enjoying herself over this.

"You two take off until Sunday. If I know you guys, and I do, you'll be in about daybreak then, anyway. And it's going to be a long day."

I nodded again. It would.

After lunch, I asked Casey if Kel and I could borrow his ATV because she hadn't seen *Bayside Club Estates* yet. Rik came along since this was "her baby;" she was doing the security plan for the properties. She pointed out various key security elements as we drove around in the rain on the newly cut road, temporarily topped with gravel. The object for the development was high security with low visibility. The underground utilities and conduits for camera cables and detection devices were just being installed.

We drove past the sites of the new spa and private club on the shoreline, then down to a huge lot on the point. This was at the intersection of the grassy shoreline and a deep creek that led back to a natural harbor that will be the private club marina. A foundation had already gone in here for a 6,000-square-foot house, the first one in the development.

"This is Eric and Candi's new place." I loved the view.

Kelly shook her head. "This is beautiful."

"Casey dreamed this development up himself. High-end, mostly three-thousand to five-thousand-square-foot houses, but professional maintenance included. And if you want a certain dinner waiting on the stove when you fly in? They'll handle it. The air charter too, if you need them to. They do all maintenance for you; the idea is to put the 'vacation' back into your 'vacation house.' Need full or part-time house staff? They'll handle it. All for a price." I loved the concept.

Rik jumped in. "And these are the high net worth individuals that are the target demographic for our private security group. Eric brought us some new customers after showing them his new home, and all the stealth security we are providing. It's another new income stream for us; security design, incorporating our ideas into new construction or even updating older developments and estates."

It caught Kelly off guard. "I didn't even know we were into this now. That's great."

Rik nodded, "And it also dovetails into your section because we'll need new systems designed to handle all this. You'll need to build a new group for this area alone for both design and installation."

I could see Kelly loved the idea. "But that's only part of why I wanted to bring you out here. With this rain, I was hoping they would be here." I pointed across the wide creek where a pair of river otters were sliding down a clay and mud-lined slide they had created. We watched, awed by the antics of these two. I could watch them for hours. Kelly melted.

"I love them! The construction won't chase them away, will it?"

I shook my head. "No. Their den is on that side which *Bayside* also owns, and that will become a wildlife sanctuary. The only thing over there will be horse riding trails."

We finished our tour, driving by the basin where the marina would be built using floating docks set out away from the natural shoreline. No bulkheads, and no disturbing the natural grasses. Casey, Dawn, and Cindy had thought this out well, wanting to be good stewards of the land. They made this a selling point of the Estates; you would live as much as possible in harmony with nature. And with the latest in stealth security from ESVA Security.

We took the ATV back to its parking spot under the carport behind Casey's office. Rik said she was taking the afternoon off too, and hoped Cindy could join her. The rain was slacking business for the afternoon, and the construction crews had taken the day off because of the weather. That, and Rik would work on Sunday along with us.

Kel and I walked back to *EMERALD IZ* in what I had predicted, that fine Virginia mist. She had her "knowing" look on.

"Okay, I saw the way you love this weather. Dawn clued me in on one of her and Cindy's favorite things; a skinny dip in the hot tub with this mist coming down. There's more, just use your imagination."

I changed into a suit in record time. We grabbed two wine glasses, uncorked a chilled bottle of white, and headed over to C3. We were, well, settled into the hot tub rather nicely with our suits piled on a chaise when we heard voices coming up the path. Kel shrieked then wrapped her arms around my neck and pulled me into a close "chest to chest" hug. Just then, Rik and Cindy cleared the trees, just as they had peeled out of their pool robes, which was all they had to peel. They stopped in their tracks as we looked over, and Kel wiggled her fingers on one hand in a wave from behind my head, "Uh, hi?"

They burst out laughing. Cindy said, "Looks like great minds think alike! You forgot to hang a tie on the gate though. Tell you what, we'll just go in the clubhouse and take our time opening our bottle of wine, take a sauna, and be back outside in say, fifteen minutes? We don't mind a communal skinny dip with friends, but that's where we draw the line." She chuckled again.

Kelly leaned back. "We can do fifteen minutes." She looked at me, cocked her head to the side, and raised her eyebrows in a challenging look. "Can't we?"

Twenty minutes later we were all relaxing in the pool. Even though this was a cool front, it wouldn't chill down until after the rain had passed. It was a tad warm for the hot tub anyway, but the view through the mist from the pool was fantastic, and the mist falling on our faces felt great. Especially after the initial surprise and embarrassment of being caught naked and well... "active" in front of my "sister/niece/partner" and our other good friend had passed. I found that downing a glass of wine helped with that. A lot. Kelly seemed to take it all in stride as well and lay next to me in the pool's recliner section.

Rikki looked over, "You might say this brings a new meaning to the whole 'partner meeting' thing."

Kelly chuckled. "This is my idea of a 'Casual Friday!' Not a good idea to expand it down to the shop though."

I laughed. "Though you've got to admit, it would liven up the end-of-year holiday party."

Rik said, "Dawn started this whole idea before the pool even had a certificate of occupancy from the county, talking Casey and his then-wife into it with her. Said it was the perfect way to relieve stress."

Kel giggled, "Uh, we ARE talking just talking about just the skinny-dipping part, right?"

"Put it this way, then he talked me into it. As much as I love Casey to death, I'm taken." She looked at Cindy. "We're taken."

"And don't you forget it." Cindy poked her playfully in her side.

"Case and I had just met. Cindy and I were just starting to date, and I was a little uncomfortable about the two of us being together around him."

Kelly looked incredulous, "Casey? Why? I thought you guys were like best friends."

"Now we are. But I had misconstrued a few things back then, and misunderstandings that don't get addressed have a habit of getting bigger. So, he made a big pitcher of his Caribbean Bloody Marias, dragged me over here, and talked me into skinny-dipping. We ended up calling it our 'hot tub summit.' He said it made us equally uncomfortable, so we could argue things out with neither of us having an advantage. Before he got together with Dawn, he was very introverted and uncomfortable around larger groups of people. He wasn't yet with her at that point. I thought I had been making him uncomfortable because I was attracted to Cindy. It turned out I couldn't have been more wrong; he couldn't have cared less, and we've been great friends ever since. So, he's the only guy who has ever talked me out of my clothes."

I said, "Whoa! Too much information, Rik. This is not Truth or Dare."

"Hah! Could have fooled me a few minutes ago, stud!"

Just then Casey and Dawn came up the walk, and Dawn said, "Stud? What did we miss?"

"More than Cindy and I did."

Dawn laughed, "Kel, when I suggested that, I didn't mean with an audience! But isn't it great?"

"The audience part was unintentional and uncomfortable, but the rest of it was fantastic," Kelly replied.

"Told you. The mist is almost magical. I love it on my face and my..."

"Whoa! We get the idea, Dawn."

"I was just going to say 'shoulders', Colt. Where did you think I was going with that?"

Dawn has this look we all call her "Challenge Face" and she was wearing it now. I hoped that by ignoring it, she would let it drop. It looked like that wasn't happening though, so I had to think fast.

"Hey! Since we will be at your favorite winery, what do you want us to bring back?"

"You're hoping I'll change the subject if you resort to bribery, Colt?"

"Pretty much."

"Well played. A case of their Albemarle Chardonnay."

"Done."

"And we'll throw in dinner tonight for all you guys, just the six of us, on our boat. Come as you are, well, maybe not as you are right now, but you get the idea. And I promise there won't be a crazy Crozetian woman in attendance this time, but we'll be dockside instead of cruising. Eric, Candi, and Elaina even flew to the west coast this weekend to avoid the whole polo debacle. It's a shame that Candi lives next door to that woman."

"She won't be for much longer unless Chris finds a gold mine on her property."

"Good." With that, she and Casey abided by the "Casual Friday" undress code and joined us in the pool for wine and conversation. Dawn had been right; it was a great equalizer and stress reducer.

After we were all getting waterlogged, Kel, and I headed back for the boat to dry off, relax, and get changed. As I opened the hatch, there was an explosive sound, and a giant six-foot plastic beer bottle inflated in the companionway. After we got over the initial shock, Kelly laughed uncontrollably.

I knew it had been Sandy. Mister 'It's on!' I yelled, "Sandy! Dammit, that wasn't funny!"

"Colt, I'm the one in here! He's over there!" Kel was pointing toward Sandy's trawler. She was still chuckling.

I stormed out into the cockpit, yelling at Sandy's boat. "That wasn't funny! I almost had a heart attack!"

"You know, you're almost as loud as your other boat. Pipe down and tell me what your problem is. The Cliff Notes version because you're prone to hysterics."

"You know damned well what I'm talking about! That giant inflatable beer bottle you booby-trapped my hatch with!"

Sandy roared with laughter. "That's PERFECT! No, I didn't do it, and I wondered what the package was. I wish I could take the credit, but I can't. I know who can though."

"Who?"

"And spoil the next surprise they might have planned? Not on your life! Hey, have you got any beer? I drank my last one."

"Yeah, hold on." I retrieved the blow-up bottle, then threw it on his boat. "There you go, suck on that one for a while!"

His laughter didn't stop until I was below where Kel was still chuckling.

"You, too?"

"Admit it, that was classic! And what a mislead, using a beer bottle to set you off on Sandy."

"Who else would have done it?"

"Think about it. Who did you warn me was the biggest prankster of all?"

"Cindy? She wouldn't have done..." Wait. It was well planned and executed, right down to deflecting toward Sandy. Cindy knew we were going into the lion's den on Sunday and knew we were trying to relax today and tomorrow because what no doubt lay ahead. This was her way of helping us lighten up. It worked on Kel, and I must admit, I'm smiling now too. Not that this will go unanswered; it will be at some point after Sunday. And the response would have to be just as well thought out.

12

FLIPPER'S REVENGE

Cocktails were on the flying bridge deck on *Lady Dawn*. The retractable center of the hardtop was closed since the mist was still falling, and it would continue until around midnight when the line moved offshore. Kel and I got there before Rik and Cindy, and she told the beer bottle story. When they appeared, the four of us gave Cindy a round of applause, as I bowed to her. She wore a huge grin.

"Well played, joke master. But the game has only just begun."

"It has and I'm only getting warmed up! We need ground rules though."

I did my best Spanish accent, which was not great. "Rules? We don' need no stinkin' rules!" I narrowed my eyes. "We play by '*Chesapeake Rules*,' meaning there aren't any."

Cindy nodded, almost slyly. "Okay, '*Chesapeake Rules*,' but with boundaries. All the areas open to the public are off-limits. We *are* running businesses here."

"Agreed. And a hiatus until Wednesday."

"Done. That gives me more time to fine-tune my next move."

I saw the look that Kel was giving her of amusement and respect.

143

The beer bottle gag had impressed her. I would need her help too if I would upstage the joke master. And I intended to.

We sat at the port side table enjoying our drinks. I spotted two figures wearing yellow slickers in the mist, one rolling and one walking toward the *Beach Café*. "Looks like Tyler and Carol are still on their way to becoming an item."

Cindy nodded. "They're cute together. He'll be sticking around now that the county agreed to sign a lease with him on Monday for his skydiving business. He also leased a Super Twin Otter turboprop that'll arrive on Tuesday. I've been talking about having them put together a jump group with smoke streamers and a big American flag that will land on the beach during our Labor Day cookout."

"That's such a cool idea! And a fun way to let our guests know this is another exciting and different thing that's available for them nearby." Dawn loved it.

I asked, "So, are you going to do it, Dawn?"

"What, jump? Not on your life! You, Colt?"

"I've done it before, and I might again. I'm not sure. But the view up there from fourteen thousand feet would be amazing. You could see Delaware, the whole Eastern Shore, the Atlantic, and the Chesapeake. I'll think about it." Kelly was shaking her head, giving me her answer before I even asked if she wanted to try it.

Dinner was fantastic, this time inside the dining area of the salon. It looked like it belonged in any higher-end home, but this one was afloat. Casey and Dawn had picked this boat because it felt less like a yacht and more like a home. A luxurious home, but a comfortable one. I was getting ideas, so Kelly and I needed to talk about boats after this weekend.

Saturday morning was perfect, the back side of the cool front was nice and calm, though the wind should pick up in the afternoon. In the meantime, the paddling was great. I loved seeing Kel with a big smile as she paddled her board alongside Rik and Cindy, chatting while they did, and I was right behind them, kind of in my own world. I was looking around, watching for fish and birds, but I saw something coming, heading for us. I kept quiet. It was a pair of dolphins, and they rolled alongside me, giving me a "once over" before they swam on ahead. They sounded then reappeared, rolling right alongside Cindy, thirty yards north of me. One exhaled as it rolled, and she shrieked, losing her balance, and ending up in the bay.

"Hey, Cindy, did you see those dolphins?" I laughed, and the dolphins must have enjoyed the joke, as they circled the boards once, rolling right next to me again. I swear they were smiling. "Thanks, guys!"

Cindy hollered, "If I didn't know better, I'd swear you put them up to that."

"Hey, they are a good omen!"

"Unless you didn't know they were there. Did you see them coming up on us?"

"Gee, Cindy, don't you think I'd have told you if I did?" By now I pulled up alongside the boards as she climbed back on hers. I gave her my best innocent look.

"Uh, huh. Kel, remember that look for later. That's his 'guilty little boy' look."

"Noted, thanks! But I'm staying out of the middle of you two. Booby-trapped inflating beer bottles, trained dolphins, who knows what's next?"

"I do! But that's for me to know, and her to find out after Wednesday." I liked this whole prank thing even if the dolphins weren't in on it. But I had always loved dolphins, which made it even better.

Later, after a great takeout lunch from the *Beach Café* that we brought over to C3, Kelly and I were lying on a pair of chaises by the pool. We continued our "non-work related" conversation, intermittently. She wondered about the name "C3." I explained it started as "Chesapeake Cool" which Casey and his ex-partner Murph originally intended to call the inn and marina. But Casey, Dawn and his soon to be ex-wife changed it to *Chesapeake Bayside* and re-christened it a resort. As Casey was fond of saying, the difference between a resort and an inn is about three times the room rate. But the private pool area and clubhouse had already been dubbed "Chesapeake Cool Club," which they decided was too pretentious for what they intended it to be, so they shortened it to "C3."

"It fits."

"They agreed, so it stuck."

She smiled.

"What?"

"I was remembering last night."

"Yeah." Now I was smiling.

"I was talking about at dinner? Not after we got back to the boat!"

"Okay, then too. What's on your mind about dinner?"

"You had something on *your* mind. You kept looking around, and I could tell you were getting ideas about something."

I sighed. "A lot has changed in a week and a half."

"Are you talking about us? What's with the big sigh?"

"Meaning my life is changing. Our life is changing. At least I think it is."

"Be more specific than that, Colt. It has been an amazing and crazy several days."

"Okay, two weeks ago I was a contractor who lived in NOVA. Then I became a partner who was splitting time over here and Norfolk, by myself. We got ourselves together, but by then I had bought a boat that was okay for me by myself, but for a couple is a bit tight over extended periods, especially for trying to entertain in cold weather. Blitz is fun, but now since I'm giving up my Wood-bridge place, I don't need it to go back and forth."

"You have so lost me here."

"I was looking around last night and thinking about winter."

"Again, you've lost me. How did we get from dinner last night to winter?"

"Bear with me. If it was January or February, do you think we might get invited to Casey and Dawn's for dinner?"

"Sure, Colt. Why not?"

"Okay, they won't be using the aft deck or the flybridge for entertaining again until spring."

"So? They have all that space inside... right, and we don't."

"And we'll be coming up once a week for meetings, and either have to beat feet back to the condo in VB or, rent a room here if we want space."

"It's not the same as having our own boat, our own home."

"Exactly. I'm trying to get you thinking of everything you would want in a boat."

"Okay?"

"Think on it for now."

"This is part of that future you were talking about?"

I smiled. "Think about it."

"I have been thinking a lot about the future, though I hadn't focused on boats."

"And?"

She reached over and took my hand. "And I hope it looks a lot like this last week. I love being here and being with you wherever you are. Do you believe in destiny, Colt?"

"Not to where we can't alter parts of our lives if we want to. If that were true, maybe we should turn the entire world over to computers with AI and let them run things. But that's not a world I want any part of. So, I think we are destined to go in a certain direction, but it's up to us to find our own way and see if we can get there. Does that make sense?"

"More than you think, Colt." She smiled, and once again her eyes did most of the talking. I liked what they had to say.

As much as I enjoy talking with Kelly, I also enjoy our periods of shared silence, like the one we started now. The kind where you don't feel compelled to talk. Where you don't have to "fill the void" because it isn't really a void. The silence that tells its own story. I'm more content to listen than talk anyway, and that's been a bone of contention in several past relationships. In fact, I don't recall another one where at this point I wasn't already being interrogated or pushed for details. Kelly had enough confidence in herself that didn't require me to babble on, which was something I appreciated. Not that I wouldn't share whatever she wanted to know, just as I'm sure she would do the same for me. Like she already did about never having had anyone stay at the condo with her before.

We had been right to be on the water with the paddleboards and kayak early this morning because the wind came up just as forecast after lunch. It was a north wind, and the trees between C3 and the parking lot sheltered us. Looking out over the bay, we could see many of the resort's fleet of small rental sailboats were out. As peaceful and serene as that scene was, and as hard as I tried to relax, I was getting anxious about tomorrow. I must have been in and out of the pool a half dozen times. I couldn't take it anymore, and I wanted boating time.

"I need to take a boat ride and get focused. Want to come?"

"Sure."

I idled Blitz out past the jetties then looked at Kelly. "Switch seats with me."

"What?"

"Switch seats with me, and you take the helm."

"I've never run a boat anywhere near as fast as *Blitz*, Colt."

"Time to learn, Kel. Oh, and just so you know, I'm the only one who has ever run *Blitz* since I've owned her." As we swapped sides, Kelly grabbed me in a tight hug for a moment. She realized that this was as big a deal to me as her having me stay at the condo was to her.

There were several reasons I wanted her to run the boat. One was for the experience because you never knew when it might come in handy. The second was I wanted her to do something I had let no one else do. I wanted a bonding moment, and to build even more trust between us. Third, I felt she too was nervous about tomorrow, and running a boat in a heavy chop at a hundred miles an hour is a major confidence builder. And, because I'd be concentrating on her and this ride more since I didn't have the wheel and the throttles. It was a great distraction for me.

I grabbed a jacket from below for Kelly because she needed more than a bikini top between her and a hundred miles-per-hour of wind. The windshield would deflect most of it, but I needed more to clip the "kill-switch" lanyard onto than a bikini strap. I made sure she wedged herself well back into the racing "wraparound style" seat. I went over all the gauges, what to watch for, how to trim the boat with the drives and tabs, and how to handle turns in this much chop. Then I turned her loose with 2,700 horsepower, but not before she pulled me to her, kissed me, and smiled.

"I won't break your baby, Colt."

"I know, or you wouldn't be sitting there. Okay, let's go!" I wedged myself in and put my life in the hands of one of the people I now trusted the most.

Kelly eased the throttles forward, and *Blitz* responded like a race-horse champing at the bit, jumping up "on a plane" as the vee-hull started slicing through the rough surface of the water. Kel took her up to fast cruise for a few minutes, to get used to how she handled. She looked over at me and winked, then advanced the throttles to the fire-wall. I loved that she had built that much confidence so quickly. Her face had an exhilaration and determination I'd never seen in her before. We raced downwind in the heavy chop that *Blitz* parted easily. Spray was shooting out to the sides just forward of us, and the engines were roaring. I was so glad I had turned over the helm; this was great for both of us. After a few minutes, Kel eased the throttles back and dropped *Blitz* down to about seventy mph. She gave me a sideways glance with a huge smile. We rode down by Cape Charles, then farther south to Kiptopeke where several huge cement ships from World War Two were sunk end to end as a breakwater, an iconic sight. From there we shot across the bay to the York River, then north to Mobjack Bay, on past Gwynn Island and Stingray Point at Deltaville, up the Rappahannock River to Irvington where we then idled up past the Tides Inn. We raced back over to the Wicomico River by Reedville, then across the bay back to our slip at *Bayside*, pulling in about two hours after we left. I had Kelly back her in as I got on the dock and tied us up. Kelly joined me on the dock and wrapped me up in a hug.

"That was amazing, absolutely amazing. What a great ride! I've never felt such power on the water before. She handled the chop and the rollers in the ship channel so well. I want to do that again!"

"I had been thinking about selling her."

"What! Why?"

"Since I don't need her to get back and forth across the bay anymore because I don't live in Woodbridge now." Kelly looked like I kicked her dog. "But, you know, that was my favorite ride in her ever. Let's keep her another summer and see how much we use her. We can always put her up for sale, and I'll never get the money back out of those new engines, so we might as well use..." I was wrapped up in a hug and kiss before I could finish my sentence. When we came up for air, I said, "I guess we could plan a few weekend trips in her, this year and next. St. Michaels, Baltimore, Annapoli..." Wrapped up again.

Kelly leaned back and looked at me. "I love keeping her, but I also love hearing you say 'we' when you are talking about plans."

Yeah, we're keeping *Blitz*, at least for another year.

I take back what I said about enjoying our periods of silence. Kelly went on and on about *Blitz*, asking about her make and model, about why I changed the engines, how long I'd had her, and was I sure I wanted to keep her.

"You, or the boat?"

"Funny guy! No, seriously?"

"I'm sure. I'm now looking forward to making trips in her with you. And before you ask, yes, you can run *Blitz* on the trips."

She grinned. "I'm taking you out to dinner again tonight."

"Has to be an early night. I want to be at the shop by 7 a.m., I need to meet with the team before they leave."

"I want to meet with my group too and make sure they're ready. Agreed, early night tonight, not like the last time I bought you dinner. We can make up for it later in the week."

"Deal. Maybe we sneak off to the Tides for spa time for you? After we get this operation completed."

"If you are trying to make yourself irresistible, it's working, Colt."

I texted Rik, and she wanted to go to the shop first thing, too. I said I'd drive us all down in the Escalade at 5:30 a.m. We'd have Shaw Air pilot Beth Powell pick us up in their Piper Aerostar at the private terminal at Norfolk International at 12:30. It should take fifteen minutes from the shop to the airport in light Sunday traffic. We'd have plenty of time to make Crozet by 1:15. Then wheels up by 3:30 at the latest, heading back to Norfolk. We'd beat the team back by two hours if all happened according to plan.

Kel and I had an early dinner and an early night. But I wouldn't rest until everyone was back at the shop and safe, tomorrow night. I slept only a few hours then got up at 4:45 a.m. and made coffee. Kel got up, came in, and hugged me from behind.

"It will be fine."

"I know. Everyone involved is a pro, and we've thought this out time and time again. But there's a lot we don't know about Heatherton and his bunch. You figure that anyone willing to sell out their country for money, not for dedication to a political ideology, would just as soon put a bullet in your back or a knife in your gut. Don't forget that today and be extra careful. I didn't just find you to have something bad happen to you."

"Ditto. And you didn't just find me, I was there all along. But you were a late bloomer. Remember, I had to ask you out."

"Oh, is that what it was."

"Yep, that was it."

13

BOMBS AWAY

We assembled the team in the briefing room just after 7 a.m.

"All right everyone, listen up, we are good to go. According to the vineyard's website, the polo match is still on for today. As soon as we finish, Kelly and her group will load Lestat. They will set detonation time for 1500 hours. IT group will simultaneously switch the auction site and monitor for any further signals between Crozet and NOVA. Hopefully, by then I will be close enough to Heatherton to take out his cell phone with Mark's 'EMP grenade' just in case there might be some signal sent by the AI. Okay, Tony?"

"Thanks, Colt. We'll be monitoring the sentry truck to watch when its system goes down. But everyone be alert for a backup system. This bunch is nothing if not crafty. That's why we won't use a drone either because I guaran-damn-tee you that would set off an alarm or increase the security level. So, once the AI is down, we breach the building, find our way into the control center, get any backup disks or drives, get the hell out of there and blow the place. We timed it, and from the vineyards entrance to the driveway of Contour Auto Tech is seven minutes. From the far side of the field to the entrance is an additional two minutes. By executing at 1500 hours, the match should be about finished, and cars should start to file out, causing even more of a delay. But no matter what we do or don't find, we will evacuate the site by 1508 hours. Two-minute chemical timers on the charges should get us back to I-64 just before detonation. If we're lucky, maybe the bastards will have enough time to get in the building before it blows." He smirked.

"There's a rest area on I-64 about seven minutes east of the Crozet exit. We'll leave right after this and head there, so we don't get caught in any interstate delays. The rest area has public barbeque grills, so we'll have a nice long cookout until closer to execute time. Nobody will think twice about us, not even the Virginia Highway Patrol if they drive by."

"Nice! Thanks, Tony. Okay, Mark, what have you got for us?"

"To start off ("off" is redundant), the 'Killer Rabbit' EMP grenade. Tony and his team will deploy that bad bunny if there's a backup AI defense system. Also, additional throwable EMP grenades you can use to clear a room without having to expose yourself to any defenses. And here are a variety of sizes of lined plastic Faraday cage bags, and everyone needs to take a couple. Before you zap everything, you'll want your phones, coms, detectors, and anything electronic inside one. That's you too, Colt, Kelly, and Rikki. I told you, Colt, that electronic grenade you'll be carrying in your pocket is no joke. It's directional up to a point, but there's no sense taking chances. And here are half a dozen trackers. The attachment strip is magnetic, but if you pull the protective cover, it exposes an air-activated glue. Again, you want these away from the direction you point your grenade, Colt."

"Mark, do you have three spare fried smart phones?"

"Sure? Oh, I get it, props! Good idea."

I looked around the room. "Okay, questions? All right, mount up and good hunting everyone!"

Kelly headed over to her section while Rik and I headed to the armory. I pulled a new 10mm Sig Sauer P220 and concealed holster from the stock, along with a box of match grade hollow points and three new replacement barrels, firing pins and ejectors. Rik and I sat side by side at the cleaning bench and donned nitrile gloves. We emptied and cleaned all six magazines, two with each weapon, then reloaded each of them with eight new rounds. The gloves would ensure no fingerprints or DNA were on the casings. The spare barrels, firing pins, and ejectors we would bring with us in a field bag. They could be changed inside of five minutes, meaning any slugs that might be recovered would no longer match any of the new barrels, any casings wouldn't match the firing pin and ejector marks, and a quick visual inspection would show none of the barrels had been fired recently.

These were just precautions in case things went south for us. Better to do a little prep work than to get in a jam over some minor detail. Next, we broke each pistol down, cleaning every working part. They had been cleaned since being fired last, but this was standard practice before a field operation. It ensured our confidence in our weapons and helped calm our nerves.

Cleaned and reloaded, we placed them along with a spare mag in each of our "small of back" holsters. Rik and I wore untucked casting shirts to camouflage the outline "print" of our pistols. Kel had on a loose-fitting summer sun blouse over khaki boat shorts for the same reason. I walked over to Kelly's workstation where she was now leaning back in her chair with her group around her, watching her screen.

As I approached, she looked up. "It's in. They haven't detected it. I mean *it* has detected nothing. The auto-communication between the sites looks normal so far."

I placed the Sig on her desk. "I cleaned and checked it. This is to replace your old 9mm, so we all have the same weapon, ammo, and mags." She nodded, and I saw several of her group look at it, at her then at me. Many of them don't shoot, they are more comfortable in the coding world than dealing with the violence, danger, and corruption that exists outside these walls. Some might not have known that their group leader carried a concealed weapon, and now the thought was colliding with their world. I could tell it rattled some of them. Not a bad thing, from my perspective, for them to see

Kel taking her share of the danger before they find out she's a partner.

"$650 million now."

"And hollow points in your pistol because of it."

She nodded. "That bit with the two congressmen has lit it on fire."

"You don't have to go. You could stay here and watch over the auction swap."

"My group doesn't need me. You might."

"We won't be programming anything from the polo field."

"How many people will Heatherton have there?"

"I have no idea."

"Exactly. And I am one great pistol shot. I need to hit the range since this is a new weapon."

I knew she was going with Rik and me, but I still wanted to give her the option. Plus, I wanted her people to see her as a badass because she was. Chances are nothing would happen, it would be a boring trip, and we'd have a nice plane ride over and back. But it's when you get complacent that things can turn ugly in a hurry. I'd be happy to have Kel watch our backs and vice versa.

I followed Kelly downstairs to our soundproof range and watched her put a box of shells through her new weapon. On one hand, I was proud of what a great shot she was. On the other hand, she beat my last score. No way in heck I would be volunteering that fact to her. We walked back up to the armory, and I watched her repeat what Rik and I had done earlier. It left no doubt in my mind about her qualifications for fieldwork, from a firearms perspective.

The three of us were waiting at the private terminal at Norfolk when Beth pulled up in the Piper Aerostar. It was one of the fastest piston twin-engine planes ever made. She came inside, paid the ramp fee, and the four of us headed out.

"Did you get it?"

"Of course, Colt. It's a lunch flight."

On each seat was a box from *Bayside* with one of their famous Seacake sandwiches, slaw, and a soda. "I knew we wouldn't have a chance to eat, and who knows how things will go over there, so this was a good option. And I'm not counting on Heatherton feeding us." I grinned as I climbed into the rear bench seat with Kelly while Rik sat up in the copilot's seat next to Beth.

Taking off and flying over the tidewater area you could see just how flat our area is. It was still flat as we passed Richmond, but thirty miles further west you could see the topography change and become more rolling. By the time we reached Crozet, I realized just how close it was to the Blue Ridge Mountains, literally at their base. We circled the vineyards while Beth surveyed the grass runway. She set up for landing with our base leg parallel to part of the mountain chain, then we dove down with the terrain over peach and nectarine orchards and the grape vineyards and then touched down on the short turf runway. It wasn't as hair raising as the approach to St. Barts, but it was a close second, and instead of water at the end, there were grape trellises. We turned around at the end of the runway and taxied back to a small grass parking area then parked next to a single-engine turbo-prop plane. Beth hopped out and placed wooden chocks in the front and back of the main gear. She stayed with the plane as Kelly, Rikki, and I walked east toward the field. An older guy with a Baltimore accent driving a four-seater golf cart pulled up and offered to give us a lift. It was almost a half-mile away, so we accepted.

"My name's Tom. Heard you all were coming in. Chris Farmington made sure of that. So, you're Casey Shaw?"

"Casey couldn't make it. Colt Toffler." I stuck out my hand which he grasped as he got a sly grin and chuckled.

"So, Shaw and Clarke both canceled on her. Can't say as I'm surprised, from what I've heard about both. Sharp operators, and they avoided her tentacles. Good for them!"

"Not a fan?"

"Have you met her?"

"Yeah. I get your drift." We both laughed. A minute later we pulled up to a caterer's tent where Chris waited.

Tom said, "Just get any of the crew to call me on the radio when you're ready to go back, and I'll give you a lift."

"Great, thanks, Tom. I need to pick up two cases of Albemarle Chardonnay while I'm here."

"I'll get one of the golf cart crews to bring it over for you. They sell wine at the field side."

"Thanks again."

Chris was all but stamping her foot. "*Where* are Casey and Dawn?"

"They asked us to apologize for them, but they had a last-minute high-profile customer for one of the Club Estates properties that flew in, and they had to deal with him."

I could see she didn't buy it, I'm sure that this wasn't the first time someone had given her the brush off. Probably not even the first time this week. She should be used to it by now. She looked disgusted but led us past the small crowd under the tent that had descended on the hors d'oeuvres table like a cloud of locusts on a field of ripe crops. Up ahead facing the field was Lloyd Heatherton. I recognized him from his file at the shop. Kelly sided up next to me on the left as Rik moved up on my right.

"Lloyd, this is Colt, Rikki, and Keiley."

"That's Kelly, Christina." Kelly said it in a sugary sweet voice, knowing it would annoy Chris, both her tone and being called Christina.

"Right. And this is Lloyd Heatherton."

Heatherton nodded at us and turned to Chris. "So where are Casey Shaw and his fiancée?"

Chris exhaled. "They had unexpected business they had to attend to."

Heatherton looked disgustedly at her then turned to us. "Please make yourselves at home and enjoy the match. I'm sorry, but I have a call I need to make." He turned and walked to the far corner of the tent. Okay, we apparently smelled like last week's fish and were dismissed. Yeah, taking this guy down would be a pleasure. I looked over and smiled at Chris. She looked like she wanted to be somewhere else.

"Well, I'm sorry that Casey and Dawn couldn't make it, but you all will have a marvelous time. Roam around, have some of our food and wine, and enjoy yourselves. I have other guests I need to check in on." She waded into their crowd.

This was about as perfect a scenario as we could have hoped for. Neither Heatherton nor Chris wanted us to be too close to them, but we were invited guests, so we were welcome to hang out. We were "flies on the wall" and could watch what was going on without suspicion. And there was no doubt I could get close enough to zap his phone when the time came.

Until then, I was getting a lay of the land. The field in front of us was 300 yards long by 160 yards wide, made of beautiful and closely cut Bermuda grass. It was ringed by wooden boards about a foot high, which would keep most of the balls on the field, except for bounces or high drives. Outside the boards was a ten-yard-wide safety zone before the tents and spectators started, and both sides of the field were lined with all sizes of shade tents, and over 1,000 people walking around, sitting in camp chairs or on blankets. Some had dogs on leads, and coolers loaded with sodas and picnic lunches. Beyond the tents, there were cars parked three deep on the grass.

It looked like tent owners had "parking rights" behind their spots. There was a late model black Range Rover backed up to Heatherton's tent with an orange traffic cone in front to keep it from being blocked in, so I was betting it was his. This narrowed down our target vehicles.

We were on the west side of the field, with the sun at our backs. The view to the east was toward Charlottesville, and it was easy to see the shorter mountains off in the distance that lined the city. Just beyond our view sat Monticello, President Thomas Jefferson's home and final resting place. Behind us, ringing the vineyards on two sides were the Blue Ridge Mountains. Part of their nearby base were the fruit orchards. The view of the rolling green Piedmont was stunning.

From here you could also see where the Blue Ridge Parkway meets Skyline Drive on Afton Mountain. The only flat area anywhere in sight other than the runway was right in front of us, and it was now covered in horses as the match started.

In so many other places, going to a polo match was just an excuse to "be seen" and there was no doubt some of that here, but most of the people seemed to be closely following the game. The audience ranged from University of Virginia college students to young professionals with their kids, and some retirees. The cars parked beyond the tents also belied the diversity of the ages of the crowd. Everything from cheap imports and minivans to Heatherton's Land Rover. The event had a great tight-knit feel to it and was no doubt the biggest entertainment on Sunday in this little town. As Tom had said, golf carts were running up and back in front of the tents selling bottles of wine. One came by, its driver asking for me, saying she had my two cases of Albemarle Chardonnay. I paid for both and a chilled bottle with three glasses. I explained that we had flown in, and the woman said she would take two cases over and put them under the plane, that they would be safe there. It said a lot about this town and this place, but I said our pilot was over there and would load them. But the trust she had in the honesty of the people in Crozet just reinforced the fact that Lloyd Heatherton and his bunch didn't belong here.

I filled the three glasses halfway and handed one to Kelly and Rik. We were just using the wine as camouflage, taking a few small sips. The three of us wandered up and down the sidelines, not wanting to be too obvious that we were watching Heatherton. He kept checking his phone, and I sneaked a look at the screen from several yards away. I could instantly recognize what he was looking at, it was the auction site. He didn't seem pleased. The last number I had seen was $650 million, but whatever it was now, he wanted more.

Polo matches are divided into six periods called chukkers, which are seven minutes long, with four minutes between them, and there's a ten-minute halftime. This match wasn't as strict and was more relaxed about the time between chukkers and the halftime. After the third chukka, most of the audience headed out on the field for the "stomping of the divots," a tradition where you replace any divots in the turf using your foot. The hooves can take a toll on a field. So as not to draw attention to ourselves we walked out in the middle of the field, giving us a good opportunity to talk without anyone close by.

"Kel, when we go back, head for one of those field bathrooms beyond the parking area, and tag that black Rover, and the cars next to it on your way back."

"Got it."

Rikki asked, "Did you see his screen?"

"Yeah. The auction. At the rate this match is finishing up, the timing should be just about right to zap his phone a few minutes before three."

"Perfect."

By the time Kel came back, there was a new black SUV parked in front of the Rover. Some guy had sidled up next to Heatherton, and he looked like he was fit. He had long sleeves on even though the day was only moderate, and I assumed it was to cover some tats. Money said they were military, probably special forces of some type. Whoever this guy was, he was trouble if he was hanging with Heatherton. Kel came up, smiling at me. Without saying a word, I knew she had tagged the vehicles we needed, including the new one. Its driver glanced over at us, and I saw a glint of recognition. That wasn't good. Kelly followed my gaze, and when she looked back, I saw concern in her eyes. I smiled and led her out from under the tent, heading over to the horse trailer area. We feigned interest in the preparations as the players each changed horses after every chukka. There were lots of horses and the grooms had their hands full with them and the tack.

"That guy talking with Heatherton? He was up at the NOVA server farm, Colt. We passed him in the parking lot there, and I'm sure he recognized me or us."

"Okay, that's not good. It's 2:48, the fifth chukka is about over, then the last one will start. I'll zap their electronics at two minutes of, so put your phone in the Faraday bag. I'll signal Rik to do the same when we get back there."

We walked back to the tent, and the new guy was watching us closely. I gave Rik a "stay back" down low signal, and the signal to bag her phone. Halfway through the last chukka, I pulled out the dead smart phone and acted like I was checking email. I reached down into my pocket and hit the button on Mark's EMP grenade while I pointed it toward Heatherton and company, which now included Chris.

Will Rhinehart, Heatherton's security chief, parked and made his way under the tent, and up to his boss. "How are we doing?"

"If you are referring to my auction, not as well as we should be. $660 million. We assured Buxton that it would be over a billion."

Rhinehart said, "It will get there, don't worry."

"You say that while not being the one who assured him of the price so he would put the Big Nile system at risk by doing this."

"It'll be fine, Lloyd... uh oh."

"What?"

"That woman that just came in, she was at the NOVA server farm last week. I think that guy with her was, too."

"Are you sure?"

"Yes. Who is she, and what is she doing here?"

"She's a friend of a big mark of Farmington's."

"I don't like coincidences."

"Me either."

As they watched, Colt tapped and shook his smart phone.

"Dammit! It had over half a charge, and now it's dead! What the hell?"

Kel looked at it from his side. "Have you tried the power button?"

"Of *course* I've tried the power button, I'm not stupid!"

The scene they were making was drawing attention, as they planned, including Heatherton and Rhinehart's. It was distracting the pair and costing them minutes they didn't realize were important. An air horn sounded the end of the match, which the local team won, six to five over the visitors from Middleburg.

At that moment the auction site was hijacked just as Lestat detonated. At the Program System site in Crozet, the sentry truck went dormant. From his position along the fence line, Tony picked up lidar and infrared going active on two of the Teslas. These were programmed to go on defense if they lost WIFI contact with the Program System. They moved out into the gravel drive, taking up positions where their detection devices would have better coverage. Tony pointed at the front gate as he Faraday bagged all his electronics. Seconds later the "Killer Rabbit" came hopping down the drive, dismissed by the two new sentries. When the rabbit was in the range of both, it stopped. One of the team waved from the gate, and Tony retrieved his detectors from the bag which confirmed the Teslas were deactivated. In seconds he was over the fence and moving to the building. Two large SUV's were pulling up at the same time. The clock was running.

Back at the polo field, Lloyd Heatherton pulled out his phone and did much the same thing that Colt had. Rhinehart checked, and his was dead, as was Chris's. By this time Colt and Kelly were in a major verbal brawl, and Rikki was stepping in the middle trying to separate the two. All eyes were now focused on them as planned. Heatherton and Rhinehart had now determined that something bad had just happened, and they went with their instincts, which was to head to the Program System site. They both bolted out of the tent and to their cars, only to find themselves caught behind dozens of other slow-moving and stopped vehicles, as hundreds of people headed down the single lane drive around the field and to the entrance. Instead of two minutes, it would take them almost seven before they got out onto the road.

Chris looked confused and took off running after Lloyd's car, catching him when he became stuck behind the line.

Colt spotted Tom going by in his cart. "Hey, Tom, that ride offer still good?"

"Hop on! You guys will be out of here before anybody else."

Tony read the text: "L delayed. You have at least four minutes extra." *Good*, he thought, because it had taken longer to find the hidden doorway to the basement, and the backups were in a safe they'd had to crack. The ceiling of the programming center was concrete pre-stressed pin-T beam construction, and a real challenge to take out. They were flooding the area with propane gas from canisters they brought and placing plastique along both sides of each beam. Once set, he pulled the pin on a two-minute chemical fuse and hauled ass up the stairs. As he jumped in the SUV, he checked the time, and it was nine minutes in. A minute over their initial plan, it was a good thing they had those extra minutes to spare.

They blew through the gate and were getting on I-64 east just as the plastique exploded and cut through the strongest part of the concrete beams. They had been designed to withstand downward force, but as the vertical sections were sheared the propane detonated, lifting the concrete upward and shattering the slabs, allowing them to collapse as their upward inertia ran out and gravity pulled them back down. The block walls above had been laid on their edges and they now buckled inward, collapsing along with the roof into the pit that was created.

Tom got them all back to the plane before Heatherton even reached the vineyard's entrance. Beth had already done the pre-flight, and they were airborne two minutes later. They took off to the south and passed by the Program System site as it imploded. They were just far enough to the side to see the roof go in as Beth banked to the east, climbing out through 500 feet.

Heatherton raced down the drive through the now open front gates, then stopping and looking into the smoldering hole where his future had once been. He walked to the edge of the hole staring down, knowing tons of concrete had crushed the racks of servers that had been there. The charging station roof had collapsed on the Teslas underneath, and the two sentinel Teslas were dead in the drive, all their electronics fried. Heatherton knew whoever could bypass both layers of AI security would have found and emptied the backups out of the safe. He looked at Chris and Will with a horrified face.

"What if they weren't after the technology, what if they were after the auction instead? This could have been a diversion!" He raced over to his Rover, followed by the other two who jumped in Rhinehart's Navigator. Together they sped to Heatherton's farm, and into his study where the landline was already ringing. He answered it as he booted up his computer which had also downloaded Lestat earlier.

"Hello. WHAT? Because it's fried, that's why! Easy, David, we don't know how bad the damage is yet... ALL of them? The backups, too? How the hell? I KNOW that's my area. I just got to my computer; I'll call you back."

Chris looked shaken. "Buxton? What did he say?"

"He said our servers are all trashed, along with all the Auto-Writer software. Whatever it was got into the backup system as well, two whole building's worth of servers are now trashed. We're out of the Auto-Writer business. No way to rebuild before the election."

"What about the auction?"

"I don't know! Give me a minute! It should have died with the server farm. Holy crap." He typed rapidly, pounding on the keys. "It's still up! Somebody else is hosting the damned thing, and they've locked me out of it! I can see it's active, but that's all!" Then the delay on Lestat ran out, and his screen went black as the hard drive shattered. He stared at the screen as it dawned on him what had just happened.

Will was the calmest person in the room, having been trained to stay this way in these kinds of situations. But even he was sweating. "Whoever they are, if they take the money after we can't produce results, that's not good."

Heatherton looked disgusted. "Gee, Will, you think so? If they are this good, you can bet your ass they will get the money, and then they will pin this on us. We're dead." The desk phone rang, and Heatherton just stared at it. Then he reached over and yanked the cord out of the back. "Chris, who were those three you brought here today?"

"Like I said, they are friends of Casey Shaw and Eric Clarke. I think they live on some boats at *Bayside Resort* on the Eastern Shore. They're nobodies."

"They were there when our phones crapped out."

"Theirs did too. They got in a big argument over it, remember?"

Heatherton took in a deep breath. "And we all stopped to watch them, which took up more time and delayed us enough to get stuck behind all the traffic and kept us from checking our phones. Which crapped out when our entire system was wiped out and my building blew up! Goddammit! Why the hell didn't you figure this out, Will? They had to know everything! Who the hell are these people? You brought them right to us, Chris! We've got to find them, and get back whatever money they steal, and we might have a chance of living through this, or we take the money and run. In any case, we've got to get the hell out of here, now. Buxton will not take this lying down, and whoever is about to lose hundreds of millions of dollars on this scam is not going to...hell, they'll kill us even if we give the money back. We've got to get that money and run. We don't have any choice now."

Will nodded. "First things first, we've got to get out of here. Then we can regroup, I'll find out who they are and where they are, but we're going to do this my way. I want to know who we're up against. Three people didn't pull this off, and I don't want to go charging half-cocked into a hornet's nest. We'll find out what we need to know, then we'll come up with a plan. But again, we need to get out of Crozet now. Let's go to your river place on the other side of Richmond until we get some answers."

14

SETTLING UP

Back at the shop, Kelly pulled up the auction, which was now running on our server. They masked the address like it had been on the server farm's. It was up to $680 million, with two-and-a-half hours left. The line from the NOVA server farm was now dead. Lestat had done its job, and Big Nile would have to buy all its books from human authors again.

The mood at the shop was jubilant, the team knowing so far they had prevented the undermining of the next national election. Now, all we had to do was ensure that the architects of this never did anything like it again.

At 7 p.m., a last-second bidder upped the price to $720 million. We now knew what an election was worth. Ironically, it was less than what the two main presidential candidates would spend, combined. The winner in China was getting a bargain. Except they weren't. We were about to steal their credit card number and head to the mall. We watched the main account as they funded it, and as the funds split and were diverted to the individual overseas accounts. Then the stealth transfers happened, the funds converging again into one after making another half dozen transfers around the world. It finally arrived in the US where $633.6 million went into a government account, and our $86.4 million went straight into our company account. No way we were sending it all to the government and waiting to get paid whenever they felt like it. This was not a tax refund we were talking about.

Kelly's group took down our cloned auction site. We wondered how long it would take the Chinese before they figured out someone had screwed them and they followed the money trail. They would also suspect Big Nile had been part of it because the original books had come from there. I wonder how long it would take before Buxton would get a call or visit. No doubt he'd deny any knowledge. Still, I doubt he'll ever stop looking over his shoulder.

We had a "burner phone" that was cloned with Heatherton's old number. I started calling the architects of the AI program, explaining briefly why they should now run for their lives. I gave them great advice because we didn't want them to get caught and take the chance they would give up the details of each of their parts in the program. They knew all too well how the money could be traced straight to them; we had left plenty of "breadcrumbs." By the last call, I guarantee there were folks already burning rubber out of Crozet. Then I broke the cloned burner phone into pieces.

Since they had all worked today, we told everyone to take Monday off, but we wanted a meeting on Tuesday at 10 hundred hours with department heads, 1015 with the tactical team, and 1030 hours with everyone else. Kelly, Rikki, and I headed back to *Bayside* because we had a full day in the office up there tomorrow.

~

The three of us sat on the aft deck of *Hibiscus* with Cindy as she made cocktails. This wasn't a wine kind of night. She knew there had been a big operation and knew of the basic overview.

"I take it that it all went well."

Rik grinned, "Textbook great. You might even say freaking amazing."

I looked at Cindy and laughed. "Ask her what her share of 'freaking amazing' is."

Cindy looked at Rik, who said, "It was a great day."

"Define great?"

"We saved the next election from being hijacked and made a little over $23 million."

"The company made $23 million? That's incredible!"

If Rik had been standing, she would have been pawing the ground with a foot in an "Aw, shucks" move. "Uh, no, that was my share."

It dumbfounded Cindy. "Your share... was $23 million."

Rik nodded. "Pre-tax. And that's after we give out half of the overall as bonuses."

Kelly looked over at me. "I haven't run the figures yet."

I smiled. "Almost $3.5 million."

"No, I mean mine."

"That *is* yours. It was a helluva day. Again, pre-tax."

"I can't... I... Wow. Did you know this was possible when you two asked me to be a partner?"

Rik smiled. "We knew a lot of things were possible with the three of us working together. Obviously, these are some big numbers. But I have to confess, we thought there could be retirement level bonuses coming from this, and we were both scared of losing you. You could still take this money and quit and sell us back your shares. But I hope you won't."

"*We* hope you won't." I wanted my two cents in.

"You guys were willing to do this to keep me." She shook her head.

I added, "It won't be the last paycheck for the year, but I can guarantee it'll be the largest one."

"I love working with you two, and I'm not going anywhere. That means work, too." She winked at me.

Okay, *this* was the best day of my life.

"And, Colt, I'll buy the guacamole for the next burrito lunch if it's extra."

It just got better... "Don't throw money around like that! We'll get the Costco bucket, and I'll bring a baggie along with us."

Later, lying in our bunk on *EMERALD IZ*, Kelly looked concerned.

"What?"

"I love the condo. I don't want to give it up."

"Why would you?"

"Because now we can afford something bigger somewhere."

"So? That doesn't mean you have to get rid of it."

"*We* don't have to get rid of it."

"Okay, *we* don't have to get rid of it. I like it too, it's so you. Everything about it reminds me of you. I've never felt like putting my mark on a place. I'm kind of envious."

"Well, I hope you will on this one, with me."

"I'm up for trying."

"Good. And Colt?"

"Hmm?"

"When you asked what I'd want in a boat, I can think of two things. One, room to entertain inside in the winter. And two, a bigger bed! One that isn't triangle-shaped."

"You don't like vee berths?" I smiled at her.

"I'd love more headroom, too."

"Okay, we'll look for one together."

"I'd love that, I've never gone boat shopping before."

"I've had fun doing it in the past. With you, it'll be great. It's boat show season."

On Monday we rechecked the figures and printed out and signed the bonus checks. There were three additional ones I wanted to deliver myself, and I had already sprung for an additional gift for someone that would be delivered this afternoon. Rik also had a big check for her dad she wanted to give him. Kelly and I knew that was a proud moment for those two to share alone, the true "passing of the torch." Rik headed for *Plan J*, but not before I invited her to join Kel and me at Rooftops for lunch, and asked her to invite Cindy, Conrad, and Janice.

An hour later Rik and Cindy joined Kel and me at a table overlooking the marina. Rik was happier than I had ever seen her before.

"Your dad and Janice not coming?"

She laughed. "He took one look at the check, said he had to go to the bank because he was losing out on interest, so he and Janice headed to town. But not before he grumbled about selling the business a week too soon. I'd say he's switched into full retirement mode!"

We all laughed and toasted his retirement with our water glasses.

Kelly said, "Speaking of retirement, I checked, and the black Navigator and the Rover are together at a farm on the James River. They hot-footed it out of Crozet like the rest. I'm surprised they are traveling together though."

"Might have had a boat on the river and figured it would be harder to track. Probably they had cash stashed there. Who knows? The important thing is they are out of business for good, and on the run." I had enjoyed helping them get to that point, too.

Lunch was a lovely relaxed affair with friends on a beautiful day and with a fantastic view. Life had taken a turn for the incredible. After lunch, the three women headed back to their offices, but I had a delivery to make.

"Hey, Sandy!"

"Come on aboard, Colt. If you have beer that is."

I climbed the gangway and found him on the back deck. "About the beer, sorry, I'm fresh out. But this'll help you buy your own." I handed him three envelopes bearing his, Carol, and Micah's names. He opened the first one, and his eyes grew wide.

"What the hell, Colt?"

"Finder's fees for you and the girls. I know that you make more off of a book, but it's found money. Oh, and Micah might want to try uploading her book again, I have a feeling that Big Nile might just be accepting new titles again starting about now."

"So, what happened?"

"This is one story I can't tell. However, I think it will be a while before you need to worry about AI written books, at least from them. But they will appear again at some point down the road, I'm sure of that. Hopefully, by then, there will be new laws in place forcing each one to be identified as machine written. Kind of like wild-caught versus farmed seafood. You pay a premium for wild-caught, and perhaps the market will dictate a premium for human-written books."

"I never thought we'd see this day, Colt. Not something I'm happy about. When you take away the need to work for a living, whether it's digging ditches, writing books, or driving trucks, you take away a bit of the collective human soul. What if factory fishing ships become unmanned? Then even that 'wild-caught' label gets worth a little less.

"I hope you're right about the laws. Then again, the only laws that can't be broken govern physics. Thanks for looking into this, and for the finder's fees. After the summer the girls have had around here winning part of Casey's tournament purse and now this, I don't think it'll be hard to talk them into coming back with me next year. Especially Carol, if Tyler is still around. We're staying until around Thanksgiving, then headed south until spring."

"Winter won't be the same without you."

"Just be sure to get more beer before then, will you?"

"Somehow, I don't think beer will be a problem, Sandy." I had spotted one of the busboys from the *Beach Café* headed in this direction with a cart. "See you later, I'll stop by for a beer."

"You'll need to bring some then. I was serious this time, I'm out!"

I chuckled as I headed down the gangway. No, he wasn't, but he didn't know it yet. I had Carlos add ten cases of Red Stripe onto the café's beer order for me, and they were now stacked on the dock cart the busboy was pushing. As I walked past the boathouse on the way over to the office, I came back within the line of sight of Sandy's boat. He yelled as I kept going.

"You're a good man, Colt Toffler, despite what everyone else says about you! But couldn't you have at least gotten *cold* beer?"

I didn't turn around; I waved and shook my head. You have to love Sandy, he's one of a kind. The world couldn't take two of him.

~

Rikki, Kelly, and I rolled into the shop at 9:30 a.m. on Tuesday, after getting caught in morning rush hour traffic. A ton of curious faces greeted us. Just before 10, the department heads all filed into the briefing room. Rik addressed them as Kelly and I stood at her sides. She explained that this was the largest fee that the company had ever earned, and it was made possible through the combined effort of everyone here, but especially Kelly. Rikki laid out how it had been Kelly's idea and plan that had allowed us to earn a huge "finder's fee" and ensure that the builders of the Program System would never come together to do anything like this again. She said it was because of Kelly's input that the company could do a one-time bonus based on that fee amount.

"Because this was such a significant accomplishment for the company, Colt and I have brought Kelly in as a partner with us in the company. When you see these checks, I think you'll agree it was a good move for all of us."

We passed out the checks to everyone, and there were some very stunned looks. Someone clapped, then they all joined in, and came forward to hug or shake hands with all of us and congratulate Kelly. She had told us on the way down it worried her about how the partner news might be received because so many other department heads had so much more seniority than her. But they were in their positions for a reason, they were smart and good at what they did. They understood that without her, there would have been no bonus. They respected that, as they also respected Kelly and what she was capable of.

The tactical team had much the same reaction when we talked to them minutes later. Then we walked into the main room where the rest of our employees had gathered. This time, however, when Rik announced a special bonus, cheers erupted. Our employees are well paid, but an unexpected windfall like this, for the younger ones with college loan debt, mortgages, and little ones to educate this was a game-changer. When she announced that Kelly was now a partner, everyone clapped, and they hadn't even seen the checks yet. When those were distributed, there were a lot of cheers and laughter. Cell phones came out, as "significant others" were called, and good news shared. I'd been having some fantastic days lately, and I added another one.

~

Will Rhinehart pulled up the satellite map of ESVA, showing *Bayside* and the middle section of the peninsula. He pointed to a spot on the Atlantic side.

"Here's what I read about, the state used this site for a portable asphalt plant, bringing in the raw materials by ocean barge into this canal and offloading them. They finished the job, the plant was dismantled, and the site should now be abandoned. It's only fifteen minutes away from *Bayside*. You two bring the Blackfin up the canal, and we can use it as a base. I'll bring your Rover, Lloyd. Once we get the money from them, we hop in the Blackfin, and a few hours later we're in New Jersey, where I've got a guy who creates bulletproof new identities, including passports. Then we go our separate ways from there."

Chris looked at him, "How can you be sure we can get the money out of them?"

Rhinehart gave her a leer that gave her a chill. "Leverage. Leave that to me. They'll pay, trust me."

Heatherton nodded, affirming this was why he brought Rhinehart in, because he was ruthless, and unafraid to act as the merciless mercenary he was.

~

After lunch, we headed back to *Bayside* and the ESVA office. Rik had a dozen calls to make, I would make a few myself. I had old customers and a few new clients to touch base with. Kelly was gathering ideas from Casey and Dawn for the system she and her team would create for *Bayside*, which would become the prototype for a package we will sell to other high-end developments. She planned on incorporating a light version of AI into the system, and yes, part of it was "lifted" from the software we "liberated" from the Program System backups in Crozet. But instead of protecting the bad guys, it would now protect our clients. I loved the karma involved in that. And yes, I know, technically this was "theft of intellectual property,' but nobody will want to come forward to object and explain how and where it had been used before, least of all Big Nile. And frankly, we didn't give a damn. We're going to patent the new system.

Another reason we wanted to be back was that Micah and Carol wanted to cook us lunch over at C3 Wednesday at noon, to thank us for the "finder's fees." They were so appreciative of receiving those checks, there's no way we could refuse. Plus, Cindy said Tyler would make a beach jump around noon. He was prepping for the Labor Day jump and said he didn't want his jump crew to try anything he hadn't already done himself. At least that was his stated reason. I'm thinking there was showing off involved, with Carol around. I think she was already smitten enough, but you have to admit, the idea was cool.

Kelly was camped out in our conference room until her new office is ready, late next week. She wandered into my office and caught me with porn on my computer. Boat porn. A boat brokerage website.

"Aren't you supposed to be making client calls?"

"Um, yeah. But I was just getting ideas."

She smiled. "Then go to ESVA Yacht Brokers. They have some great inventory." Evidently I wasn't the only one whose mind had been drifting today.

"Anything in particular you liked?"

She replied, "I'm not saying. I want to see what you like, then we can compare notes. Let's talk about it over cocktails in the cockpit tonight."

"I'll make guacamole appetizers."

"How did I know something like that was coming?"

I grinned as she smiled and headed back to her office.

I lied. Other than grilling, I don't cook. And I haven't owned a grill in years. I haven't even looked on the condo balcony to see if Kelly had one. Okay, another thing just got added to the boat "Wanted" list. I could use the grill at C3, but I want one of my own now because I'm with Kelly. I want to cook for her, on our boat. Maybe it's just the macho "I want to show off my grilling" gene kicking in. I didn't care. Grill. Check.

Okay, back to what I was admitting; I didn't make any appetizers, instead I picked up something from the *Beach Café*. Unfortunately, they had nothing with guacamole. But they had steamed North Carolina shrimp and Carlos's take on cocktail sauce, very Chesapeakesque, with tons of crab seasoning and horseradish, and it was a good second place choice. And I should get the credit because I picked it all up. Maybe.

"Well done, Chef!"

"Smartass."

She laughed. I'd have caught the damned shrimp myself to hear her laugh.

"No guacamole though. Point deduction."

"I'll make up for it later."

"You know, I think I'll hold you to that."

I nodded. "Deal."

"So, did you find anything on ESVA's website?"

"Yessss, I did. The question is, did you?"

"I did. So, here's the deal. We each bring up our choice on our smart phones and compare. You show me yours, and I'll show you mine."

I grinned, "We *are* still talking about boats, right?"

"Yes! We can discuss other things... later."

We each shielded our phone screens as we pulled up our choices and turned the screens simultaneously.

"Colt, are you getting a funny feeling?"

"Not all that surprised." We had picked the same boat, an older forty-three-foot Saberline. Plenty of time left on her 3208TA Caterpillar diesels, a nice salon for entertaining, great master stateroom with a queen-sized bed, guest stateroom with a huge vee berth, a large galley, a grill on the flybridge deck, along with a great table and booth seating, both in the salon and up on the flybridge. Well maintained and lying at a marina just up the river from the shop. And the price was half of what I was asking for my condo. I loved that Kelly wasn't interested in a brand-new boat, and even though we both just made a pile of money, she wasn't in a hurry to spend any of it.

"It has everything that we want! I love the pictures; I hope it looks this good in person."

I nodded. The Mainship was a great single person's boat, or a younger couple's, but there were reasons Conrad wanted something larger after he and Janice got together. But at this point in my life, I also wanted more room and comfort. "So do I."

Kelly drew a deep breath. It didn't go unnoticed by me.

"Getting real, isn't it Kel? It's one thing to have your flirts get returned, and another to invite some guy to move in with you, but this isn't just picking out draperies together."

"Is that how you think I see you? As 'some guy'? If you do, one or both of us has made a huge mistake, Colt."

"No, I didn't mean it that way." I stopped, gathering my thoughts carefully before continuing. I was on the verge of hurting her with that comment, and it was the last thing I wanted to do, "I'm sorry about how that came out, Kel. This is new territory for me, and I'm a little nervous. I've never picked out a condo or a boat with anyone else's input before. Because I've never wanted nor needed anyone's input. Before, it was all about my needs, just me. Frankly, this was all new to me, and for lack of a better word, it's a little scary. I haven't been here before, thinking about the long-term. I never wanted to look that far before, beyond just now. That's always been enough."

She smiled, and her eyes showed relief. "Then I'm not the only one feeling this way. Good."

"Are we making a mistake then? Too far, too fast? Without even an 'I love you' spoken?"

"You'd have made a good lawyer, Colt. You're right, neither of us has said those exact words, but I think if we both didn't feel that way, I doubt either of us would be sitting here. We'd be crazy to be looking at boats together. So, do you still want to look at boats?"

I reached over and took her hand. "More than I ever have before. How about you, still up for looking at that Saberline?"

"I am." She squeezed my hand. "I like looking down the road and seeing you there, too."

15

———————

PAYBACKS

I called the broker Wednesday morning and arranged to tour the
Saberline Thursday in the late afternoon. We planned to finish
up at the office, go have lunch with Carol, Micah, Rikki, Cindy, Sandy,
and Tyler at C3, then head down to the shop and spend the night at
the condo.

A little before noon, Rik, Kel, and I walked over to C3, thinking we
would collect on our free lunch. Instead, we walked into a firestorm.
When we emerged beyond the trees on the path, ahead was Chris
Farmington, holding a pistol to Carol's head. Before any of us could
even reach for our pistols, Rhinehart and Heatherton moved up
behind us from spots in the trees on either side of the path, with their
pistols trained on us. Rhinehart took all our weapons, unloaded
them, and dumped them into the unused fire pit. Cindy and Micah
were over next to the clubhouse tending to Sandy, who was sitting on
the ground with blood running down his forehead where he had
been pistol-whipped. Tyler's dog Kaili was lying next to Sandy. Farmington looked over at me with a scowl.

"We want our money."

I smiled. "I didn't think you were here for lunch."

She snarled, "Not smart to be so bold with guns on all of your friends. Maybe you need to understand we're serious." She cocked the hammer back on her pistol, which she now moved closer to Carol's head. Carol was shaking, with tears running down her face, and she sobbed. Kaili started a low growl down deep in her throat. "And you need to keep that dog calm, or I'll shoot it."

Horse person my ass; horse people love their dogs. "The problem is, the government confiscated the auction money, so we don't have it. Why don't you put down your guns before you make things any worse for yourselves?" I didn't expect them to put their guns down, I was only buying time until I could evaluate the situation and come up with a plan.

Heatherton's eyes narrowed as he looked at me. "That's too bad because the only way you are all going to get out of this alive is if you can come up with cash, and a lot of it. And I figure someone with your connections to people like Eric Clarke and Casey Shaw should be able to come up with a lot of cash. Enough so we can get out of here and start over. And we want the backups for my AI system. I know you have those."

"I can get you those, but they aren't here."

"Where are they?"

"In Hampton, in a bank vault."

Heatherton said, "Now that wasn't hard, was it? All you need to do now is come up with the cash component."

"How much?"

"Thirty million. It's a fraction of what you cost me, but it should be a doable amount in a short time frame."

"You're nuts! I don't have that kind of money."

"I figured as much. But I bet your two friends have that much in 'walking around' cash. I'm sure when you explain the situation to them, they will be happy to help if they want to see you again. And I imagine someone like you who can wipe out our phones, blow up my building, and take out our AI system will have all kinds of tricks up his sleeve, so we will need an insurance policy. Two in fact. Chris?"

"Those two are together Lloyd, and those two." She indicated Kelly and me, and Cindy and Rikki.

Heatherton nodded at Rhinehart who smiled cruelly and moved toward Cindy. Rik started for him, but I grabbed her arm, holding her back. She glared at me, but I looked pleadingly at her. Rushing them now would only get us all shot. Rhinehart pulled two pairs of flex-cuffs out of his pocket, and cuffed Cindy's hands in front of her, and dragged her with him over to Kel, doing the same to her. Kel looked over and locked eyes with me, and I could see she was scared. I hoped that she couldn't read in my eyes I was as scared for her if not more so.

Rhinehart motioned to Heatherton, "Give me the car keys." He took the keys and smiled at Carol. "Thanks for the gate card." He walked down the path, coming back two minutes later. "Rover's at the gate, let's go."

Kelly looked over at me, and mouthed, "I love you" and I did the same back. I silently prayed it wouldn't be the last time I'd get to tell her that. I've never felt as helpless in my life as I did right then, as Rhinehart led her away. Heatherton led Cindy as she turned to Rik. "Do your thing. I know you, and I love you."

"Count on it. I love you, too, and I'll see you soon."

Farmington addressed Rik and me. "Well, that was a touching little scene. I figured that you two would need encouragement, and if you truly want to see them again, you won't screw around." She shoved Carol over toward the rest of us which sent her sprawling onto the paver bricks. Kaili came rushing over to Carol while growling again at Farmington.

"I told you to keep that dog quiet. Next growl out of it earns it a bullet!" She motioned for all of us to sit on the curved benches on the east side of the fire pit, while she remained standing on the west side, preventing any of us from rushing her. Micah had one hand putting pressure on Sandy's cut on his forehead, which had stopped bleeding. I raised my hands above my head and motioned for the others to do the same. Chris Farmington didn't notice as she was too wrapped up in herself. I had seen something in the sky behind her she missed.

"But the show's not over. Will is an expert at leverage. Leverage, meaning as in making something happen more easily than it would have otherwise. I guess that's why he loves backhoes because they are based on leverage. And he has this 'thing' for hydraulics. I guess you saw our AI sentries at Contour. Will was the one that came up to use the backhoe to dispatch any trespassers. The bucket of a backhoe can squash a human skull like a ripe melon. AI knew the best places to dig graves, and it even cleaned up after itself.

"Will gave me a lesson with the backhoe and showed me how by barely moving a lever, you can have the bottom of the bucket restrain someone. With ever so slightly more pressure, you can crush bone and finally organs. It's not pleasant, and we're going to demonstrate it for you. How far we have to take it will be up to you." She held up her phone. "We're 'borrowing' a backhoe... never mind where it is, but when they get there, they'll set up a live video shot, so you can see that we're serious. You need to get those backups and cash together, and I mean before the sun sets, or your two ladies will end up as flat as pancakes. Now, none of us want that, except Will, he gets off on it. So, for the sake of those two, I suggest you make some phone calls."

Tyler perched on the edge of the door of the leased Super Twin Otter turboprop at 13,500 feet on a "severe clear" day. He was looking down over *Bayside*, just west of their airport drop zone. He pitched forward and splayed his arms out to his side. His two legs, weakened by surgeries to counteract the effects of the muscle tightness caused by his cerebral palsy, were bound together with Velcro straps to prevent any joint damage on landing. If all went well, he would slide on his behind across the sand.

The drop was incredible, and when his wrist altimeter read 2,500 feet, he pulled his ripcord. The chute opened, and the slider moved down in place, preventing the four sets of steering lines from being tangled. It fluttered above his head as he relaxed and enjoyed the view. He had about two-and-a-half minutes left in the air.

Tyler scoped out the beach, making sure he had a clear landing zone, then his focus drifted over toward C3, where Carol and Micah would cook everyone lunch. He saw a black SUV pulling through the security gate, and as C3 came more into focus, he realized that something was very wrong. A figure on the west side of the fire pit shoved someone, who ended up on the ground. Now at 1,000 feet, he couldn't be sure, but that person looked a lot like Carol, and Kaili rushed over to her. The person who pushed her was holding something that looked like a pistol.

Several people sitting on the bench now raised their hands above their heads. Tyler realized that he had to get down there and fast. It meant losing altitude quickly, so he executed a "hook turn," something that they teach every skydiving student that you *never* do, especially at low altitude. It has sent more skydivers to the hospital and the graveyard than any other maneuver. He pulled hard on his right steering line, and the canopy dipped below his body as centrifugal force spun him outward. Only his skill and experience allowed him to recover a second later and 250 feet above the ground in a classic "swoop" maneuver, propelling him forward, way too fast for a safe landing. He never flared, or hit his "brakes," counting on hitting the person full force with his feet. He knew it wouldn't end well for him, but it should give his friends a chance to rush the intruder who he now saw was a woman.

I saw Tyler go into a spin at low altitude and thought for certain he would fall into the bay, but at the last second, he recovered, coming at us, but way too fast to land, in a shallow trajectory. I don't know if it was the flutter noise from his slider or his yell of "Hey!" that made Chris Farmington turn at the last second. He hit her full force in her side, kicking her with his boots, causing her to discharge her pistol toward the bay as she was knocked off her feet, her head colliding with the edge of the fire pit with a sickening snapping sound, which was followed by a second snap as Tyler tumbled across the paver deck exclaiming, "Ow, that's gonna leave a mark."

I rushed over to disarm Farmington, while Carol rushed to Tyler's side. I could have taken my time with Farmington, as I saw her head was now at an unnatural angle from her shoulders, her neck having snapped on impact with the fire pit edge. I turned toward Tyler, who I could see through a rip in his trousers was bleeding from one knee, and he was holding an obviously broken arm. Rik was already pulling our pistols out of the fire pit and in the process of reloading them. She handed me mine and Kelly's. I had Farmington's phone in my hand. We were now racing against time. Once that video call came and Chris didn't answer, Cindy and Kelly were as good as dead. "Rik, go get your tablet and pray that beacon on Heatherton's Rover is still active. I'll pick you up in the Escalade." Rikki took off, and I turned to the group. "Carol, get Tyler to the hospital. Do not mention that this was skydiving related, say he crashed his Segway. Take Sandy and get him stitched up, too. Leave the body here, we'll take care of it. No police and say nothing about this to anyone." With that, I took off too, picking up Rik by the office as she was pulling up the tracker which thankfully was still working. They had a five-minute head start on us, and I was determined to make up as much time as I could.

~

"Sorry about this, ladies, but we can't have you shouting out any clues about where you are over the video call." Heatherton was fastening two strips of extra adhesive duct tape across their mouths. He had already taped their knees and ankles, immobilizing them. They were both now lying on the ground next to a large deep hole that had been dug by an ancient backhoe. By a stroke of luck for them, the asphalt plant's crew had yet to remove it. Heatherton motioned to Kelly, "We'll start with this one."

Rhinehart grinned evilly as he climbed into the backhoe.

~

Rikki studied the satellite view as we raced down US-13 then turned off toward Quinby. Two more turns and we were on a narrow two-lane. I was going faster probably than anyone had ever driven before on this road. When we were about one minute away Rik advised me to slow down so that they wouldn't see us speeding past. "It's lined with trees, but there's still no way to keep from being seen if we go in the entrance road. The whole clearing is ringed with trees. Go past the entrance, and there will be a narrow drive back into the woods. Take that."

I turned where she directed and drove back in about 150 yards before she said, "Stop." We climbed out, communicating with hand signals as we made our way about 200 yards through the trees, our pistols up and ready. When we reached the edge of the tree line, we could see that the area beyond it was a flat graveled open area about 300 yards across with a canal cut back into it. An older thirty-two-foot Blackfin sport fisherman was tied up to the bulkhead to the right. About thirty yards ahead in the gravel was the Rover, and ten yards beyond it was a backhoe, next to a pile of dirt and what appeared to be a deep hole. Heatherton was next to the hole, holding Kelly down as Rhinehart was climbing into the backhoe. I motioned "go," then Rik and I took off across the open gravel area between the trees and the Rover, taking cover behind it. Seconds later I heard Rhinehart start the backhoe. He operated the levers and foot pedals, extending the boom and curling the bucket so the flat part of the bottom was parallel to the ground as he swung it toward Kelly and started to lower it. Rik crept around the front of the Rover while I moved around the back. I wasn't about to let Rhinehart keep operating those controls or reach for his pistol. I shot him in the upper right arm, shattering his humerus, making him release the right lever. He screamed in both agony and frustration, as he let go of the left lever, reaching for the wound, to try to stop the blood flow. He looked over at me as I raced forward toward him.

"You bastard!"

"Don't move!" I saw him glance at the lever that would lower the boom, crushing Kelly with the bucket. I guess he didn't realize I meant don't move your eyes, either. Before he could do what I knew he was about to, I shot him just above the right eye. A 10mm hollow point from five yards away likes to keep traveling, even after it comes in contact twice with the human skull. The first contact is only a third of an inch across, but as the bullet passes through the bone it mushrooms and slows somewhat, turning the brain into gray jello for half an inch in any direction around its path. Then when it exits, it makes a hole in the skull about the size of a golf ball, and it takes a lot of blood and brain tissue with it. So, I guess it was kind of redundant when I shot him in the head the second time, but I was really pissed, and yes, it *did* make me feel better. I turned and saw that Rik had disarmed Heatherton and had him standing in front of her at gunpoint. I went up to the backhoe and saw that Rhinehart had used a screwdriver jammed into the keyhole to start it. I pushed a foot pedal to make the bucket swing away from Kelly before I shut it down, and was I glad I had. Without the hydraulic pump operating, the worn-out hydraulics allowed the boom to slowly sag to the ground. Its deadweight alone would have crushed Kelly. I dragged Rhinehart's body out of the backhoe, allowing it to fall to the ground in a heap.

I walked toward Heatherton as he looked over at Rhinehart's body then back at me.

"I want my attorney."

"Oh, we passed the attorney stage a long time ago, Lloyd. About the same time that you decided to sell out my country for money, you damned greedy bastard."

I shot him in the thigh, and he crumpled to the ground, screaming.

"Lloyd, I just hit you in your femoral artery. You'll be dead in just minutes. Do you think I believed for a second you wouldn't kill Kelly and Cindy? That you dug that hole for fun? Don't worry, we won't put you in it, I want to make sure there's no chance you'll ever be found. So, screw your attorney, and screw you." Then I shot him in the head, too.

I walked over to help Rik who was using her knife to free Cindy and Kelly. I helped Kelly up, and hugged her, she was shaking.

"You killed both of them." She was in shock and the way she said it was almost matter-of-factly, not like she was accusing me of murder.

"They were going to kill you, Kel. No way I would let that happen, and no way we would be spending the rest of our lives looking over our shoulders. They murdered people, using the AI system and a backhoe. Only this time they were going to do it personally." I searched her eyes for acceptance and agreement, and after a moment, I found it. She wrapped her arms around my neck and pulled me to her.

"I love you, Colt."

"And I love you. I'll always protect you, no matter what I have to do." It sounded corny as hell, but it was how I felt, and I'm glad I said it. We stood there a minute hanging onto each other because we could. That wasn't such a certainty just a short while ago.

Rik walked up holding Cindy, who looked shell-shocked. She looked over at Heatherton's body, then back at me. The look she gave me had fear mixed in it. I guess it was hard to process that a guy you were going to have lunch with just shot two guys in the head even if those guys planned on killing you. I understood though, and I'd give Cindy plenty of space. And I hoped that she would come back around, eventually. We all walked back through the woods to my Escalade. I grabbed a pair of nitrile gloves and shoe covers from a "go bag" that I kept in it. I passed the keys to Rik.

"Get them both back to *Hibiscus*. I'll come over and take care of

Farmington, then I'll fix things back here. They are all going for a last ride on that Blackfin."

I walked back through the woods and retrieved the Rover's keys from Heatherton's pants pocket. I locked the seat's position with the memory button number one after I got in, now wearing my gloves and shoe covers. Then I adjusted the seat for me. Heatherton was a few inches shorter, and when I abandon the car, I wanted to make sure that the seat is set back to him, and now all I needed to do was hit the button again. After they find the car and they link it to a missing man, that's one of the first things they would check, was the last driver the same height as the missing person.

I drove over to *Bayside*, backing up to the security gate by C3, and opening the Rover's rear hatch. The SUV blocked me from being seen by anyone in the marina. I retrieved Chris Farmington's body using a fireman's carry, then dumped it in the cargo area of the Rover. I found Rik on *Hibiscus* and gave her a list of things we'd need, and the first thing on the list was Casey Shaw's help. Then I took off for the old asphalt plant site again. I backed up to the bulkhead by the Blackfin and hit the seat memory button. Then I unloaded Farmington's body, dumping it in the cockpit. I opened the boat and checked it over. Besides three bags of clothes, there was another bag with just over $95,000 in cash. It was one thing that would come back off the boat.

I put the body in the vee berth, then walked over to the bodies of Rhinehart and Heatherton. Using the backhoe, I scooped them up, dumping them in the Blackfin's cockpit, then I dragged them up into the vee berth too. I used the saltwater wash-down hose to get rid of the blood trails in the cockpit because I'd be passing close to a marina in Wachapreague. No sense in raising anyone's suspicions. Then I took the backhoe over and dug out the bloody areas in the gravel where the bodies had been, dumping it all into the hole. Then I used the front loader section to push the dirt pile back from where it had come. There was a small mound of gravel left over from the asphalt production, and it covered the raw dirt and holes perfectly.

Now to remove the tracker from the Rover and it would be time to go for a boat ride.

The canal connected with Bradford Bay, and from there I headed north in the inside channel that runs past Wachapreague. After it dumped me out into Burton's Bay, and I saw Casey's big Jarrett Bay sportfish, *Predator*, idling out of the *Bluffs Marina's* channel. I idled up to her after I got close, and Rik transferred to the Blackfin, bringing a small black field bag with her. Then I took the lead and headed out the inlet channel into the Atlantic Ocean. The waves were about four feet, not too bad for running, but making transfers between the boats dicey, especially when you have two prostheses for feet. I'd worry about that though when the time came.

We ran southeast, away from any of the popular fishing canyons and spots. There weren't any other boats in sight offshore. Rik went below with the bag and reappeared five minutes later with it and the bag of money.

"Give me your Sig. Did you pick up your brass?"

I handed her my pistol, and from my pocket I fished out the spent cartridges I had picked up as well as the tracker. She threw the cartridges and the tracker overboard and replaced the barrel on my pistol. She threw the old barrel over the side, eliminating the last link between my gun and the two men's bodies, not that they would ever be found. It doesn't hurt to be cautious, but with no shell casings near the bodies there was no need to change the ejector and the firing pin.

I throttled back to idle, and Casey eased up alongside as Rik took the helm. I stood on the gunwale's covering board with the two bags in one hand while grabbing the flybridge cap for stability. Timing it perfectly, I crossed over to a similar spot on *Predator*. Rik then eased away, taking the Blackfin back up to cruising speed, and setting the autopilot. Casey matched her speed, staying about fifty yards behind and twenty yards to her side. From the cockpit I watched Rik go down below, reappear seconds later, then dive over the side. Casey steered over to her, slowing as he did. I pulled her aboard handing her a waiting towel. We climbed up to the flying bridge, as Casey raced to catch up to the Blackfin, then staying back about 500 yards.

Rik had set charges forward of the center bulkhead on either side of the boat and well below the waterline. They simultaneously blew a pair of two-foot diameter holes in the hull that also took out the cabin windows. Still running at cruise, water now poured into the hull. Within seconds, she was straining to keep up on a plane, settling down as the cabin filled with water. The bodies would stay put as the anchor line locker was behind the vee berth's forward bulkhead. I had pulled it through the access hatch and secured them with it. With the end attached to a "pad eye" in the bottom of the locker, they weren't going anywhere.

We watched the death throes of the Blackfin as the engines kept trying to push the boat forward, that bulkhead keeping the water away from the engine compartment, just as we'd planned. The bow deck finally dipped below the waves, and water came flooding over the cockpit's forward-most gunwales. It reached the engine intakes within seconds, shutting both down. Less than a minute later she disappeared, heading bow first toward the sandy bottom almost 160 feet below. This spot was too deep for recreational divers, and with no reef or structure around, it was too sandy for bottom fishermen. So, it would be a long time if ever before someone would discover the wreck.

16

LICKING WOUNDS

Casey headed *Predator* back to the *Bluffs* as Rik went below to shower and change into the dry clothes she brought with her. I sat in the seat next to Casey's helm seat.

"Thanks for this, Casey. I owe you one."

"You don't owe me anything, Colt, Rik told me a little of what happened. Thanks for saving Cindy and Kelly, you two put yourselves in a hell of a lot of danger to do that. I didn't like Chris, but if you two hadn't told me, I'd never had any idea she could be so dangerous."

"The most vicious ones sometimes hide it the best. Their group was dangerous to the entire country." I knew that Casey would love more details, but the less he knew, the better off he would be. This was something the government wanted erased, so the fewer people who knew the whole story, the smaller the chance it would resurface. There was one more loose end in NOVA that needed tying up, and it would require some additional help from someone who already had a security clearance. We would take care of that shortly.

"And thanks too, for keeping *Bayside's* name out of the news. If it got out that armed thugs got into our secure area that no doubt would hurt our business."

"That was our fault, and we'll make sure that never happens again. First, we should have told your office to change the gate access code after Eric sent Farmington packing. They would never have gotten near C3 without it."

Casey shook his head. "It wasn't just you guys; we missed that one too."

"At the time we only thought she was acquainted with those bad actors; we didn't figure she was partnered with them. But it all makes sense now since that's where her money went. She and Heatherton put everything into this operation, including building a legitimate server farm. That was the 'great tech investment' of Heatherton's she talked about over dinner. By then she was out of cash, mortgaged to the hilt, and betting on a windfall from another scheme they were both involved in. The server farm had an unfortunate event that probably won't be covered under insurance, and they lost their largest customer, the one which had been paying the bills. When that happened, they had no choice other than to run." I left out the part about the Chinese also looking for them.

And speaking of running, we had the matter of the bag of money that was onboard the Blackfin to discuss, Heatherton's river house escape stash. Only the three of us were aware of it, and now we needed to decide what to do with it. Rik came up the ladder and rejoined us, so I brought it up, asking for their thoughts.

Rik said, "I've made a ton of money off this job already, so I don't need a cent of it. Without Tyler, that hole they dug would have held a few of us. With a broken arm, that means no canes for him for a while, and he's working so hard to get his skydiving business going. What do you two think about giving it to him?"

Casey said, "Good choice. That's my vote."

I was smiling because I was thinking the same thing. He was in for a rough couple of months until those bones mended. "Done deal. I like him, I hope he ends up staying in the marina."

Casey nodded. "Everyone who meets him likes him. I'm going to make sure he stays here on the South Dock; we're going to cut him a great deal, and let's give him a C3 card."

We all nodded, knowing everyone else would agree.

Back on *Hibiscus*, Cindy and Kelly were sitting in the salon, talking. Kelly had always been around members of the operations group through her job. She understood between their military service and some rougher assignments for the company, all had killed people that needed to die. This was the first time though that she had been present when that happened. She had known this was a possibility when she told Colt she wanted to do some fieldwork. Still, seeing what Colt had to do had come as a shock at first, but she understood it, and ultimately, she approved. She would've done the same thing if her hands hadn't literally been tied at the time.

Cindy was still shaken, more by Colt's actions than even her own abduction. Less about what happened to Rhinehart, but when Colt shot Heatherton, he knew Rik had already disarmed him. She told Kelly she liked Colt, but never dreamed that he could be that cold and ruthless. It was a hard memory to erase.

"If he wasn't, Cindy, we'd both be dead. There is so much more to this business than you know, or that you'd want to. Trust me, given a chance, both men would have done the same thing to all of us, with no hesitation. Colt did what I would have done if I had been standing where he was." She looked in Cindy's eyes. "I can guarantee Rikki would've done what Colt did too, and she'd have never lost a minute's sleep over it. I understand it's tough, but you need to get past this. We're alive right now because of Colt and Rikki."

"I understand, it's just that I have never seen Colt so much as get angry. And he seemed so cool when he shot Heatherton." She shuddered.

"Trust me, he was anything but cool, he was as mad as he could get. He shot him in the thigh for revenge." Kelly thought a minute before deciding to level with Cindy. "He wanted revenge because Rik told me they planned to crush us slowly on camera with that backhoe to force a ransom payment, and Colt knew that and they still would even after they got the money.

"By shooting him in the femoral artery, he also knew there was no way to get him to a hospital in time to save him. He wanted Heatherton to feel just as helpless as we would have as they slowly crushed us to death with that machine. Shooting him the second time was an act of mercy, putting him out of his misery. He could have just let him continue to bleed to death. If it had been up to me I might have, to tell you the honest truth.

"It wasn't because I was there, Cindy, he'd have done the same thing if it had just been you there alone. I know it's weird, he's such a quiet person, always listening and seldom talking. But most of his friends, and all his closest friends, are right here in this marina, and he'd do anything he could to protect us. That's Colt, and I guess it's part of why I love him; he's so loyal to those who are loyal to him. I've known that about him from the time we first met. If you have his back, he's got yours. When you think about it, I trust him with my life, because he already saved it once. Yours, too. So, please work on getting past this. He's more than worth it."

When we got back to *Bayside*, we all walked straight over to *Hibiscus* where we found Cindy and Kelly in the salon. I could still feel the weird vibe coming from Cindy, so I didn't plan to stay long. I sat with Kelly for two minutes, then said I needed to check on Tyler and Sandy. Kel and Casey left with me and we walked to Sandy's trawler, finding them all in the salon. Sandy had a large bandage on his forehead, and Tyler had a fiberglass cast on his arm. Sandy looked at me with a wry smile.

"I already know, it can't go in a book. But you got those two bastards, right?"

I nodded. "They'll never bother any of us again."

"Are you okay?" He looked worriedly at Kelly, who smiled at him.

"I'm good, Sandy, thanks to Tyler. How's your head?"

"Seven stitches. The scar will be another true story I can't ever tell, so I'll make up something good. I'm a fiction writer, it's what I do best." He grinned.

I looked at Tyler, who had Carol hovering over him. I was glad they were together; he is going to need a lot of help to get around until that cast comes off. "How's the arm?"

"Clean break. Should be good to go in six weeks. I'll be back in the sky in two."

Carol jumped in, "Maybe, or not. One day at a time, pal."

Tyler rolled his eyes, "Yes, nurse."

"I saw that!"

"You were supposed to!" Everyone chuckled, a good sign that things would get back to normal soon.

I said, "Tyler, that was the worst skydiving landing I've ever seen, and the most accurate one as well. Everyone in this room owes you a huge debt. We found something we figured you ought to have. It came from those three, and it's only right that you have it." I handed him the bag of cash and watched as his eyes popped when he opened it and pulled out a few bundles. "This should help hold you over until you get the skydiving operation up to full speed."

Casey chimed in, "And your dockage is comped through the end of next year, so you don't need to worry about that, either."

I didn't know Casey would do that, but I'm glad he did.

"I don't know what to say other than thank y'all. But I don't feel right about taking this and the free dockage."

Sandy put his hand on Tyler's good arm. "A bit of advice, Tyler. Not accepting all that would make the rest of us 'not feel right.' I can speak for all of us when I say we're damned glad to know you, and happy that you'll be around. And we are still around because of what you did, so thank you."

I could see it choked Tyler up, so he replied with an exaggerated nod of his head. Couldn't blame him, it had been an emotional day. And it wasn't over yet, I still had one last loose end to tie up.

Back on *EMERALD IZ* with Kel, I called Candi Ryan's cell phone and arranged to meet her in her office on Capitol Hill the next morning. I called Beth Powell and booked an early morning charter on the Aerostar to DC. Then I called the boat broker and rescheduled our appointment for Friday.

Business now completed, I poured two glasses of wine for Kel and me, and we sat in the cockpit. I didn't want her out of my sight, and she thought the same about me. We had finally gotten our timing right, then we almost lost each other. It made me appreciate her that much more. We sat in a very comfortable silence, communicating so much without ever saying a word. I hadn't ever found that with anyone before, and I silently vowed never to lose it.

17

DINNER DEALS

The next morning, I walked into Candi's office and briefed her on everything that happened, leaving out the parts about how Chris and her partners were dead, leaving her to connect the dots on her own with no confirmation. I wanted to give her plausible deniability while getting across the fact they were no longer a threat. I gave her a list of board members of Big Nile, and she knew or had met most of them including James Bowman the vice chairman, who turned out to be a close friend of hers. His office was in Fairfax, close to Big Nile's headquarters. She made a call, had her office assistant cancel the rest of her schedule, and we headed over to meet with him.

Candi introduced us, then we sat across from him in his office.

I looked straight into his eyes. "I understand you had trouble with your new AI Writer system at Big Nile." And I saw it caught him off guard.

"How did you know about that?"

"I know a lot of things about it; much more than even you. Like how you've probably tried using your backups, with the same result. And I know why." I filled him in on how the system had been hijacked by Heatherton's crew, and how David Buxton had been in on it from the beginning. From his reaction, I saw he hadn't known, and the news shook him. Then I figured we had an ally.

"I was against that damned project from the beginning. It was David's project. I thought it was misleading and fraudulent, but they outvoted me. Now I understand why he was pushing so hard for it. If that gets out, Big Nile is finished."

"None of us want that. So, if you want to save Big Nile, here's what you need to do..."

~

It started as a whisper on Wall Street and turned into a roar by the end of the day. Something bad had happened at Big Nile, there would be a massive write off, and the chairman was involved in a scandal. The rumor stated the Security Exchange Commission was gearing up for an investigation, focusing on David Buxton. I already knew about it because I'm the one who started it, through some friends in New York.

~

Early that afternoon, James Bowman, flanked by several other board members barged into David Buxton's office. He looked up from his desk, taken aback.

"What is this, James?"

"This is us saving the company." He pushed two pieces of paper across the desk. "This top one is a letter of resignation we had drawn up for you. Sign it, David."

"Like hell I will! I'm the only one that can lead this company out of this mess!"

"You're the one who created it. Sign that and leave, or the story about your AI auction and your involvement in Contour Auto Tech goes public, and the company will come after you for the losses incurred because of this fiasco. You'll be lucky to avoid jail time. It's up to you."

Buxton's eyes went wide. "How did you know about Contour?"

"*How* isn't important, it's enough that we do, and we know everything. This statement also declines any severance pay, and you agree to divest yourself of all stock in the company you own within the week."

"You can't do this! I'm margined to the hilt, and I'm close to the minimums now after today's drop. I've used this as collateral for loans for personal projects; those get called, and this will ruin me!"

"I don't give a damn. We can do this, and we will. Your days of using Big Nile for your personal piggy bank are over. You've got two minutes to sign it and clear out, or I'm calling the SEC myself."

❧

We watched CNBC in Eric's office. At 4:02 p.m., two minutes after market close they read a press release from Big Nile announcing the departure of David Buxton, and the planned divestiture of his stake in the company. Several other board members had also resigned. James Buxton, the vice chairman had taken over as temporary chairman until there could be a formal meeting and vote on a new slate of directors. The stock had been in free fall all day, and this hurt the after-hours price. Eric grinned.

"Glad you all didn't tell me more about what led to this, because I'm going to buy a ton of the stock tomorrow afternoon. The hysteria should die down by then, and I bet it'll rebound next week."

Candi smiled. "I can't say anything to anyone about that right now."

Eric's eyes narrowed. "Can't? As in restricted from saying anything by law?"

Candi's smile got wider. "I can't say."

"In that case, I will double what I was thinking about buying! With you leaving public office and a board shakeup underway, there's only one reason I can think for you to stay quiet. James asked you to join his board."

Candi was silent, but I figured Eric hit it on the head. I wasn't sure either as she and Buxton had talked for five minutes in private before we left. But I would also call my broker tomorrow. First though, I had a few things to tell my client, Eric, that Candi now couldn't know. I made sure Eric was looking straight at me, then I looked at Candi and tilted my head. He got the hint. We were all going to be flying to *Bayside* in Eric's Sikorsky S-76 helicopter in a few minutes, so he asked if she would mind checking to see how his daughter was coming with packing.

"She doesn't need my help unless this isn't about packing at all. As in, you two need privacy." She looked at Eric questioningly.

"As in, I have no knowledge of that." Eric smiled back at her.

"In that case, I better make sure she packs plenty of fishing clothes. See you two upstairs." She smiled as she left, showing she didn't take exception to it, but in fact appreciated being protected since she might join Big Nile's board.

Without going into deep detail, I assured Eric the threat from Chris was over, and that she would not be bothering them anymore. Then I added that it was complicated, but she had threatened both Cindy and Kelly's lives.

"I'd guess she's on the run."

I shrugged. "I wouldn't worry about her anymore, Eric."

"Colt, if anyone threatened Candi, I'm not sure what I could be capable of."

"I think you would take whatever measures were necessary to protect her and do whatever you felt was called for to make sure she could never threaten Candi again. It's part of what I do, Eric, and why you don't need to worry anymore. Did I mention that Tyler got hurt? Broken arm."

"Uh, no you didn't. Skydiving accident?"

"Kind of, but let's say it was much more heroic than that. I'm not sure what the cover story will be, but let's say things wouldn't have turned out well without his help, and he made a bodily sacrifice to save others. He's one heck of a guy."

He raised his eyebrows. "One heck of a guy that needs a cover story, that says a lot, coming from you. In that case, I hope he stays around."

"Casey's already made sure he will, at least through next year."

Eric paused for a moment, thinking. "Would you and Kelly like to be our guests for dinner tonight on *Miss E*?"

That was Eric's vintage seventy-five-foot Trumpy yacht, and where they stayed at *Bayside*. "I'll check with Kelly, but I'm sure we would."

"Do you have Tyler's number? I'd like to invite Carol and him as well and get to know them both a little better."

I sent Tyler's contact info to his phone, then we headed to the helipad.

~

Kelly was already having a glass of wine, sitting in the cockpit of *EMERALD IZ*. There was another full glass next to the empty chair beside her. I sat down, and she leaned over and kissed me. "I saw the Big Nile news. So, everything went well?"

"I don't think they'll be in a hurry to get back into the AI writing business. And while she can't confirm or deny it, Eric and I suspect that Candi is about to be put on their board after she's out of office. No doubt a 'Thank You' for helping straighten up their mess. I'm buying some of their stock right before the closing bell tomorrow."

"Sounds like a good idea, I think I will, too. It's taken a beating, but their core business still looks good. Speaking of looking good, I can't wait to see that Saberline tomorrow."

"Me, too. And I've been thinking about that empty slip at the condo. I have an idea." I laid out my thoughts, and I got a smile and a kiss.

We saw Tyler, Kaili, and Carol making their way to *Miss E's* gangway. He was on his Segway, which he could operate single-handedly. It was when he transferred off it and could only use one cane that things got dicey. Fortunately, Carol was there to support his other side. Been there, done that myself, and I guarantee it's no picnic for either of them. Carol was a special young woman, but then again Tyler had already proven himself to be quite a guy.

Over cocktails in *Miss E's* salon, Eric coaxed Tyler's story out of him. He had become interested in skydiving after getting involved with off-road endurance and obstacle racing in a specially designed hand lever propelled wheelchair. Many of the participants were wounded veterans who also skydived, and they found a kindred spirit in him. He became friends with many of them and helped talk quite a few through some tough periods in their lives. While many had lost mobility they once had, Tyler had never had it to begin with. More than one found new inspiration through his contagious enthusiasm for life, despite his having daily physical challenges.

Over the years Tyler fought hard to find solutions and create innovations to help him stay in the mainstream, his modified Segway being an example. He told Eric that he had fallen in love with skydiving because between jumping from the airplane and landing on the ground, he was on a level playing field with every other jumper. No special equipment was necessary, other than the Velcro leg straps.

He said his goal though was to create a place where other people with mobility issues could come vacation with their families and be in a comfortable environment designed for ease of them getting around. Give them access to skydiving, fishing, horseback riding, all while being surrounded by their families. He had fallen in love with ESVA, saw it as a great place for this, and his skydiving business was the first link in the chain.

While Eric had been talking to Tyler, Candi and Kel had been chatting with Carol. As usual, I was staying quiet, getting the gist of both conversations. It turned out that Tyler and Carol had talked about her coming back up for the winter after she helped Sandy and Micah take his boat to the Keys. But they decided that his Bertram would be just too small for the two of them for that many months. I looked over at Kel and winked, and she beamed. We had a surprise in mind for those two.

Eric had stepped out on the aft deck to make a phone call. When he came back in, he asked Tyler if he could spare an hour or two tomorrow.

"Sure, but for what?"

"I just spoke to Greg Sawyer, an attorney friend who owns a farm over on the Atlantic side. He knows of an eighty-acre farm by his that's for sale which would be perfect for what you want to do."

"I haven't raised the money for that yet."

"Yes, you have. I think your idea is great, and I'm going to start a foundation to fund it if you and Carol will oversee the construction and the operation. Those would be paid positions, and we'll fund trips for folks that can't afford it. I've got friends that plan on building houses here at *Bayside* too, and I think I can twist arms to raise even more money. It will help connect them further with ESVA, just like it will with me. Maybe we'll even throw an annual benefit at the new club here. You'll still have time to run the skydiving operation too if Carol agrees to be full time at the foundation's farm."

Tyler was speechless as Carol came over and hugged him. "Say something!"

He looked at Eric, "Uh, that's amazing. I don't know what to say."

Eric grinned. "You both just say 'deal' and we'll do it."

They both grinned and said in unison, "Deal!"

Kelly came over and wrapped an arm around mine. "Tyler, Colt and I are going boat shopping tomorrow for a new home base."

I jumped in. "And we also love your Bertram. I realize it has a special meaning to you, but it's too tight for two people for the winter.

EMERALD IZ is tight for entertaining in the cold, but it might just be a fit for you two if you wanted to swap your Bertram even for it, as the next step for you. We have an empty slip at our condo in Virginia Beach that will fit a boat lift. Tough to leave a boat like the Bertram with its outdrives in the saltwater for extended periods without having electrolysis issues, and the lift would solve that."

He looked at me and said, "Colt, you understand how much that Bertram means to me and why. But my dad always said things are just things and making memories is what's most important. However, your Mainship is worth several times what my Bertram is."

"So is having Carol come back up and help you put this organization together. Plus, the Mainship has a shower, and your Bertram doesn't. It's a long way over to the marina's showers by the *Beach Café* in January. Tyler, if you hadn't done what you did, Kelly wouldn't be here, and I can never repay you for that. I'd like to think this swap is a small down payment though. And while we'll give her a good home, if we ever want to get rid of the Bertram, we'll sell her back to you for a dollar."

Carol looked at Tyler with big "doe" eyes. He nodded, and she hugged him. "Deal, Colt. Thank you. Thank you both, er, thank you all."

There's something about *Bayside* that brings people together, and great things get accomplished. But I think this was the biggest thing I've seen come out of it yet. And I hadn't seen Eric so happy. He was excited about Tyler and Carol's project, and what it would mean to so many families.

Kel and I were excited about having the Bertram behind the condo. It was quiet, almost twice as fast as the Mainship, and would be fun to take to the Outer Banks on weekend trips, or just on after work cruises. I loved the vintage design.

The rest of that evening it was impossible not to get caught up in the enthusiasm that was being generated by Tyler, Carol, and Eric. It was so much fun watching the three over dinner. Eric was putting down more ESVA roots, as was Tyler, and now Carol, too. All the bad that happened earlier in the week was now being replaced by hope for things that were about to happen. Kel and I left after dinner filled with a renewed optimism. We were all putting down ESVA roots together. I could see this group would all have some fun times ahead, together.

18

NEW DIGS

The next morning Kelly and I ran down in *Blitz* to look at the Saberline, and yes, she ran *Blitz* both down and back. The Saberline was perfect for our needs; we took it out on a sea trial and then were able to make a deal. Later that afternoon we both bought in heavily in Big Nile. We would watch it rebound over the next two months, our profit at that point almost enough to pay for the new *EMERALD IZ*.

We invited Tyler and Carol over that afternoon to have a closer look at their "new digs" over glasses of wine. They were blown away with how much more room they would have. Kaili went throughout the cabin, up on the bow, then out on the diving platform, and walked back through the transom door and onto the dock. It got her seal of approval.

I helped Tyler remove and reinstall his Segway hoist on *EMERALD IZ* over the weekend. Okay, he supervised while I did the installation. Kind of hard to do all that with a broken arm. The Main-ship would be perfect for him, Kaili, and Carol. I was glad we could make that happen for them.

Kelly and I got Rik to run us down on Monday to pick up the

Saberline. I even got to take her downriver until Kel mutinied when we hit the Chesapeake, taking the helm for the rest of the trip. Not only didn't I mind, I planned on it. For the first time in my life, I found someone whom I was completely comfortable with, from watching my back to running our boats. Yes, our boats. We'll have challenges ahead, we're both old enough to be set in our ways, but so much has changed in our lives that's all new, and we'll find our way together.

One thing that won't change is keeping a floating home at *Bayside*. But I needed to fix something there, and I wasn't sure how to go about it. I talked to Kel on the way back, and she made a call. After we tied up, we moved our things over from the Mainship and made another fun grocery run. We had company coming for dinner that evening.

Rik and Cindy showed up at 6:00, and there was wine waiting in the salon. I excused myself to go heat the grill, leaving Kel to give them the full tour. Yes, I am going to cook. Okay, more accurately, I will grill lobster tails and beef tenderloins. Kel was making all the sides. I am still the chief cook though because I was doing the main course. It's a guy rule... so sue me.

Yes, I'm babbling, but I'm nervous. That's why I wanted to hurry to the flybridge by myself to figure out what to say. The most important person in the life of someone who is one of the most important people in my life had just come aboard. I know she no longer thinks of me like she once did, and if that wasn't bad enough, I haven't figured out how to fix that, if I even can. I'm not worried just because she is important to an old friend, but because I like her, and we're friends. What I did over at the asphalt plant site was partly because of her. If it had been only her, and Kel hadn't been there, I'd still have done the same thing. Truth is, if neither of them had been there, I'd have done things differently, and it would have been far uglier than it worked out to be. Heatherton and his crony deserved it; they were evil personified, period. The only reason I'm losing any sleep over this is not directly because of what I did, but because of how it has affected my relationship with Cindy.

I lit the propane and used the brand-new grill brush I bought at the grocery store to clean the grate. While I stood and watched the temperature rise on the thermometer two arms encircled me from behind, and two lips touched my cheek. When the arms released me, and I spun around, it surprised me to see Cindy standing there alone, looking me straight in my eyes.

"I never thanked you properly for saving my life, Colt, I'm sorry."

I exhaled loudly as I hadn't seen this coming at all. "Uh, you're welcome?" I didn't know what else to say. Like I said, I'm a better listener than a talker.

"Rikki and Kelly both talked to me quite a bit over the past couple of days. I never understood everything that Rik had to do in her line of work. I never wanted to think about it I guess. She told me she's done similar things to what you did, for similar reasons. So, it upset her over how I reacted to... what happened, and how it made her afraid of how I'd react over some things she's done. It led to some long talks between us. She told me she thought about shooting him too, but she wouldn't have ended it so quickly for him." She took both my hands. "Then she told me you were there when her mom died, and you killed the man who murdered her."

I nodded, not trusting my voice or words right now. This was the last place I expected to revisit tonight, but I understood why Rik had gone there with Cindy. It was a tough memory for both of us, but this might be the only way she could get across to her why she was okay with what I had done, by exposing her own raw pain to her.

"She told me what happened to her mom before she died, and how you made sure that sadistic bastard paid for it afterward. That you, Conrad, and her mom had been so close, and this must have felt almost identical to that night, bringing back the pain you felt then. I didn't understand, Colt, I had no way of knowing how scared you two must have been for Kelly and me because you had been through it before with a very different outcome. I saw you take two lives, and it's only recently that I've understood you knew what they planned, that they never intended to let us go. What you did to them was more than justified, and I'm sorry that I reacted the way I did. I misjudged you, and what you had done, without having all the facts first."

Cindy hugged me again, and this time I hugged her back, both of us communicating more than we could with words. I looked over her shoulder and saw Kel and Rik standing on the lower deck, and both were smiling.

Our relationship and our dinner were both back to being relaxed and casual like it had always been before "that day." Kel and Rik had known it would be, but Cindy and I had to figure that out for ourselves. Now that we had, there would be a lot of dinners ahead with the four of us together. And these could happen on our boat even in the cold weather now. "Our boat," that had a nice ring to it.

After dinner, we walked Cindy and Rik back out to the dock and said goodnight before they headed back to *Hibiscus*. Kaili passed them alone, heading toward the Mainship where Tyler and Carol had settled in. She must have taken herself for a walk over at the grass strip. I swear she smiled at us as she passed, and when she stepped onto the swim platform, she looked back and "chuffed." I don't know if it was "*good night*," but it made us both spontaneously wave back at her. Yes, I know she's a dog, but it felt like the right thing to do. I swear she was waiting for it to happen before she would go bark at the hatch to be let in for the night. It was just another sign that everything was right with the world, at least here and now. But we'd be ready whenever it wasn't. That's our job, and Kelly and I would do it together from now on, no doubt with some help from our friends. Bring it on world, we're ready.

A FEW AUTHOR NOTES

One thing I need to point out is that there *is* a company based in Crozet, VA (which is pronounced Kro-Zay) that is working on self-driving automobile technology. It is *not* in any way, shape, nor form related to, connected with, nor supposed to be the company represented in this book, which is entirely fictional. In fact, in this book, I deliberately placed the location of the AI company miles away from this business's location, on the opposite side of town. I've never researched that company, and to my knowledge, I've never met anyone even remotely associated with the place. I developed the construction equipment idea on my own after seeing GPS equipped farm tractors working in a field near here.

The National Ground Intelligence Center (NGIC) is real and is located just north of Charlottesville, part of the "Post 911 Dispersal From DC" of strategic operations centers. But to the best of my knowledge, there is no clandestine intelligence facility located in Afton Mountain. Then again, it wouldn't be clandestine if I knew of it. There *is* however fiber optic internet service available in certain parts of the tiny little town of Crozet.

Crozet Vineyards is also a product of my imagination as is their Albemarle Chardonnay. Crozet is located in Albemarle County, and that's where that label name came from. It's kind of a tip of the hat to President Thomas Jefferson, who is believed to have been the first person in America to cultivate grapes for wine, right here in Albemarle County.

There are a few private polo fields near Crozet, including one at King Family Vineyards which has matches that are free to the public for viewing on Sundays throughout the summer, weather permitting. You can find out more about the polo matches, their award-winning wines, and their vineyard tours at KingFamilyVineyards.com. And while it was the inspiration behind Crozet Vineyards, there is no runway there, and I've yet to meet any villainous neighboring tech gurus at any of the matches I've attended. But once there was a family with a devious plan on the sidelines that I met (not the Kings). As they unloaded their SUV, they asked various people to hold a pile of golden retriever puppies "Just for a minute, while we get things out of the car." Kaili, our last golden, came from that litter that day. I told you they were devious.

However, I *did* base the character of Tyler MacKenzie on a real person. He is now twenty-nine-years old, was born with Cerebral Palsy, and has been a true inspiration to many people with disabilities including many wounded veterans. He uses canes and a Segway that's identical to the one in the book, carrying it around on a Segvator lift on the back of his Jeep. Ty has been involved with **Segs For Vets** (a non-profit group providing mobility equipment to wounded veterans), **Adaptive Anglers, Oscar Mike,** has completed many **Spartan** races, become a skydiver, and was interviewed on ESPN. He's been an advocate for people with disabilities for well over a decade. I'm very proud to call him my friend, as well as my son.

A point of clarification is that while there is an industry leader in the independent self-publishing distribution world today, there are also several other major players in that arena. The company represented in this book is <u>*not*</u> based on any of them. It is a product of my imagination invented to fit within this emerging industry, as was its chairman. Back when I wrote *AI Politics*, the book that became the basis for **GhostWRITER**, I had no way of knowing that the largest seller of books on the internet would announce a year later that they were relocating their headquarters to Northern Virginia. It turns out that the truth sometimes *IS* stranger than fiction...

During my research for *AI Politics*, I discovered references to some companies that are working on AI-based writing, however none of them appeared to be in any way linked to existing publishing or distribution houses. So, my job is safe, at least for now. But always bear in mind from now on what Chief Justice Roberts said, *"Beware the robots."*

If you enjoyed **GhostWRITER**, I'd be grateful if you would leave a review on GoodReads.com or Book Bub. And please email me at contact@DonRichBooks.com if you would like to let me know what you think about this book or any of my other books. I'd love to hear from you!

Don Rich

ABOUT THE AUTHOR

Don Rich is the author of the bestselling Coastal Adventure Series. Three of his books even simultaneously held the top three spots in Amazon's Hot New Releases in Boating.

Don's books are set mainly in the mid-Atlantic because of his love for this stretch of coastline. A fifth generation Florida native who grew up on the water, he has spent a good portion of his life on, in, under, or beside it.

He now makes his home in central Virginia. When he's not writing or watching another fantastic mid-Atlantic sunset, he can often be found on the Chesapeake or the Atlantic with a fishing rod in his hand.

Don loves to hear from readers, and you can reach him via email at contact@donrichbooks.com

ALSO BY DON RICH

Check my website www.DonRichBooks.com for the current list of all my book titles.

The Coastal Beginnings Series:

(The prelude to the Coastal Adventure Series)

- **COASTAL CHANGES**
- **COASTAL TREASURE**
- **COASTAL RULES**
- **COASTAL BLUFFS**

The Coastal Adventure Series:

- **COASTAL CONSPIRACY**
- **COASTAL COUSINS**
- **COASTAL PAYBACKS**
- **COASTAL TUNA**
- **COASTAL CATS**
- **COASTAL CAPER**
- **COASTAL CULPRIT**
- **COASTAL CURSE**
- **COASTAL JURY**
- **COASTAL CURRENCY**
- **COASTAL CRUISE**

Other Books by Don Rich:

- **GhostWRITER**

Here's A Tropical Authors Novella by Deborah Brown, Nicholas Harvey, and Don Rich:

- **Priceless**

Go to my website at www.DonRichBooks.com for more information about joining my **Reader's Group**! And you can follow me on Facebook at: https://www.facebook.com/DonRichBooks

I'm also a member of TropicalAuthors.com, where you can find my latest books and those by dozens of my coastal writer friends!